Miss Whitaker

OPENS HER HEART

OTHER BOOKS AND AUDIO BOOKS

BY JENNIFER MOORE

A Place for Miss Snow

Lady Helen Finds Her Song

Simply Anna

Miss Burton Unmasks a Prince

Lady Emma's Campaign

Becoming Lady Lockwood

Miss Whitaker

OPENS HER HEART

A Regency Romance by

JENNIFER MOORE

Covenant Communications, Inc.

Cover image © Mark Owen / Arcangel Images

Cover design copyright © 2017 by Covenant Communications, Inc.

Published by Covenant Communications, Inc.
American Fork, Utah

Printed in the United States of America
First Printing: April 2017

23 22 21 20 19 18 17   10 9 8 7 6 5 4 3 2 1

ISBN 978-1-52440-217-4

For Marshy V,
who always has the golden gun.

Acknowledgments

How can I begin to say thanks to all the people who bring a book to life?

I'm so grateful to my parents for the use of their cabin so I could squirrel myself away for some good writing time.

And thank you to my family, Frank and my boys, who made do on their own for a few weekends while I escaped.

My critique group: Josi Kilpack, Nancy Allen, Ronda Hinrichson, Jody Dufee, and Becki Clayson. Thank you, girls, for listening to a first draft and helping me make it better.

Thanks to Sharon Robards, whose fabulous book, *A Woman Transported*, gave me inspiration and a taste for life in the penal colony of New South Wales. I'm so grateful to you for your research tips, your willingness to look over my manuscript and give advice, and your patience with my questions. One of my favorite things about writing is all the wonderful friends I make on the journey.

Margot Hovley and Josi Kilpack, thank you for setting aside your own projects and giving this a read-through. I appreciate your input so much.

Thank you, Jodie Sanders, for setting up an appointment, going with me to the sheep ranch, and spending the day tromping around in the mud and documenting the whole thing on your phone. You're such a good friend.

Thanks to Chad and Ann Edgington for showing me around your ranch, answering questions, sharing your expertise, and giving me a taste of the nitty-gritty parts of sheep farming. I loved it.

Madison Kilpack, thank you for taking pictures, answering questions, and letting me experience Australia through your eyes.

Carla Kelly, thank you for your excellent advice on research and for letting your fabulous character Lord Ragsdale make an appearance in this book.

And my crew at Covenant, thank you for taking my manuscript and making it into a beautiful book. Stacey Turner, I'm so lucky to have you for an editor and friend. Thank you for making the words sound pretty. Thanks, Michelle Pipitone, for the cover art, Stephanie Lacy for your marketing skills, and everyone else who gives their expertise to make me look good.

Prologue

1804—South Atlantic Ocean

"Good afternoon, Miss Whitaker," Captain Ainsley said as Sarah stepped out of the companionway onto the deck. His thick white hair blew in the warm sea breeze as he tipped his head toward her.

Sarah dipped in a curtsey. "Hello, Captain. Mr. Thackeray told me we will cross the equator today, but I have not seen him, have you?"

The captain seemed to pause for an instant before answering. "I've not."

Sarah felt a bit disappointed. The first mate had made crossing the equator sound very exciting, and yet her closest friend aboard the *Coeur D'Alene* was nowhere to be found. Mr. Thackeray never treated her like a child—she was eleven years old after all—but instead made her feel like one of the crew.

The captain excused himself, and Sarah walked to the rail, marveling at the vastness of the ocean. In the six weeks since they'd left Portsmouth harbor, they had seen but one other ship and, aside from the Canary Islands, not one speck of land.

Mr. Thackeray had shown her the sailing route on the captain's large map. Each morning, after the deck officers made their calculations, he'd tap his finger on a spot, indicating the ship's position. She thought they were moving dreadfully slow. And according to the first mate, they still needed to stop for supplies in Rio de Janeiro, then sail southeast, beneath Africa and through the Indian Ocean, rounding the southern point of Port Jackson and then north, past Botany Bay to Sydney Cove in the colony of New South Wales.

This morning he'd pointed to a spot near the thick line that split the map into the Northern and Southern Hemispheres. "We're entering into

Neptune's kingdom, Little Minnow," he'd said. His eyes were bright as if they held a secret. "Only the most seaworthy of sailors are permitted in his domain."

"I am seaworthy." Sarah held up her chin, considering the past weeks aboard the ship. Unlike her aunt Hortensia and many of the other passengers, she'd not been seasick for an instant. She did not like to remain all day in the passenger dining room or her small cabin and much preferred to assist the sailors with their duties on deck. Her aunt had not been pleased with the idea, but since the older woman typically chose to remain below decks, Sarah had found if she listened to her aunt's admonishments with a thoughtful expression then promised to behave, she could do as she pleased.

Just as soon as she'd come aboard, Sarah and Mr. Thackeray had become friends. He told her she reminded him of his daughters. To keep her occupied during the long weeks, he had assigned her various tasks: scrubbing the wooden decks with a slab of limestone he called a holystone, unraveling yards of rope to make oakum for caulking, polishing the bulwark rails until they shone. As Sarah worked, she chatted with the other seamen who told her tales and taught her shanties that she learned quickly not to repeat in her aunt's presence.

Aunt Hortensia would disagree, but Sarah had found the voyage to be anything but dull, in spite of the duration. The sea was full of surprises. Sometimes, she found she could stare at the changing colors of the water for hours on end. Mr. Thackeray had pointed out schools of porpoises and allowed her to look through his spyglass. The only time he'd forbidden her from assisting the deckhands was during a storm or when the sailors climbed aloft to trim or reef the sails.

She heard footsteps approaching and turned, hoping Mr. Thackeray had finally been found. But she saw with some disappointment that it was only Aunt Hortensia. Sarah straightened her shoulders, smoothed her skirts and curtseyed.

Beneath the shade of her parasol, the woman's eyes were squinted in a look of disapproval, and Sarah was relieved to be found merely standing on deck instead of sitting on a crate, swinging her legs as she chatted with Mr. Owen while he mended sails or taught her to tie knots. Though she was not cruel, Aunt Hortensia had a disposition that was far from warm, and since Sarah's father was away for years at a time and her mother had died at her birth, her aunt was the nearest thing to family that Sarah knew.

And the woman was determined that her young charge should act like a lady in all circumstances.

"A fine day to be at sea, is it not?" Sarah said by way of greeting. Mr. Thackeray often used this very same sentiment, and Sarah thought it was the perfect way to describe a sunny sky glistening on the water and a slight wind blowing the sails.

"If you mean the waves are not tossing the boat about making passengers ill, then I suppose it is fine." Aunt Hortensia curled up her lips. "But one day at sea is very much the same as another. When I consider we are to be aboard this ship for over five ghastly months . . ." She closed her eyes as if it were too much to bear.

"But just think of it!" Sarah clasped her hands in front of her breast. "In New South Wales, we shall see a real kangaroo and native aborigines with dark skin and throwing sticks. And koalas climbing in eucalypt trees. We shall hear a kookaburra and finally visit the property in Paramatta." She swallowed a thickness in her throat. "And Papá! How I have missed him." She had not seen her father for nearly three years and felt a mixture of sadness and anticipation that very nearly overwhelmed her. "I shall be glad to see Papá." She spoke in nearly a whisper, pushing the words through a tight throat and rubbing her itching eyes.

"When we return to London, you will need finishing school lessons more than ever." Aunt Hortensia's voice snapped Sarah out of her ponderings. "Why your father thinks a young girl should be taken to a savage, inhospitable land is beyond me. Certainly, mingling with sailors and convicts will do nothing to forward you in society—"

"But they are not all convicts," Sarah burst out. The look of disapproval she received at interrupting only made her talk faster. "Papá says many free settlers have come to make a new life. And he believes convicts can be reformed. Some even have a pardon from the governor—a ticket-of-leave. They own land and farms and live honestly."

"And these are the sort of people with whom your father associates." Aunt Hortensia sniffed. "If my dear sister were alive to see this . . ." She closed her eyes again and blew out a breath through her nose as if she needed to calm herself. Sarah would not be surprised if even the mention of their destination proved too much for her aunt and she took to her cabin with smelling salts.

Sarah turned her attention from her aunt and watched curiously as a group of sailors stretched a large piece of canvas sail over the deck. Ropes stretched from the corners and were tied to the rails and mast to form a basin into which buckets of water were poured, making a shallow reservoir. She wondered if the crew was planning to wash their clothing.

A cry from the bow drew her attention, and she moved with the deckhands toward a commotion at the front of the ship.

She looked through the cluster of men until she found Mr. Owen. "What is happening?"

"An ol' sailor tradition, it is, miss. The crossing of the line ceremony." Mr. Owen grinned, showing gaps in his smile where teeth were missing. He pointed a knobby finger toward the bow. "Go on, there, ye'll not be wantin' to miss this."

Sarah moved to the front of the crowd and saw a group of crewmen hauling something from the sea. Perhaps a large marlin or sea turtle? When they pulled it onto the deck, Sarah gasped. It was not a fish but a man. She drew back.

The man stood straight with strands of seaweed draped over his shoulders and a dented metal crown on his head. His matted beard reminded her of a dirty mop. She squinted. It looked *very* much like a dirty mop.

He took a step forward, dripping water onto the deck, and raised a staff with prongs on the end. *A trident*, Sarah realized. *Is this truly a magical monster from the deep?* Another dripping figure was pulled over the rail, then another. Both were draped with seaweed and wore shapeless robes. One appeared to be a woman with long matted hair. The other's face was nearly obscured by a wet strip of cloth that looked a bit like a dirty cravat.

Sarah glanced around, searching for Mr. Thackeray but could not see him anywhere. She backed up, thinking she would run toward the companionway and hide in her cabin, but she stopped when Captain Ainsley stepped forward and bowed to the sea man.

"Welcome aboard, King Neptune."

Sarah froze. Was this real? The captain did not look afraid, but could it truly be King Neptune? And what harm was he capable of with his weapon? Hadn't Mr. Thackeray warned her they were entering into the sea king's realm? Would they be punished for trespassing?

She looked at the deckhands and saw that they were smiling. Some actually looked excited. Her fear started to melt, and she looked back toward the strange figures.

King Neptune swept his eyes over the sailors and the passengers that had joined them on the deck. "Captain, I have a subpoena from Davy

Jones for the uninitiated pollywogs aboard this ship to stand trial in my court." He spoke in a loud, deep voice.

King Neptune took a seat on a crate as if it were a throne, and the other two flanked him. He motioned to one of his companions with a sweep of his hand.

The creature with the wrapped face stepped forward. "I am Davy Jones. Let it be known that you are now in the realm of the king of the sea. And slimy pollywogs are required to prove their seaworthiness before Neptune."

Sarah glanced to her side and saw that Mr. Owen stood near. She scooted closer to her friend. "Mr. Owen, what is a pollywog?"

"One whot 'as never crossed into the Southern 'emisphere, miss."

"Then am I a pollywog?" Sarah asked, a nervous thrill moving over her.

"Aye, that you are." The corner of Mr. Owen's mouth quirked into a crooked smile. "Most certainly, miss."

Sarah glanced back to where Aunt Hortensia stood beside other passengers. Her parasol shaded her eyes, but her lips were tight in an expression of utter disapproval. "And is Aunt Hortensia a pollywog too?"

Mr. Owen glanced over his shoulder then quickly back. His smile grew. "Maybe she ain't a pollywog."

Davy Jones read off names of the novice sailors. The men stepped forward and knelt in a line on the deck before King Neptune.

He lowered the paper and looked as if he'd say something else, but instead he leaned close and listened to the king before he turned back to the crowd. "Sarah Whitaker." His raspy words carried over the hushed voices and the whisper of the waves against the hull.

Sarah's stomach tightened with both nervousness and excitement. She glanced back toward Aunt Hortensia. Her aunt's face was pulled into a scowl of disapproval, and she shook her head.

"Go on," Mr. Owen whispered. "Yer shipmates'll not allow any 'arm to come to ya, miss."

Sarah pushed down her shoulders and held her head high. She stepped forward, kneeling beside the other pollywogs.

"You pollywogs are charged with posing as true sailors without paying tribute to the god of the sea." Davy Jones paced before them, water dripping off the tips of the seaweed leaves. He motioned to the first person in the line with a sweep of his hand and ordered him to present himself to

Neptune. The man rose and bowed to the sea king, kissing his extended hand. When he stepped back, three sailors grabbed him and tossed him into the pool of seawater they had created on the deck.

The sailors cheered, and when he climbed, sputtering from the pool, Davy Jones announced that he was now a "trusty shellback."

Sarah was still trying to make sense of what had happened when she heard Davy Jones call her name. She walked forward.

King Neptune stretched out his hand, and Sarah hesitated. She was no longer afraid but uncertain.

"Not to worry, Little Minnow," he said in a low voice.

Sarah looked closer into Neptune's face. She gasped when she recognized the smiling eyes of Mr. Thackeray behind the filthy costume beard.

He winked. "You claimed to be seaworthy. Shall we find out?"

Sarah grasped his hand, planted a kiss on it, then ran to the canvas pool, laughing when the sailors lifted her over the side. She splashed into the cold water, slipping as she tried to stand. Strong arms pulled her out and set her onto the deck. Her gown was dripping, her slippers squishing out water, and she could not hold back her swell of pride when her shipmates proclaimed her a shellback.

Captain Ainsley shook her hand, offering congratulations, and she glanced once more at Mr. Thackeray in his costume that now looked comical instead of frightening. He wiggled his eyebrows, and she grinned, knowing he was proud of her bravery. *How much I will have to tell Papá.*

That night, after her aunt was asleep, Sarah lifted a long wooden tube that leaned in the corner of the cabin and sat upon her berth, turning the instrument over and listening to the sound of falling rain. Papá had told her small rocks and seeds made the sound by sliding over obstacles inside the tube. She studied the markings, rubbing her finger along a line of white dots on the dark wood and wondering about the hands that made them. Her father had told her stories—both on his visits and in letters—about the aboriginal people in New South Wales. The Eora, he'd told her, were the indigenous people that lived around the area of Sydney Town. He'd even become friends with a man named Bennelong and his wife, Barangaroo. In the darkness, Sarah whispered the names, liking the strange feel of them in her mouth, and turned over the rain stick again.

She'd imagined the land on the bottom side of the earth—with its backward seasons, unpredictable weather, and animals that sounded like mythological creatures—for so long that it felt to her like an enchanted world from a fairy tale. And soon, she'd not have to imagine anymore.

Four months later, Mr. Thackeray stood beside Sarah on the port side of the ship watching across the sparkling blue water as a flag was raised on a rocky hill high above Sydney Town. "Cover your ears," he warned.

The cannons of the ship boomed in salute, and blasts from the shore fired in response.

Sarah clapped her hands. After months at sea, the last hours had seemed like an eternity. "Just wait, Mr. Thackeray. You shall love Papá. You must come to Parramatta for supper at Sarah Hills." She smiled, thinking how much her father loved her—he'd named his sheep farm after her to feel close to her while he was all the way on the bottom of the world.

"Of course you will be welcome anytime," Aunt Hortensia said, joining them.

Sarah gripped the rail, leaning forward. "A boat is approaching!" She took the offered spyglass from Mr. Thackeray. "Perhaps it is Papá." But squinting through the lens, she could not recognize any of the men on the small boat rowing toward them. Where was her father? He'd promised to meet them as soon as they arrived.

Captain Ainsley came to stand next to his first mate. "The governor of the colony coming to greet us personally?" His voice was low and the tone seemed uncertain.

Sarah saw Aunt Hortensia exchange a look with the captain and, though she didn't understand what it meant, felt a foreboding chill. She rubbed her arms.

Once the men climbed on board, a short, balding man with white hair and a soldier's uniform strode forward and bowed a greeting to the captain. "Welcome back to Sydney, Captain Ainsley."

"Thank you, Governor King."

"And Mr. Thackeray, you are welcome too."

"It is always a pleasure to return to your beautiful colony." Mr. Thackeray bent his head forward in a bow.

Sarah thought Mr. Thackeray's face held a question. Aunt Hortensia's looked similar. What was it about the appearance of these men that made the sea air feel heavy?

Governor King shook the first mate's hand. He glanced around the deck until his gaze landed on Sarah. The corners of his eyes tightened, and something in his expression made her stomach feel sick.

Captain Ainsley followed the man's gaze. He lifted his arm toward the women. "Governor King, if I may introduce Miss Hortensia Blakemore and her niece, Miss Sarah Whitaker."

The governor stepped closer and took Aunt Hortensia's hand. "Very nice to meet you, Miss Blakemore."

"A pleasure," Aunt Hortensia said.

"And Miss Whitaker."

Sarah curtseyed.

Governor King studied Sarah and cleared his throat, then he shifted, running his palm over his head.

The sick feeling grew, and Sarah moved closer to Mr. Thackeray, who put a hand on her shoulder.

"I am dreadfully sorry, ladies." The governor's cheeks pulled in a grimace. "But I am afraid I bear bad news. Miss Whitaker, your father died, nearly two months ago."

The deck shifted beneath Sarah's feet, and her thoughts turned sluggish. "Papá?" Her head felt light, and she swayed. *How could this be? She had come so far. He had died two months ago, and she didn't know?*

Mr. Thackeray caught her before she fell. He knelt, pulling her close. "I am so sorry, Little Minnow."

Sarah turned her face against his shoulder and wept in earnest.

He patted her head, letting her cry as the governor continued to talk to Aunt Hortensia. She heard them as if they spoke from a great distance and only vaguely understood their words.

"Inherited extensive property . . . wool . . . wealthiest young lady in the colony."

Chapter 1

1814—London, Newgate Prison

DANIEL BURTON HEARD THE CELL door creak on rusty hinges but didn't lift his gaze from the stones of the floor. Since his arrest three days earlier, he'd ignored both the gaoler, who had brought his food, and the attorney, who had visited twice. His cell was located on the master's side of Newgate prison, thanks to the sixpence he'd given the gaoler. Daniel had paid the extra fee to avoid the commoners' side with the majority of the prisoners. He wished to be alone. If he had his choice, he'd never speak to another person as long as he lived. Which, according to the magistrate would be a few days at most.

How had he come to this?

Wagering had ruined him. Attempting to fix the race had been the most foolish action in a long string of foolish actions. The thought of the horse dying sickened him. When did he become this man? He never intended for the situation to get so out of control.

Footsteps drew closer, and he closed his eyes, pressing his back against the rough rock of the wall. The bumps dug into his muscles, and he welcomed the discomfort. A wooden chair sat beneath the small opening that served as a window, but Daniel sat on the floor in the darkest corner, his legs pulled up against his chest and his shackled arms resting on his knees.

"They tell me you've not eaten nor spoken."

Daniel recognized the voice and instead of being grateful to see his relative, the Duke of Southampton, his shame grew until he nearly choked on it. He stared at his boots. A piece of hay caught between his sole, and the soft leather served as a further reminder of his disgrace.

The wooden chair scraped over the floor, then groaned as the duke sat. "What have you done, Daniel?" The duke's voice was soft, filled with a disappointment that was much worse than if the man had shouted.

Daniel didn't respond. Truly, what was there to say? He'd made a hash of everything: his reputation, his financial standing, and his very life, which was now worth less than the few coins remaining in his pocket.

The chair groaned again as the duke shifted. "I have repaid Lord Hughes for the loss of his animal, as well as the other creditors that have come forward with claims. As you are undoubtedly aware, most of your liabilities were accrued through wagers. The *financial* damage at least has been repaired." The duke's voice sounded as if he were leaving more unsaid.

Daniel's stomach burned at the unspoken implication. His actions had not only damaged his own reputation, but as the duke's guest, a member of his household, Daniel's misdeed had hurt the entire family—Serena, the duchess; Little James, the heir; and Daniel's sister, Meg, and her husband, Rodrigo. He'd besmirched all of their good names. His death would be a blessing to everyone.

The duke cleared his throat. "I spoke at length to the magistrate, but as an American and with the ongoing war, you are technically an enemy to the crown. The best I could manage was to convince the high judge to remit your sentence."

Daniel glanced up. Seeing the finely dressed man amid the squalor of the prison was such a contrast that Daniel was taken aback for a moment. The duke's face held such an expression of concern that Daniel could not bear to look at him and was forced to turn his gaze back to the ground. The man was actually trying to help him—even after all the disgraceful things he'd done.

"You will not hang," the duke continued. "But the court considers your crime so heinous . . ." He rubbed the side of his face. "Daniel, I cannot fix this. I have tried everything, but I cannot save you from punishment."

"The punishment is justified." Daniel ground out the words through clenched teeth.

The duke blew out a breath and leaned forward, resting his forearms on his knees. "You are to be transported to serve a fourteen-year sentence in the colony of New South Wales."

A surge of fear shot through Daniel. Immediately, images of criminals—scarred, tattooed, dangerous—appeared in his mind. He could not live among these people. But just as quickly, he realized he was every bit the criminal they were, and worse. By the law, larceny of property valued at more than one shilling carried the penalty of death. Daniel's crime had destroyed much more than that. His stomach twisted as he realized that none would have a crime as serious as his to their name. Without the duke's interference, any regular man—like Daniel—would have been hanged. Daniel was the guiltiest of all.

"I have spoken to the captain of the convict transport ship, Captain Seymour. He will ensure you are treated well, and he carries a letter for Governor Macquarie in Sydney. I hope to convince him that you will be a benefit to the colony. Perhaps he will consider your experience of farming in America to be an asset." The duke removed a billfold from inside his coat and held it toward Daniel. "Take this. It should be enough to start you off once your sentence is served. Buy some land, livestock, or seeds. I've heard—"

"Why are you doing this?" Daniel's words came out in a choke. He stood with a clank of chains. His head was light from rising so quickly and from lack of food. He leaned a shoulder against the wall to steady himself. "Did you not say yourself that my crime was despicable? You do not know the half of it." He breathed heavily as he thought of his dissolute existence over the past two years. Humiliation rose sour in his throat. "I deserve to hang," he said in a low voice.

"And how would I face Meg if I did not do everything in my power to save you?" The duke's tone remained calm.

Thinking of his sister made Daniel's eyes burn. "Does Meg know?"

The duke shook his head. "She is in Spain with her husband, or you can be certain she would have hatched a grand escape plan by now, probably involving disguises and ambushing the guards." The duke's words were no doubt intended to cheer Daniel. The man smiled fondly as he described what they both knew would be a completely believable reaction from Daniel's audacious sister.

Daniel's chest ached. His sister's imagination and grand schemes had been a source of amusement and sometimes frustration, but thinking of her now, of the hurt she'd feel when she discovered what he'd done, filled him with the most bitter shame.

Oh, Meg. I have let you down. He pinched the bridge of his nose, smashing his eyes shut against a wave of emotion. He'd let everyone down.

The duke rose and laid a hand on Daniel's shoulder. "It is not for your sister alone that I would save you. You are more than this person you have become. I see a man who is creative and intelligent but has indulged too much in vices. You have been given more than most people in this world, and yet you've made less of yourself." He remained silent until Daniel raised his head. "You can change."

He set the billfold on the chair and walked toward the door. "This is the last money I will give you, Daniel. You must choose whether to gamble it away or use it to start a new life. You lost some of your freedom when you poisoned that animal, but concerning your future, you have a choice." The duke opened the door. "There is always a choice."

"Your grace," Daniel called suddenly.

He turned, his brows raised in question, and Daniel was struck again by how out of place the nobleman looked in his surroundings. The duke had made a great effort on his behalf.

"I did not mean to kill the horse, only to make it sleep—I needed it to lose the race." It seemed vital that the man understand his motive, that he knew Daniel was not fully corrupt. He'd been desperate but not malicious.

The duke dipped his head once and left, the door clanging shut behind him.

Daniel sank back to the floor and thrust his fingers through his hair. He reached for the billfold and then hung his head, surrendering to the despair that fell over him like a dark fog. He was not the man the duke believed him to be. The duke's coming, his efforts on Daniel's behalf had been meant to give hope, but in truth he'd only extended Daniel's miserable life.

What hope was there for him? And how was it to be found in a penal colony in an untamed land on the other side of the world?

Chapter 2

1815—Colony of New South Wales

SARAH URGED HER HORSE FORWARD over the rolling pastureland. As she crested another hill, she glanced back to make sure her foreman was close behind. Bill Hawkins was a fine worker and knew more about sheep than most men, but he was still a convict, and therefore Sarah knew she needed to keep a close eye on him. Over the last ten years, she'd repeatedly learned that lesson—and never in a painless way.

They rode down into a valley near the very edge of the Sarah Hills property. It was still early in the summer, and typically the heavy rainfall wouldn't come for a few weeks, but she'd not risk losing her livestock to flooding. In merely a few hours, one storm could raise the water level over ten feet from the narrow creek that bordered her acreage. And so, as a preventative measure, she'd ordered the shepherds of the different flocks to move the sheep to higher ground.

The sun was hot, and the buzz of cicadas surrounded them. The sound could lull a man to sleep, especially in the heat, and she'd need to make doubly sure the convict workers that tended her sheep were alert and not dozing.

A cloud of white cockatoos burst noisily from the thick screen of trees that ran along the creek. Sarah studied the tree line, wondering what had startled them. It could be nothing more than a 'roo, but she knew to be cautious.

She slowed her horse and reached into the pack on her saddle to take out a pistol. Holding it low in front of her, she turned, motioning for Bill to join her.

He raised his chin toward the flock of screeching birds and glanced at the pistol. Sarah knew the man must feel frustrated at not having a weapon, but convicted felons were not permitted to carry firearms.

The foreman nodded as they urged forward their horses. His jaw was set. Bill was not one to use unnecessary words, and Sarah appreciated this about him. They both understood the danger and that Sarah would be the one to defend them, should they meet with trouble.

A trickle of sweat ran along her hairline beneath her wide-brimmed hat, and her hand tightened on the weapon. Wild dogs, hostile aborigines, or fleeing convicts could be hiding in the thick trees. Any of them posed a threat both to Sarah's animals and her workers.

They rode closer, and she saw something move in the thick grass.

A chill ran over her skin, but as the mistress of the farm, she had a duty to investigate.

She heard a splash and jerked her head around so quickly that her braid flipped over her shoulder. Something was definitely near the creek, and it did not sound small. Clutching the pistol tighter, she continued down the hill, her heart pounding as they moved into the dappled shade. The horse's steps were muffled by the soft ground.

As she drew near, a man rose to his feet. He rubbed his wet face and shook his head. Water dripped from his light auburn curls. He wore only his trousers. Sarah's cheeks burned in embarrassment, and she fought against the impulse to turn away. But now was not the time to worry about propriety. She forced herself to assess the situation with a detached eye. In spite of his reddish hair, his skin was quite tanned and his face extremely handsome. Out of habit, she looked for shackle scars on his wrists but could not make any out.

When the man saw Sarah and Bill, his eyes grew wide. His gaze moved to the pistol, and he held up his hands, glancing to the side. A coat hung from a branch of a gum tree; beneath it, a musket leaned against the peeling trunk.

"What are you doing here? Are you alone?" Sarah held the pistol steadily and spoke in the most forceful voice she could muster. She moved her gaze over the area but saw no one else.

"Yes. My billfold is in my coat, but I think you will be disappointed at the contents."

For a moment she stared at the man until his meaning became startlingly clear. "We are not going to *rob* you." Sarah allowed a huff of indignation into her tone. "*You* are the one lurking about this property."

The man's brows rose in a look of surprise. "I beg your pardon. I should not . . . I am only newly arrived and still learning the ways here. I assumed you were, ah, bushrangers."

"You assumed?" Sarah blinked in astonishment, feeling insulted. "What would possibly have led you to that conclusion?"

He shrugged, and a side of his mouth lifted in a crooked smile. He raised his brows and nodded toward her.

Her outrage dissipated. She thought how her appearance must look to him: a woman wearing trousers and thick boots, holding him at gunpoint. He thought she was dangerous? A bandit? She could not help but be amused and even a little flattered at the supposition that she was an outlaw. Her aunt would have had a fit had she still been alive to hear his conjecture.

Aunt Hortensia had insisted Sarah dress like a lady no matter what the circumstances, but with her aunt gone and Sarah taking on more of the farm's responsibilities, it became apparent that she could not efficiently manage the operation from the dainty velvet chair in her drawing room. Sarah had found it utterly inconvenient to ride on a silly sidesaddle while directing the workers and inspecting the herds, and her fine gowns and slippers were not only impractical but treacherous. Snakes lurked in the thick grass, just as likely to bite a horse as a person's legs. She'd been thrown once when her horse startled, and the next day she sent her lady's maid into town to purchase a pair of trousers and work boots.

Her mouth quirked at the idea that she'd given the man a fright. She lowered her weapon but kept it close. "Sir, who are you?"

"My name is Daniel Burton. At your service." He bowed from his position on the muddy riverbank then grabbed his shirt and slid it over his head.

"And you are from America." With the amount of new immigrants aboard every ship, Sarah had come to recognize the various accents.

"Yes. But I came by way of London."

"On which ship?" Captain Thackeray's ship, the *Coeur d'Alene* was due to arrive soon. Had this man traveled with her friend?

"The *Bellerophon*."

A convict ship? She tipped her head. It was not unheard of for captains to take on other passengers, but she did not think it was the way most men would prefer to travel. Perhaps Daniel Burton was simply frugal. He was not a convict, obviously. His skin was tanned, which would not be the case if he'd been chained below decks for half a year. And he did have a weapon. He did not wear the coarsely woven gray convict uniform. His clothes seemed to be well made, if not in the best condition. Hardly surprising after a long voyage. She scrutinized him a moment longer then twisted and slid the pistol back into the pack.

"And if I might be so bold, what is your name, miss?"

"Sarah Whitaker." She inclined her head, pleased that she kept her voice steady. Daniel Burton put her off balance.

"Miss Sarah Whitaker of Sarah Hills?" He gave that crooked smile again and cocked his brow in a tease.

"My father named the farm, of course." She felt her cheeks heating as she always did, being the owner of a property that bore her name. As if she would do something so vain as name the property after herself.

"A lovely name that suits both the farm and the woman."

She did not respond, unsure if he were speaking with sarcasm, or was he in earnest? *Lovely* was not a word she'd use to describe her name. She'd always considered it to be practical at best. But at the way he spoke, his voice low and sincere, she couldn't help but feel flattered. And a bit agitated at the attention. The farm on the other hand . . . She was convinced there was no place lovelier.

"Governor Macquarie mentioned you, Miss Whitaker. When he learned I'd purchased a flock of sheep, he told me you have the most successful farm in the colony."

Sarah dipped her chin, feeling a swell of pride at the governor's praise. The new governor was a good man, and despite his tolerance for freed convicts, she considered him honorable. He, at least, respected her position as the manager of the farm. Many of the men she was forced to work with in government offices did not. "The majority of the success is due to my father's initial investments nearly twenty years ago."

He nodded. "Perhaps that is part of it. But the governor attributes much of it to you. Made you out to be a very capable manager."

"That was courteous of him."

"He also invited me to a ball in two weeks time at Government House in Parramatta. I assume you will attend as well."

Sarah nodded. "When the governor and his family are at their country home, the neighborhood is glad for any excuse to assemble. We do not get many chances for society out here in the bush."

"And he assured me there will be dancing." His blue eyes sparkled as his smile grew.

"Very likely." Sarah lowered her gaze, feeling shy at his attention and unsure how to respond. She did not know this man and could not trust his outright friendliness, and besides, she did not have much experience speaking with a man in a situation that did not concern money or sheep. A drip of sweat rolled between her shoulder blades, but since she was in the shade, she knew the sun was not the cause.

"If you will allow me, I should like to take this opportunity to claim your hand for a dance."

A funny feeling moved through her middle, as if she'd ridden the horse over a jump. She reminded herself to be cautious of the stranger but could not help but smile and found it difficult to look him in the eye. "Yes. I would be delighted." Sarah stumbled over the words then, in her embarrassment, turned quickly, motioning toward her companion. She'd all but forgotten Bill was there. "I beg your pardon. This is Bill Hawkins. My foreman."

"Pleased to meet you, Mr. Hawkins."

"And you, sir. You've a new flock, ya say? What breed?"

"Saxon Merinos. Mr. Orton at the stockyard claimed they've the best wool." Mr. Burton rolled down his sleeves as he spoke.

"He speaks true," she said. "The wool of that breed is very fine. Strong yet soft." So he wasn't raising the animals for the meat, only fine wool. Sarah had a flock of Saxon Merinos herself and knew the sheep were quite valuable.

"I hope after the first shearing, I'll be able to purchase some horses." Mr. Burton kept talking to Bill, and Sarah noticed a decided change in his tone and demeanor as he spoke of business matters. It only served to heat her cheeks further when she realized he had been *flirting* with her. "That is my intent, to breed horses from fine bloodstock. The sheep are just a means to an end, you see."

"The colony can always use more horses, but they can be right difficult to raise. A bit more finicky than sheep, they are." Bill scratched his cheek as he spoke. "Have ya experience then?"

"My grandfather bred horses in South Carolina."

"Very good, sir."

"And where is your farm, Mr. Burton?" Sarah asked.

"I'm standing on it." He spread his arms and grinned. "Apparently this little creek marks the boundary between our properties. You and I are neighbors, Miss Whitaker."

Sarah felt a cold stone settle in her stomach. "You were granted this property?"

"Yes." Daniel could obviously sense the tension in her question. His face clouded, and he spoke tentatively. "Apparently it just became available with the new bridge providing access to the road. Mr. Campbell of the governor's office assured me the property was perfect for livestock as well as agriculture."

She gritted her teeth. It *was* perfect. Which is precisely why Sarah had offered for years to purchase it. On the north side, the land was raised and flat with rich soil, good drainage, and plenty of sun—exactly right for growing feed. A deep pond in the middle of the property provided fresh water and rainbow fish. The acres of flat grassland didn't need to be cleared for planting, and the hills would accommodate a large flock. But the main reason she'd wanted the land was, with the new bridge, the direct accessibility to the road that led to Parramatta. It was much more convenient than driving lambs and leading bullock drays filled with wool from her outbuilding across miles of hills to market. She'd mentioned at least once a month to the colony secretary, John Thomas Campbell, that she was anxious for the land, and he'd assured her that as soon as the bridge was built, the property was as good as hers. The heaviness in her stomach heated until her hands started to shake.

That was, until Mr. Burton *came to town.*

Sarah's mind whirled. She needed to speak to the colony secretary, to plead her case. She was angry but not surprised that he would choose to give the land to a man. So many men in the colony thought it was unbefitting for a young lady to manage a farm.

She considered her options. If she left now, she wouldn't be able to make it to Sydney Town before nightfall, but she could reach Parramatta, spend the night at a guest house, then continue on.

First, she would need to return home to pack and change her clothes. She couldn't arrive in town and ask for an audience with Mr. Campbell dressed like—well, like a bushranger. And she could not go alone. Even carrying a weapon, a lone woman wasn't safe on the isolated roadways. Bill could not be spared from the farm. He would need to remain and continue to direct the shepherds to move the flocks.

Tom had probably already left for the afternoon to tend to his own small garden and wouldn't be able to prepare the carriage.

Drat that Mr. Campbell. Her visit would need to wait until tomorrow. And drat Mr. Burton. Sarah tapped her fingers on her knees, anxious to return home and prepare for the journey. She turned her attention back toward the men, who had continued their conversation.

"The flock will be delivered in a few days." Daniel was saying in answer to a question Bill had asked. "I hope to have at least a paddock constructed by then."

"You'll not need it. Sheep only require a tender to keep away wild dogs and prevent any of 'em from wandering. Surely you've been assigned workers."

"Yes. They're coming early tomorrow morning." Daniel chewed on his lip. "As you can probably tell, I have much to learn."

"Not to worry. You'll pick up the way of things right quick."

Daniel's gaze moved to Sarah. "And if I have questions, my closest neighbor is an expert. Might I presume to call on you, Miss Whitaker, should I need advice about my flock?" His smile seemed hopeful, as if he was worried she'd not return it.

"What?" Sarah had to focus to remember what he'd asked. "Oh, yes. That would be fine." Her voice was clipped, and she knew she was not disguising her irritation with any amount of grace. She nodded her head in farewell. "If you will excuse us, I've suddenly remembered I need to go to town."

She glanced at Bill and saw his gaze rise to the sun as if calculating the time. He frowned and looked as if he might pose some argument. Well, it was none of his business anyway. Sarah turned her mount and started up the hill.

Behind her, she heard the men exchanging farewells but did not stop. She was acting rudely, but this was not an assembly hall or a garden party. She was not a demure debutante who smiled and pretended as though everything was all right. It was most decidedly not all right. And as mistress of Sarah Hills, she was going to do what she could to correct it.

Chapter 3

THE SUN SHONE BRIGHTLY, A slight breeze stirred, and in all, it was a very fine day as Daniel turned his mount up the road toward Parramatta. If one could call it a road. He thought it was better defined as a track: distinct but rough. Riding this way in a carriage would be murder on one's spine. He crested a rise and let his gaze travel over the miles of thick forestland surrounding him. A feeling of nostalgia washed over him as he thought of his grandparents' farm outside Charleston. The warm sun, the smell of animals, and the satisfaction of working with his hands over the past days brought back a flood of memories. How had he forgotten? A smile spread over his face as he rode down the hill.

He passed beneath a wide gum tree. The tree was strange-looking with smooth skin where the bark had peeled off. The bends in the branches looked like an old man's wrinkled elbows; the leaves were thin and pointy.

That morning, Daniel had asked the supervisor who'd delivered his convict workers where to inquire about a housekeeper. Even though he had only a small shelter, his clothes were in dire need of washing—by someone who could do a proper job—and the meals he made in the open fire pit were beyond terrible. The man had directed him to the Female Factory in Parramatta, where he could find an unassigned convict woman to employ as a domestic servant.

Following the path around a turn, he came upon a labor gang working on the road. Acid churned inside his stomach, bringing his pleasant thoughts up short. The bright sunlight seemed to darken.

He should be among those men. By rights, Daniel should be living in a bark hut, wearing gray duck cloth, and performing manual labor like the other criminals. It was only because of his wealthy cousin's generosity that he was not.

He did not know what the duke had said to Captain Seymour of the *Bellerophon,* or what money was exchanged, but based on his resulting treatment onboard, Daniel thought it must have been significant. A wave of gratitude mingled with the bitter shame.

In spite of his convict status, Daniel had been granted some leniency at sea. His chains had been immediately removed when he came aboard, and though he was still under guard, he'd been allowed to leave his cell and operate as part of the crew.

Since Daniel had no experience working on a ship, Captain Seymour assigned him the most menial of tasks, but Daniel had jumped at the opportunity—anything was preferable to sitting in the dark, foul-smelling cargo hold with the other prisoners. Daniel watched the gang now, wearing ragged clothing and grim expressions as they leveled out a section of road. The clank of the fetters attached to their wrists and ankles sounded unnatural mixed with the call of birds and the rustle of leaves.

He shivered as he remembered laying his arms over a barrel in the ship's carpenter's workshop and watching as shackles were re-attached to his wrists for disembarkation in Sydney Harbor. The cool iron bands were not tight, but it still gave him a panicky feeling of being trapped, just as it had in Newgate Prison six months earlier.

"I'm sorry. Standard procedure, ye understand." The marine standing behind him had spoken the words in an apologetic voice that intensified his thick Scottish brogue. "Once yer processed and assigned, ye'll probably never see chains and fetters again."

Daniel's mouth pulled into a smile as he thought of the man speaking the words. Over the months of the voyage, he and Sergeant Conall Stewart had become close friends, and when the marine's duty had required him to treat Daniel like a prisoner, Conall became uncomfortable.

Daniel tipped his hat to the labor gang's supervisor, exchanging a greeting as he passed, and tried to keep his guilt from showing on his face.

Conall had been right. Within an hour of Daniel's arrival, Governor Macquarie himself had granted Daniel a full pardon. The governor had explained that convicts who showed promise, who came with money and could provide for themselves, were often freed, thus easing the burden on the government for their food and housing. But the action, Daniel knew, was again due to the duke's influence. The status of convict would remain on his record for the entirety of his life, and he could not leave New South Wales until his fourteen-year sentence was completed. But he could move about without a writ from the warden, could own land, mingle among society, and be considered a free settler. The hopeless punishment had disappeared with a few strokes of the governor's quill.

Daniel had been granted a parcel of land, much larger than the typical thirty acres given to an unmarried freed convict. With Conall's help, he'd purchased a horse, a gun, and a flock of sheep, and his future plans, which had seemed so distant hours earlier, were set into motion.

Daniel should have been thrilled at his freedom and good fortune, but the guilt continued to gnaw at him. He'd not done penance for his crimes. Another had paid, and Daniel was left feeling as if he owed a debt he was unsure how to settle.

Daniel rubbed his wrists absently, glancing at the silvery-leafed tree overhead, searching for the bird whose cry sounded like maniacal laughter.

As he rode toward Parramatta, he shifted in his coat, which was much tighter around his arms and across his shoulders than it had been when he'd boarded the *Bellerophon*. The journey had wrought a change not only to his body but inside him as well. The hours and hours of mundane tasks and time alone had given him the opportunity to think, to consider his life and the direction of his path.

You lost some of your freedom, but concerning your future, you have a choice. He'd realized the value of the duke's words and made a promise to himself. He was finished with wagers. To forego gambling would be difficult, but if he was to become a new man, that was an aspect of his life that he'd not return to. Labor gave him a distraction when the impulse to wager nagged at him. Daniel also gave himself a strict rule to avoid places where he might be tempted to gamble, and found himself challenged nearly every day aboard as the officers, sailors, and even convicts indulged in card games. But he'd remained strong. The memories of the cold of Newgate prison cell and the duke's disappointment gave him the will to forego what was once such an enticement.

He continued to ponder as he rode, frustrated at the disconcerting feeling that his good fortune had come at cost to others.

Most recently, the cost had been to his new neighbor, Sarah Whitaker. By her reaction yesterday, he'd felt certain she'd hoped to obtain his land to add to her own. And it was not difficult to ascertain the reason. The accessibility to the road and the fine water source made the land extremely valuable. She'd not been able to hide her anger as she left their meeting. He didn't think she'd even bothered to try.

He felt sorry they'd gotten off on the wrong foot, especially when the encounter had started out so nicely—at least, once he realized she wasn't planning to shoot or rob him.

A smile spread over Daniel's face as he thought about his attractive new neighbor. She was unlike any woman he'd ever met; she appeared extremely independent and clever, yet at the same time, her smile had carried a hint of uncertainty, even shyness. She spoke as an educated woman of breeding yet wore men's clothing, brandished a weapon, and managed her horse with a casual confidence.

Daniel had never met a woman with attributes that seemed so contrary to one another, and the combination fascinated him.

He continued to mull over the thoughts as he rode along the dusty road. Even though the journey to Parramatta took a few hours, he did not mind. Not after months in close quarters aboard a prison ship. He hoped he would not take something as simple as fresh air and freedom for granted again.

Once he arrived at Parramatta, it was easy to find the gaol. The Female Factory was exactly as the convict supervisor had described: a long two-story stone building on the north side of the river. Two smaller buildings sat on each side. Daniel dismounted and tied his horse's reins to a tree. As he approached, he saw women of all ages tending to babies, carrying buckets of water, or visiting in groups. The only indication that this was a prison were the soldiers stationed at the outer gates, lazily watching the small children play in the hard-packed dirt of the yard.

A few other men walked in or out of the gate, and Daniel wondered at the apparent lax security. Were visitors free to come and go as they pleased?

He approached the guards. "Excuse me, is this the women's factory?"

One of the soldiers, a heavy-set man with drooping eyelids gave a flat look, as if Daniel's question was absurd. The other, a tall man with a thick mustache, smirked.

"Yes, well." Daniel shifted, unsure how to proceed. "Might you direct me to the supervisor? I am in need of a housekeeper."

The mustached man's smirk grew. "Women's section is atop the gaol. You'll find plenty o' *housekeepers* inside, working the looms." He put unnecessary stress on the word, as if sharing a joke. "Go on now, and choose yerself a pretty one."

Daniel's insides grew cold at the man's implication. "Sir, I am actually looking for a woman to cook and do my laundry. To whom should I speak about acquiring an employee?"

The soldier cocked a brow, his expression indicating that he did not believe Daniel's intentions to be the least respectable but he would play along all the same. "You'll be wantin' Mr. Oakes then." He squinted and glanced at the stone building. "'E's gone home for his midday meal. Should return in an hour or so."

"Thank you." Daniel looked back toward the town, thinking he'd not mind a midday meal himself.

He made his way back to his mount and rode across the wooden bridge toward the cluster of buildings that made up Parramatta. Barracks, businesses, shops, cottages that likely belonged to town officials, and a few quaint public houses lined the dusty roads. Cages containing colorful birds swung outside doorways, and pots of flowers sat on porches. Chickens, dogs, and pigs moved freely through the town. He heard the clanks of a blacksmith and smelled fresh-cut wood as he passed a tradesman's workshop. The town reminded him of a frontier settlement in America.

He scanned the area, located a spot for his horse, and made his way toward a building with a swinging sign: Yorkshire Grey. *Fine name for a pub.*

As he crossed the hard-packed road, he saw a familiar man approaching. Miss Whitaker's foreman. Daniel searched his mind for a moment, then remembered the man's name. He waved. "Mr. Hawkins. A pleasure to see you again."

Bill Hawkins smiled a greeting, pulling down on the brim of his cap. "Good afternoon, Mr. Burton."

Bill was of average height, lanky with a round nose and bushy brows. From their brief interaction the day before, Daniel thought he seemed to be a listener instead of a man who spoke too freely, the sort that immediately earned a person's trust. "What brings you to town today?" Daniel asked. He was pleased to have someone to talk to in the unfamiliar place.

Bill looked worried, perhaps fearing Daniel was thinking to turn him into the authorities for being away from his assigned position at Sarah Hills. He raised his chin in the direction of the bridge leading to the women's factory. "I've authorization. A ticket from Miss Whitaker, sir. Today's the day I visit my wife. Her workday ends at three o'clock."

Daniel was surprised. Not that it was surprising to know the man had a wife. Bill Hawkins seemed to be quite a regular person. But one considered a man differently when one realized the man was a husband. For some reason it made him seem all the more dependable.

Daniel looked at his pocket watch. "Then you've still over an hour. Perhaps you'd allow me to buy you a meal?"

Bill blinked, opening his eyes wide. He pulled back his chin. "I'd not want to impose on ya like that, sir."

Daniel removed his hat, pushing his hand through his damp hair. He suddenly felt exhausted. "Mr. Hawkins, it has been nearly a year since I took a meal with a friend in a pub. I am hungry and tired and within a four-thousand mile radius, acquainted with close to eight people. And as you are one of them, I'd be extremely grateful for the company."

Bill's lip lifted in what Daniel thought was the equivalent of a smile. His heavy brows relaxed. "In that case, sir, I thank you. But I should recommend Freemason's Arms Inn." He pointed up Back Street to a brick building. "'S the most popular place in town."

Daniel followed him to the hotel. Once they were inside, he inhaled the familiar smells of smoke, food, and drink and heard the sounds of conversation, clanking dishes, and laughter, which he imagined must be the same at any public house in the world. Women in aprons moved among the wooden tables carrying drinks and smiling at the patrons, some of which were red-coated officers; others looked to be gentlemen. Still others were typical working men with dusty boots, tanned faces, and worn coats. It seemed people of all types frequented Freemason's Arms.

Daniel and Bill took a table near a window. He appreciated that Bill was a quiet person, a comfortable companion that allowed a man to enjoy the atmosphere and eat his meal without too much chatter. As he ate, Daniel listened to the blend of accents: Welsh, Scottish, Irish, and the distinct inflection of those born in the colony.

"Your wife, you say," Daniel began, once their dishes were cleared away and their drinks refilled. "She works at the factory?"

"Aye, that she does. Her name's Winnie. She's a weaver."

Daniel leaned back in his chair. He studied the liquid in his cup for a moment, unsure of exactly how to frame his next question. "I don't mean to sound rude, but I'd been led to believe that even government men are permitted to live with their families." He spoke carefully, hoping not to offend and using the more polite term for *convict*.

Bill shifted. His finger tapped on the base of his cup. "Aye, that is true, Mr. Burton." He kept his gaze firmly on his drink. "But it depends on the employer, you see."

Daniel leaned his arm on the table, feeling a wave of indignation rise hot inside him. "Are you saying Miss Whitaker doesn't allow you to cohabitate with your wife?"

"No, that's not it at all." Bill's eyes darted to the side, and his face paled. "I'll not speak ill of my mistress. Treats me fairly, she does. Every week on Thursday, I leave after half day and visit my Winnie."

Daniel could tell the man was worried about being overheard, so Daniel kept his voice low. He didn't like to pry but felt a need to understand not only the situation of the convicts but also the character of his new neighbor. What could possibly be her justification for not allowing a man to dwell with his own wife? "But Winnie is unassigned, is she not? She could easily live with you at Sarah Hills."

Bill scratched his cheek. "Aye, sir, but 'tis more to it, you see. The factory's not just for unassigned women. It's for ladies what are expecting babies or them who have small children. I've a daughter, Mr. Burton. Most employers don't take on women with children. Keeps 'em from working."

"That is preposterous," Daniel said. "The woman is separating a family. It's utterly intolerable."

Bill's eyes were wide with worry. "Sir, if you please. When I was assigned to Sarah Hills, it was the aunt that made the arrangement. Miss Whitaker's only taken full control of the farm these last two years, since her aunt died. She's been a fair mistress, sir. More than fair." Bill's brows were pulled together. The man looked uneasy, and Daniel realized he needed to temper his reaction.

"I am sorry. I am just learning the way of things here. Do not fear; I'll not breathe a word of what you've said to anybody."

"Thank you, sir."

Daniel slid back his chair and crossed an ankle over the other knee, hoping to look relaxed, even though inside he was fuming. Perhaps he could imagine himself in Bill's shoes because his fate could have so easily been the same. How dare anyone separate a family just because a child was inconvenient? His impression of Miss Sarah Whitaker had just taken a plunge into the realm of his thoughts reserved for self-centered tyrants. He took a drink. "Tell me about your daughter, then, Mr. Hawkins."

Bill's face softened into a smile. "Trudy's bright as a new penny, she is. She'd talk and sing the whole day long if her mama allowed it. A happy girl, that one."

"Is there a school for the children near the factory?"

Bill's smile faded as quickly as it had appeared. "No, sir. She'll be taken to the orphanage once she's four. Then Winnie can be assigned to work duty."

Daniel's stomach froze. "They take away the children?"

Bill gave a tight nod. "Until their parents can care for 'em, you see, until their time's served."

"How much of your sentence do you have left?"

"I've three years. Winnie's five."

Daniel tapped his finger on his lips. The idea of a child being taken from her mother made the mutton and potatoes he'd just eaten feel like lead inside him. Was there nothing that could be done? Could he perhaps help this family?

"Is there hope of reassignment for you? Perhaps to someone who will employ Winnie and allow your entire family to remain together? Is that a possibility?"

"Only if another private employer offers and the local superintendent agrees to the change."

Daniel continued to tap his lip with his forefinger. If Sarah Whitaker was angry with him before, how would she react if he were to offer for her foreman? But the desire to help was so strong, he felt he couldn't ignore it. This family needed him. He was in a position to change their lives for the better—to do what they couldn't do themselves—just as the duke had done for him.

He put both feet flat on the ground and leaned his forearms on his knees. "Bill Hawkins," he leaned his head to the side and waited for the man to meet his gaze, "I'm looking to hire a housekeeper, and I also need someone who knows how to raise sheep. If you and Winnie would consider working for me, I'll speak to the convict superintendent today."

Chapter 4

SARAH HELD HER TEACUP IN her lap, crossing her ankles beneath the chair on the shady lawn in front of the Government House. She dabbed a napkin on her mouth to make sure there were no remaining crumbs from the biscuit she'd eaten and tipped her head as she regarded her companions. She reminded herself how fortunate she was to be invited to tea by the governor's wife with a small group of local ladies. Sarah kept her back straight—Aunt Hortensia would have been proud—and tried to hold a pleasant expression on her face while wondering how much longer until she could graciously make an excuse to leave.

She looked across the patch of lawn, green against the brown dirt that covered the rest of town. The Government House was situated on a rise, giving a splendid view. From here, she could see the river winding between clusters of trees. In the distance, the rocky mountains with their green slopes were stunning against a clear blue sky.

Smoke rose from the blacksmith's forge in town. The lack of a breeze left it hanging over the grouping of wooden structures and stone houses that made up Parramatta. Above, a crow cawed in the large gum tree that gave shade to the women. It was answered by the shrill notes of a caged parakeet on the porch. She watched a tall crane stalk across the grass. Spring was in full bloom in Parramatta. Geraniums and other bright flowers grew in the beds surrounding the house. Orchards bore blossoms on their branches, filling the air with perfume, and tall Norfolk Pines towered like sentinels above the thick canopy of the gum trees.

Elizabeth Macquarie was a fine hostess. She served real British tea instead of the usual colonial brew of "sweet tea" made from eucalyptus leaves. As she poured out, she spoke of her new son, born only a few months earlier, and of the changes she planned to make to the residence during the summer. The other ladies nodded and commented. Sarah pretended to listen to the conversation, but her mind had wandered back to her farm. Being away for an entire day this time of year was extremely inconvenient. Not just for her, but the journey into town had required two men to accompany her, along with Molly, her lady's maid. Tom drove the carriage, and Walter rode along with him to ensure they weren't set upon by bushrangers or hostile aborigines.

She knew those remaining at the farm would have to compensate by working longer hours today. With new lambs and spring shearing, every person was needed. And now that Bill was gone . . .

She tightened her jaw as she remembered the frustration of returning from an unfruitful meeting with the colonial secretary in Sydney to find that Mr. Burton had not only taken the land she'd wanted but had appropriated her foreman as well. It seemed her new neighbor was determined to make himself her nemesis. She reached forward and snatched up another biscuit, biting into it a bit more forcefully than was necessary.

"Have you made the acquaintance of Mr. Daniel Burton?"

At the question, she started and nearly choked. Her gaze snapped toward the woman who'd spoken, and Sarah realized her face had flushed with heat. But an innocently curious expression convinced Sarah that Dorthea Iverson hadn't seen her thoughts.

Dorthea was not the sort of person to have a hidden agenda in her words. She was a young woman close to Sarah's age, married a few years earlier to a lieutenant in the local regiment. Sarah relaxed and chewed the crumbly bite. The mention of the very person she was thinking of was only a coincidence. Hardly unusual within such a small society. Dorthea's brows rose as she took a sip of tea.

"Oh yes." Minerva Pierce shifted her ample backside in the delicate armchair, reaching herself for another biscuit. Minerva's husband was the supervisor of the local government farm, and she had taken on herself to be the supervisor of the local gossip. "What a charming young man. And so handsome. Mr. Pierce and I were introduced to him after Reverend Marsden's service on Sunday. I think we are likely to become good friends with Mr. Burton. Mr. Pierce is already talking about inviting him for a 'roo hunt with the officers next week—"

"Have you met him, Sarah?" Dorthea cut off what was certain to be a flood of words by Minerva. A small tick of her brow was the only indication of a shared annoyance with their companion's tendency to chatter long after anyone had stopped listening.

"Yes, I've met him." Sarah said. She brushed crumbs from her fingers.

A servant came from the house and whispered to their hostess. Elizabeth excused herself to attend to the baby.

Dorthea's gaze hadn't left Sarah's face. "He is very handsome, don't you think?"

"He?" Sarah asked, turning her attention to folding her napkin.

"Mr. Burton." Dorthea tipped her head, lowering her eyes to half-mast as if she didn't believe for one second that Sarah had forgotten who they were speaking about. "A land owner, polite, unattached—even you can have no objections, Miss Whitaker."

"He's American," Sarah said.

"Well, then *that* is surely his only flaw. If D'Arcy Wentworth—a highwayman, if you can believe it—can be the new Sydney police chief, surely you can see past your handsome neighbor's unfortunate origins." Dorthea winked.

Sarah opened her mouth to deliver a witty comeback at her friend's audacity—the mere implication made her fume. As if she would *ever* consider that man to be the slightest bit acceptable.

"Mr. Pierce and I think Governor Macquarie has lost his mind," Minerva broke in before Sarah had a chance to speak. Her eyes darted toward the door Elizabeth had just entered. "Appointing such a man as police chief. We are utterly furious that he's assigned thieves to serve as magistrates. Did you know former convicts dine here at the Government House? They own fine homes and land." She shifted again, making the wooden chair creak ominously and leaned forward, no doubt worried her words would be overheard. "They think themselves worthy of equal status with the rest of us. Really, it is too much to be borne. You, of all people should be of the same mind, Miss Whitaker. After what you've endured . . ."

Sarah felt a flush of heat in her cheeks at the reminder. "I—" She realized she had twisted Mrs. Macquarie's napkin into a tight ball. She smoothed it on her legs. "We should be wary when trusting anyone." Her answer was trite, but she feared if she said more, she'd unleash a torrent of angry words. Or emotion would get the better of her, which would be equally uncomfortable. Best to remain quiet.

She'd met D'Arcy Wentworth and thought him a polite, capable man, but that didn't mean she trusted him. As a child, she'd believed all people to be inherently good, but now . . . Now she bestowed her trust but seldomly, being especially cautious around those who'd made a career out of deception and been sent to the penal colony. It was a lesson she'd learned repeatedly over the years. Those who seemed to have her best interest in mind were just waiting for a chance to take advantage. She'd found the truth of this painfully for the last time two years earlier. Now she trusted very few—and never criminals, no matter what the governor might say.

Sarah folded her hands together and gave the ladies a polite smile. "I am sure the governor did not just appoint Mr. Wentworth without giving the decision proper consideration."

Minerva Pierce gave a snort. "What consideration would possibly lead to such a reckless decision? It is insufferable, I tell you."

Dorthea rolled her eyes when Minerva looked down at the plate of biscuits. "The governor believes in reform, Minerva. When a person's time is served, their record is clean."

"Once a criminal, always a criminal, Mr. Pierce and I agree on that fact. We utterly refuse to do business with felons, and we recommend you do the same."

Another tick of Dorthea's brow had Sarah fighting to hold back a smile. They had both heard rumors about Mr. Pierce's dealings with convicts, especially those ladies with less than honorable morals. Sarah avoided the man and his leers at all costs. Thank goodness for her friend's humor. In truth, former convicts owned more than half the property and private businesses in the colony. If the free settlers really did refuse to do business with them, the economy would collapse. But from experience, she and Dorthea knew Minerva Pierce was more interested in gossip and indignation than business reasoning, and so neither posed an argument.

"This is why it's so nice to have people like Mr. Burton come into the neighborhood. Respectable men." Dorthea's smile bordered on a smirk as she wagged her brows. "I wager he'll dance with you at the governor's ball next week, Miss Whitaker."

"We will see." Sarah lifted a shoulder in a shrug. She was glad for the change of topic, although she wished it hadn't moved in the direction Dorthea had chosen. The heat threatened to rise back in her cheeks. She hadn't told her friend how Daniel had asked for a dance nor how she'd felt a connection to the man that day at the creek. And she was glad only Bill knew of how foolishly she'd acted.

"Mr. Pierce and I plan to have Mr. Daniel Burton to supper. He must be lonely with only servants and sheep to talk to all day," Minerva said.

How tragic, indeed. Sarah closed her eyes and tried not to let her irritation show. She didn't mention that on her farm, she was every bit as isolated as Mr. Daniel Burton. And far too busy to feel lonely. But, she reminded herself, she was perfectly happy living alone. A fact that seemed unfathomable to the ladies with whom she associated.

Sarah took another bite of her sweet biscuit. She was used to the married women trying to play matchmaker, especially now that she lived alone. It seemed these women couldn't be satisfied while there were still unattached persons among their acquaintance, making it their personal business to resolve the travesty.

Sarah had entertained various offers during the last few years. With twenty men to every woman in this part of the colony, she'd had her pick of suitors, but each man she'd seriously considered had promised to take over the maintenance of the farm so she could concentrate on throwing garden parties, serving tea, and having babies. Even amid her protests that she loved managing the farm, they'd all wanted her to change.

Why must she become a different person just to be a wife? Why couldn't a man see that she managed the farm because it was her duty, a legacy begun and left to her by her father? It gave her purpose and made her feel close to a father taken too soon from her life. She did it because she loved it not because there was no husband available to do the work.

Sarah was certain that a man didn't exist who would understand her desire to be something so unladylike as a farm manager, and so she resigned herself to being an improvement project for the married women.

She looked up when Elizabeth returned, glad for a distraction. Sarah set her tea cup on the low table and spoke before anyone brought up Mr. Burton again. "Mrs. Macquarie, tell us about the Great Western Road over the Blue Mountains." Sarah was fascinated and a little frightened by the idea of the colony spreading to the areas beyond the ring of mountains that surrounded Port Jackson and Sydney Town.

Elizabeth seemed happy to describe her husband's project to settle the farmland to the west of the mountains and the expedition that had discovered a path through the deep gorges and thick scrub to the arable land beyond.

As she listened to the women talk about a proposed settlement in Bathurst, Sarah saw a trio of red-coated officers approaching the house.

She recognized two of them. Lieutenant Mason and Major Blackhurst of the Seventy-Third Regiment were long-time residents of the colony, but the third man was a stranger.

When the officers drew near, the ladies rose.

Elizabeth held out a hand in welcome. "Good afternoon, gentlemen. The governor told me you would be meeting with him today."

"Thank you, Mrs. Macquarie," Lieutenant Mason said, clicking his heels together sharply and bowing. "If I might introduce you to Sergeant Conall Stewart, lately arrived on the *Bollerophon*."

Elizabeth greeted Sergeant Stewart, and the ladies curtseyed in turn as they were introduced.

"From whence did you arrive, Sergeant?" Minerva asked.

"Most recently from Portsmouth, madam. But before tha', my regiment fought at Mauritius."

Sarah liked hearing the way he pronounced the name of the French island with his thick Scottish brogue. She studied him. Sergeant Stewart was tall with wide shoulders and a broad chin. He carried himself with an air of authority befitting of his rank, but there was gentleness about his eyes that made Sarah think he was a kind person.

"I heard a plot was discovered in Mauritius." Dorthea pushed her hand against her heart and leaned forward as if she might be overheard. "The emperor planned to invade Sydney. We owe you our thanks, Sergeant."

"Aye, I've heard the rumors as well, Mrs. Iverson. But I'm afraid I can't verify. You'd need to ask the commissioned officers. My job was tellin' the men which way to shoot."

"And are you from Scotland, Sergeant?" Minerva asked.

Sarah nearly rolled her eyes at the stupidity of the question. She didn't think the sergeant could act any more obviously Scottish if he carried bagpipes and wore a tartan kilt.

Sergeant Stewart smiled, but his eyes dimmed the slightest bit. "Aye, though 's been ten years since I've seen me Highlands. If only we'd defeated Napoleon himself, instead o' a small French island, I might be home by now."

"But at least he's on Elba," Sarah said.

"And with any luck, there he'll remain." Sergeant Stewart nodded. He glanced at the other officers.

Major Blackhurst tipped his head toward the house. Sergeant Stewart bowed again, and the men excused themselves to meet with the governor.

Sarah thought about what an amiable man Sergeant Stewart was. Surely he would be at the governor's ball next week, and perhaps she would have another opportunity to talk with him. It was nice to meet a new person who didn't seem determined to destroy her life. Maybe Mr. Burton could take a page from the sergeant's book.

She sat back in her chair. The sergeant was no doubt acquainted with Daniel Burton. They had arrived on the same ship. She wondered what the marine thought about him.

Sarah pressed her lips together, annoyed. Again her mind had turned to her neighbor without her permission. She'd have to watch her thoughts more closely because thinking of Daniel Burton and his deceptively handsome smile and teasing words had the unwelcome effect of making Mrs. Macquarie's imported tea roil inside Sarah's stomach.

Chapter 5

DANIEL WOKE EARLY, USING THE faint light in the purple predawn sky to keep from tripping as he found his musket and made his way from his partially constructed house. Walls and a section of roof were the extent of the shelter, but it was enough to keep him mostly dry during the spring rainfall. He estimated the house would be complete in a few weeks—or at least watertight.

As he walked down the path toward the forest, past the bark shelters of his workers and the wooden shack Bill had built for his family, he placed his feet carefully, trying to be silent. In just a few hours, the camp would be a flurry of activity, and he wanted the others to sleep as long as they could. Winnie would wake soon and move into the kitchen building to bake bread.

He smiled as he thought of the small family. Bill and Winnie Hawkins were hard workers, and not a day passed when he didn't think how much easier they made his life. Winnie prepared marvelous meals with the primitive rations and facilities. Bill had directed the planting in the fields and prepared a schedule for the sheep tenders, instructing them in duties Daniel did not even know existed. He could not have begun to manage his farm without the man's expertise.

And Trudy. He felt a tug on his heart as he thought of the little girl with her wispy blonde hair and rosy cheeks. She was pure joy. When she saw him, she always called, "Mr. Burt!" and ran to embrace him as if he were her dearest friend. Her laughter brought smiles to the faces of even the most surly workers.

The atmosphere of the camp had altered as soon as Trudy and Winnie had arrived. Their feminine influence changed the mood of the group. He would never underestimate the effect of a woman's presence. The workers were well behaved and courteous now, whereas before they'd been rough men, cursing and brawling at every opportunity. They all took particular care to keep Trudy safe, checking for hourglass spiders and venomous snakes where she played.

Seeing Trudy fall asleep in her father's arms after supper warmed Daniel's heart, and any uncertainties he'd had about bringing the family to his property vanished. They loved one another, needed one another, and knowing he'd been the means of keeping them together eased a bit of guilt for his misdeeds. As he worked each day, his mind had begun to develop a theory. Perhaps by improving the lives of others, he might begin to alleviate some of his remorse. Maybe helping those in need was a path to self-forgiveness.

His stomach growled, and he turned toward the forest. He'd purchased essentials at the dry goods store in town, but they were basic: flour, sugar, rum, salted pork. Physical labor had begun taking a toll on his men, and he noticed some had become lethargic. If his workers were to maintain their strength, they needed meat. And with the equipment and additional horses he'd had to purchase, he couldn't afford to slaughter one of his sheep.

He stepped into the darker shadows beneath the leafy canopy, his mind still deep in thought as he planned his strategy. Hunting in Australia couldn't be much different from shooting pheasants on the duke's park. Same basic principles, he figured. He hoped to find a kangaroo or another large mammal, but fowl would be welcome as well. Listening to hear where the larger birds might be roosting, he kept his gaze on the canopy above him, So when he rounded a tree trunk and came face to face with a man, he jerked back, and his heart raced. The man's skin was dark—nearly black—and Daniel had almost collided with him in the shadows.

The aboriginal man's eyes grew wide, and Daniel realized he had been startled as well. He took a step back, hefting a long, pointed spear. In his other hand, he gripped a thick wooden wedge, bent at an angle. Both weapons looked equally capable of killing a person.

"Wait." Daniel held up a hand, realizing the man was staring at his musket. "Listen, I've no intention of hurting you." He bent down slowly, set the gun on the ground, then raised his hands, palms forward. "I'm just looking for food. Sorry to have surprised you." He was shaking.

The man pointed his wedge-shaped weapon toward the gun and grunted, a noise that sounded like a mixture of a question and a threat.

"For hunting food." Daniel touched his fingertips to his mouth. "I'm hungry."

The aborigine man stared at him for a long moment, his spear cocked back, the tip aimed directly at Daniel's chest.

Daniel's heart pounded so forcefully he thought it might give out before the spear had a chance to pierce it. His fingers itched to grab the musket, but he knew he wouldn't be able to lift it and fire before the man skewered him. He'd seen a few of the dark-skinned natives in Sydney and been told they weren't allowed to carry weapons, but Bill had warned him that the aborigines in the mountains distrusted white men. Was this man a member of one of the fierce tribes?

They stared at each other across the dimly lit space with only the sound of their breathing and the buzz of insects intruding on the silence. Finally, the man lowered his weapon.

Daniel's shoulders sagged in relief.

The man touched his fingertips to his mouth. "*Bada?*"

"That's right, food." Daniel repeated the motion. He placed a hand on his chest and tried to look as nonthreatening as possible and keep the trembling out of his voice. "My name is Daniel."

"Dan-ya?"

"Yes. Daniel." He patted his chest for emphasis.

"Charrah." The man placed a hand on his own chest.

"Pleased to meet you, Charrah." Daniel held out his hand to shake, then wondered if it was the appropriate action. Hopefully the man had had interactions with white settlers and knew the offer of a handshake was not a threat.

Charrah took his hand, holding firmly as he looked into Daniel's face. Daniel felt as if he were being sized up.

"Dan-ya." He pointed to the musket, then pointed forward with the wedge-shaped tool. He said something and made a motion for Daniel to follow.

Daniel clutched his gun, walking behind and looking over his shoulder to see if they were alone. Charrah showed immense trust, turning his back on a stranger with a weapon. The idea that there might be more people hiding out of sight made Daniel uneasy. But if they were there, he had to trust that they wouldn't hurt him. And his best chance was remaining on good terms with Charrah.

Charrah walked on bare feet over the forest floor, making no sound. Daniel thought each of his own steps sounded like cannon blasts in the quiet. He tried walking on his toes but still cracked sticks and rustled leaves. A few times Charrah glanced back, shaking his head.

When they emerged into a clearing, Daniel realized the sun was close to rising. He could see his companion clearly. Charrah was bare except for an apron of animal skins tied around his hips. He was perhaps a few inches shorter than Daniel, well built, with lean muscle and an intelligent face. Although his teeth looked healthy, he was missing a front tooth, leaving a dark gap in the row of white. Clay was smeared over his chest, legs, and arms, and dried to a gray powder. Daniel wondered if it was to keep away mosquitoes or perhaps protect his skin from the sun's rays. A mass of black wiry curls spread from his head and followed his cheek line down to his chin.

His appearance reminded Daniel a little of the African slaves sold at the Exchange Building in Charleston. The color of Charrah's skin was the same, but that is where the resemblance ended. He stood tall and unafraid. In the eyes of the slaves headed to tobacco and cotton plantations, Daniel had seen defeat and confusion. And fear.

Charrah seemed to be studying Daniel as well. He wondered what the man saw. Could he tell Daniel was uncertain? That he had no idea how to survive in this land, how to manage a farm? Could he see that Daniel was not the man he pretended to be?

He shifted his weight under the man's scrutiny.

Charrah pointed toward the trees directly above them. "*Weerambi.*"

Daniel looked up, squinting as he tried to make sense of the dark masses on the thin upper branches. Most were moving. They looked like large birds but sat on the branches strangely. One opened its wings, and he realized they were hanging upside down. Not birds at all, then. Enormous bats, the size of large rabbits.

Charrah spoke, waving toward the bats.

Daniel lifted his musket, aiming upward, but Charrah rattled off a string of words, waving hands in a gesture for Daniel to stop.

He lowered the gun.

Charrah showed Daniel the wooden tool. Up close, he could see it was smooth, bent at an angle with tapered edges. The flat sides were painted with black and white designs. Charrah pulled back his arm, flicked his wrist, and threw the weapon. It spun upward end over end, making a whirring noise before it hit one of the bats with a thump. The animal fell to the earth.

"Weerambi." Charrah grinned and ran to fetch his weapon and the carcass. When he returned, he held the wedge of wood to Daniel. "*Bou-mar-rang.*"

Daniel took the bou-mar-rang, hefted it to check the weight, and threw it upward. It flew nearly as high as the bats. Then dropped.

Daniel grimaced, scratching his throat. Using the tool was more difficult than he'd assumed.

Charrah gave a flat look that was recognizable in any language then ran forward, picking up the weapon and returning. He lifted Daniel's hand, putting the bou-mar-rang's long side against his palm, nodding to make sure Daniel understood that this was the proper way to hold it. Charrah bent his wrist quickly, motioning for his student to mimic the movement.

Daniel obeyed.

Charrah said more words, standing with his left side toward the trees and indicating for Daniel to copy his stance. He pulled back his right arm then inspected Daniel's position, showing him how to move his arm forward, elbow first, then at the last moment flick his wrist as he released the weapon.

Daniel practiced his form a few times until Charrah nodded for him to throw. He flung the bou-mar-rang into the trees. The flick of his wrist sent it whirling end over end, until it smacked into a bat, dropping the animal from the branch.

"Weerambi." Charrah lifted the animal and brought it to Daniel with a grin. He spoke another string of words in an excited voice, motioning to Daniel and nodding.

Daniel couldn't help but smile at the man's praise, even though he could not understand a word of it. He was reminded of a fencing instructor in Charleston, an equally cheerful man who took pleasure in seeing his students perform a well-executed maneuver.

Daniel and Charrah took turns throwing the bou-mar-rang, which Daniel now understood was not just a strangely shaped wedge of wood but an instrument crafted with precise balance. He realized if he had shot at the bats with his gun, the report of the musket would have frightened the animals away, but this silent weapon worked perfectly. How much could he learn from people who had survived on this land before the British ever arrived? Charrah would be a valuable friend to have.

Once they'd each killed four bats, Daniel followed his friend's example and lifted the animals by the feet. Carrying them along with his heavy musket was a bit tricky, and he wished he'd thought to bring a bag or some string to make it easier.

The two walked back through the thicker forest, and Daniel felt a swelling in his chest. He was immensely grateful to Charrah. He'd never have thought of shooting bats or even looking for them. If he'd managed to stumble upon them and recognize them for what they were, he'd have been lucky to hit one with a musket ball before the others flew away. He felt the familiar unease of owing a favor, wishing he knew how to repay the man.

Charrah stepped into a space between the trees, stopping suddenly. He tipped his head to the side as if listening then turned to Daniel. He rattled off a string of words, his brows drawing together in a way that looked as if he were worried. He glanced over his shoulder then back to Daniel. His gaze dropped to the gun.

Daniel felt a spike of fear. Were they in danger? He dropped the bats and lifted the musket in both hands.

The motion seemed to alarm Charrah. He pushed the gun down, his eyes wide, and he spoke quickly in a soft voice. He rubbed a spot over his brow in a nervous gesture. "*Magura*," he said.

"Magura?" Daniel shook his head, not understanding his companion's behavior. "I'm sorry I don't—"

"Magura." Charrah said the word slowly, then dropped the bats and made a waving motion with one hand. He pointed toward Daniel's farm then wiggled his hand again. "Magura." He touched his fingers to his mouth. "Ngununy." Then pointed again toward the farm.

"Fish?" Daniel said. "You want fish?" He copied the man's gestures.

Charrah nodded. A bit of the tension left his face.

"Of course." Daniel nodded then pointed in the direction of the pond. "Magura. You are welcome to fish all you like."

Charrah looked relieved. He glanced back at the forest and grimaced.

Daniel was still trying to make sense of his friend's strange behavior as he bent down and picked up the bats. When he straightened and lifted his gaze, he took an involuntary step back.

A ring of dark-skinned people surrounded them, brandishing spears.

Daniel's insides froze. How had they all approached without him hearing?

Charrah stepped in front of Daniel and spoke rapidly to the group. Daniel heard his name in the torrent of words.

A man with wild gray hair, a thick beard, and a fierce scar on his face spoke in a low voice. He pointed at Daniel's gun and scowled. The others muttered.

Daniel felt his pulse racing. His muscles were clenched so tightly it was painful. His gaze darted around the group of aborigines. He counted twelve men with sharp spears pointing directly at him. Others—men, women, and children—stood behind them. Some looked frightened, some angry. Daniel's mind churned frantically, but he knew escape was impossible.

Charrah continued speaking. He turned to Daniel and made a downward motion with his hand. His expression clearly told him not to try anything foolhardy.

Daniel set down his weapon. He realized his chance of survival depended on the man's ability to convince these people that he meant them no harm. He wished he had any idea of what Charrah was saying. From his motions, he appeared to be describing their hunt. He continued speaking, pointing toward the pond. The others glanced in that direction. In Charrah's flood of indecipherable noises, Daniel recognized the word *magura. Fish.* The older man's scowl softened, and his face grew thoughtful instead of angry.

Charrah was apparently telling the people that they could fish on the pond. Daniel's tension relieved a slight bit. Charrah was a smart man. A brilliant negotiator.

The man who appeared to be the leader gave a grunt and spoke a word in a bark. The others lowered their spears.

Daniel let out a trembling breath. He couldn't help but admire Charrah's foresight in finding an advantage when he knew his people were approaching. By making a deal, he had demonstrated that an alliance was beneficial to both parties. Daniel felt a chill when he thought he could have very well come upon them on his own this morning. Without Charrah's intervention, he would have surely been killed.

Charrah motioned for Daniel to join him. "Obing," he said, indicating the older man.

Daniel held out his hand, which he was proud to note wasn't shaking. "A pleasure to meet you, Obing. My name is Daniel."

Charrah gave another flat look that Daniel interpreted as, *You know he can't understand you, so just keep it simple.* He put a hand on Daniel's shoulder. "Dan-ya."

Obing took Daniel's hand. His dark eyes peered from a weathered face, furrowed with wrinkles. "Dan-ya," he said in his low voice. Obing's expression did not change. He dipped his chin the slightest bit then released Daniel's hand.

Daniel thought the man would not be convinced of his peaceful intent with words alone, not when he was carrying a gun in their homeland. He made a note to speak to the men at his camp, instruct them to behave civilly to the native aborigines, not only for their own survival but for Charrah's sake. The man had taken a risk befriending Daniel, and he could not let that trust result in harm to his new friend's people.

The others gathered around. Most stood silently, while others spoke in low voices. One man fiddled with the buttons on Daniel's jacket. Another kicked his boot with a bare toe.

"Dan-ya."

He turned when Charrah spoke his name and saw that a woman stood beside his friend. She held an infant in her arms.

Charrah touched her shoulder, and she stepped forward. She lifted her gaze with a shy smile.

"Kiturra," Charrah said.

Daniel didn't need a translation to understand who this woman was to Charrah. The soft way he said her name and the expression of pride as he looked at the baby said more than any language could. Daniel felt a pang of something very close to jealousy, but it was overtaken by happiness for his friend. "Hello, Kiturra." He gave a bow, which elicited strange looks from the other members of the group.

Charrah cocked a brow in a look of good-natured tolerance at the white man's strange ways.

Daniel smiled sheepishly. He was starting to become accustomed to the man's dry sense of humor and found that he was pleased to have a friend. Even if their communication was limited. He liked Charrah and wished he had more to offer in thanks than a pond full of boney fish.

Obing said something, and the others turned to go. A few lifted their hands in farewell, but most just disappeared into the trees. Seconds later, only Charrah and Daniel remained in the clearing.

Charrah picked up the musket and handed it to Daniel. He carried two of Daniel's bats. The others must have taken his away. They walked silently until they reached the edge of the forest.

Charrah handed him the bats and turned as if to leave.

"Wait." Daniel wished he could say anything his friend would understand. He owed a huge debt, not only for his life but for the hunting lesson as well. "Thank you, Charrah."

Charrah's squint indicated his puzzlement at the words.

Daniel set the animals and weapon down. He took Charrah's hand and clasped his shoulder, looking directly into the man's face. "I owe you my thanks. And I will find a way to repay you."

The man seemed to understand the sincerity of Daniel's words. His own expression became solemn, and he placed a hand on Daniel's shoulder.

Without words, the men made a pledge to one another. The moment was witnessed by only the two of them, but Daniel knew they both felt the significance of their promise. Charrah had proven in only a few hours to be a loyal friend, and Daniel vowed to himself that he would never break the man's trust.

Chapter 6

SARAH REINED IN HER HORSE at the top of the rocky hill at the edge of her property where she had a good view of the road to Parramatta. The day before, she'd sent two workers to collect a shipment of lumber and cut stones, and she was anxious for it to arrive. The new storehouse she'd planned needed to be completed within the week in order to be ready to store fleece from spring shearing. The men she'd sent had been employees for years, and she'd never had any trouble with them, but she felt her usual uncertainty about whether they'd return. Would they escape into the hills? Sell the lumber and make off with the gold? Should she have gone herself? Well, worrying about them now would do no good. All she could do was wait.

She twisted in the saddle, looking back at a flock spread over the meadow. From her vantage point, she could see across the hills, dotted with sheep, to the smooth brown fields where workers were planting barley, maize, and wheat. Turning the horse, she squinted at a black wisp of smoke that rose from the other side of the land. The sight of smoke always sent a chill through her, even though she knew this fire was nothing to be alarmed about. Every spring a crew was sent out to burn away some of the thick dingo scrub that encroached on the grassy hills. The dense undergrowth stretched for miles, providing cover for wild dogs that preyed on the flocks.

Sarah breathed in, feeling a swell of satisfaction at how smoothly the farm was running. This time of year was especially demanding. The schedules she'd made and the improvements to the routines seemed to be working perfectly. And Tom had filled the role of foreman splendidly.

The view of Sarah Hills, green hills surrounded by forests and craggy mountains, made her heart feel like it was inflating. The landscape was striking; the smooth blue sky only seemed to magnify the colors and contrasting textures of the earth beneath. She felt a connection to her father here. She considered how he would have managed different concerns and felt close to him as she worked the land. Had he stood in this very spot and gazed over the property, marveling at the wonder of the prospect?

She looked back to the hard-packed road and saw a cloud of dust in the distance. Her mind moved back to the matters at hand. The workers had made good time. She squinted, looking closer, and instead of a bullock dray within the dust cloud, she saw only one red-coated man on horseback. Sarah studied him as he rode closer. The familiar feeling of suspicion rose inside her, setting her nerves on edge and increasing her awareness. For a soldier to ride alone over the remote roads was unusual. Typically they rode in groups on official colony business or even heading off to the outback on a 'roo hunt. What could be one man's reasons for traveling alone? And who was he?

As he rode toward her, she compared his features with the officers she knew—sandy hair, broad shoulders. Finally, he drew near enough that she recognized him as the man she'd met a few days earlier at the Government House. Sergeant Conall Stewart. Was he coming to call on her? A flurry of uncertainty moved inside her. She was unprepared for a caller—not only was she sweaty, dressed in trousers with her hair braided, and had no refreshment ready—she'd not mentally prepared herself to entertain. Her experience with gentlemen courting had left an unpleasant taste in her mouth, and she would have liked to have time to make arrangements, consider what to say, and maybe invite someone else to join them.

The sergeant raised his hand in a greeting.

His presence could mean news from town, or perhaps he was indeed coming to call. Either way, she should find out his reasoning for traveling this far into the back country. She waved back and rode carefully down the rocky hill toward him, reminding herself how she'd enjoyed speaking with him a few days earlier. She had no reason not to trust the sergeant, but she reminded herself to be guarded. Even the most seemingly trustworthy person could end up seeking to exploit her or her money.

He swept off his black shako hat and bent forward in the saddle when they met. "Miss Whitaker, I didna recognize ye."

"Sergeant Stewart, how nice to see you again."

"What are ye doin' so far away from Parramatta?" He smiled and returned his hat.

His question surprised her. "I live here, Sergeant Stewart." She waved a hand to the land behind her, wishing she didn't feel a sting of disappointment. He hadn't come to see her after all. "What brings you out into the bush? It's not safe on the road alone, you know."

He shrugged and let a smirk pull up his lips. "Not to worry, miss. I've a reliable weapon." He patted the pistol at his waist. "I've come to visit a friend, Mr. Daniel Burton. Are ye acquainted with him?"

Sarah felt the smile fall off her face. She turned her eyes down, pretending to be adjusting something on her horse's saddle. Naturally the man had come to visit Daniel. It seemed everyone in the colony was enamored with him. "Yes. I have met Mr. Burton."

"And am I close to his land then? His directions were a bit vague."

Sarah nodded, pointing to where the road curved. "The road splits a bit farther ahead and crosses a bridge. His property is just on the other side. You'll see a large pond past the trees."

"Aye, his letter did mention a pond. I'm much obliged, Miss Whitaker." He looked forward along the road then up to the hill she'd ridden from.

He didn't voice the question, but she thought he was wondering why she'd been watching the road. "I'm waiting for a shipment today, Sergeant. Did you pass a wagon carrying building supplies? I expected them to have returned by now."

He squinted and nodded. "Aye, they're not far behind. Perhaps half an hour. The men were resecurin' some o' the ropes. I offered assistance, but they assured me 'twas all in hand."

"Thank you."

He looked back up the hill, pointing with his chin. "A fine view o' the road from up there. Your land continues in tha' direction? Over the hills?"

"Yes."

He rose in the stirrups and moved his gaze over the area. "'Tis beautiful here. The grassy hills remind me o' the highlands. Though there's a definite lack o' fortress ruins."

"True." She smiled at his jest. "The oldest structures in the colony aren't yet thirty years old. The aboriginal natives don't construct dwellings."

"What are ye buildin' then?" Seeing her confused expression, he tipped his head back toward the road behind him. "With the lumber and stone?"

"A new storage barn. I hoped to have it finished before we started to shear—to keep the wool dry. The old one has a terribly leaky roof, and this one will be much closer to the road."

"Och, 'tis a pity. I hoped ye were plannin' to construct a mighty castle."

Sarah laughed. "I wouldn't even think to undertake such a project without asking for your advice first, Sergeant."

His face took on a solemn expression, though his eyes were merry. "I should hope not, lass."

Sarah smiled, quite comfortable with Sergeant Stewart. She glanced up the hill and then back to him. He didn't seem to be in a hurry to continue to Mr. Burton's, and his easy manner gave her courage. "Would you like to see Sarah Hills, Sergeant?"

"Sarah Hills?" His brows rose, and his eyes twinkled.

"Yes, my farm. My father named it before I came to the colony. Of course I wouldn't have—"

"'Tis a fine name." He spoke with a smile.

She felt her face burn red and was glad for the shade of her hat. She was acting extremely inappropriate, inviting a man to visit. She didn't get many opportunities for callers. She enjoyed the sergeant's conversation and hoped for a friendship with the man. But if she were to be truly honest with herself, a part of her wanted him to stay, to prefer her company to Daniel Burton's. A coil of shame twisted her stomach at the realization. "I don't mean to keep you if—"

He held up a hand to stop her words and leaned forward in his saddle. "I would love to see Sarah Hills, Miss Whitaker."

They rode up the rocky hill, leading their horses carefully around scraggy bushes and trees. Sergeant Stewart let out a low whistle once they reached the top and he could see the entire view.

Sarah couldn't help but grin. "The house and farm buildings are in that direction." She pointed toward the far end of the property, near the mountain foothills and untamed forest. "There's a road for wagons and carriages where the land is level, but it's much faster to ride over the hills on horseback." She waved her hand in another direction. "And over there are the crops, and of course, the sheep graze on the slopes and valleys." She was pleased to see Sergeant Stewart nodding as he took it all in.

The horses walked at a leisurely gait along the tops of the hills, stopping to sniff at tufts of grass growing between red rocks. Sarah and the sergeant chatted amiably about the farm and the surrounding area until finally a dust cloud on the road beneath announced the return of the lumber wagon.

The bullocks pulling the wagon lumbered along at their typical slow speed. Martin, the bullocky, lifted his hat and waved as they passed.

Sarah returned the wave, glad they'd finally arrived.

Sergeant Stewart frowned, following the road with his eyes. "How much farther is the access from here?"

"About a mile."

He twisted around and pointed. "And you've not considered making a road on that side o' the hills, near to the forest? 'Twould be much faster."

"I have, of course," Sarah said. "Until recently, the road didn't continue in that direction. But now with the new bridge, it would be possible." She pursed her lips and breathed out through her nose. "Those trees there, they line a creek marking the property boundary. The land on the other side belongs to Mr. Burton." She tried to keep the familiar frustration from showing on her face, but glancing at Sergeant Stewart, she could see he definitely noticed, though he pretended not to.

He urged his horse forward, and she rode next to him.

"A good man, that Daniel Burton. I've not met many better." Sergeant Stewart spoke in a conversational voice, as if the thought had just occurred to him.

Sarah wasn't sure how to respond. The sergeant was obviously attempting to make a point of defending his friend. And truly, Sarah knew his being granted the land was not his fault. Taking her foreman though . . . That was clearly ill-mannered, especially because it portrayed Sarah as a heartless supervisor for not permitting her workers' families to live on her property. But once Daniel Burton lived in the colony longer, he'd learn the difficult truth—criminals cannot be trusted. Even if they have wives and children. But for now, she felt discomfort, knowing he considered her cruel. The feeling nagged like a splinter beneath her skin.

She realized Sergeant Stewart had remained silent, apparently awaiting a reply. She thought back to what he'd said. "Yes, Mr. Burton seems very likeable," she said. "Although I have only one encounter to judge by." She turned away her face lest he see the blush that covered her cheeks as she remembered the meeting. Especially the part where Mr. Burton had been somewhat incompletely dressed.

"That he is, miss. 'Tis lucky the two o' ye are neighbors." He crossed his wrists on the pommel of the saddle. "Ye'll have plenty o' chances to become better acquainted."

Sarah wasn't certain how to respond, and conversation focusing on the one person she didn't wish to speak about made her feel cross. "And what about you, Sergeant? With Napoleon in exile, the war could soon end. Do you plan to return to Scotland? Or will you take a land grant here in New South Wales? Marines are given incentives to remain, you know. And you seem knowledgeable about farming. You'd do well here."

His eyes lost some of their light. "My heart longs for my homeland."

Sarah could feel the pain in his words. She turned toward him and saw that he studied her with his head tipped to the side.

"Ya know how I feel, Miss Whitaker. I can see it in yer face when ya look at this land."

She nodded. "It's true. I don't think anything could convince me to leave Sarah Hills. My father started the farm after my mother died. He loved it here, and keeping the farm productive is my way of honoring his memory."

"And what happened then? To yer da?"

"He was killed two months before I arrived, found on the road with a spear in his chest." Sarah tried to keep her voice from shaking. She'd said the words often over the past ten years, but each time she couldn't keep the image of her papá dying alone and frightened—killed by those horrible dark-skinned savages—from her mind.

"How old were ye?"

"A few months shy of eleven."

"I am so sorry. I wish he could see what ye've done here. He'd be proud of the farm—and his daughter—tha's for certain."

"Thank you." Sarah whispered the words through her tight throat.

They sat in silence, each lost in thought as they gazed over the vista. The quiet wasn't uncomfortable, but the air felt heavy. Sarah wondered if Sergeant Stewart was thinking of his home.

A dust cloud appeared behind the hills, indicating the wagon had circled around and was approaching the farm buildings. She glanced at her companion and saw that his gaze was focused on the cloud too.

"I thank ye for the visit, Miss Whitaker. I'll continue on now. Ye've a castle to build." He spoke with a teasing tone, and she was grateful that he lightened the solemn mood before his visit ended.

"Thank you for the fine conversation, Sergeant. As you can guess, I don't receive many visitors out here."

"'Tis a shame. But now I know where to find ya, I'll call again."

"And I promise to have tea and cakes and greet you like a proper hostess."

"I should hope not. I much prefer ridin' than sittin' straight in a dainty chair, holdin' a fragile cup, and tryin' to think o' somethin' polite to say." He winked. "But I'd not say no to cakes."

"Then I'd be pleased to ride with you again." Sarah smiled, a genuine expression that didn't have to be forced.

"I assume ye'll attend the governor's ball?" Sergeant Stewart leaned in his saddle, offering his hand.

Sarah placed her hand in his. "Yes."

"'Twill be a pleasure to see ya again, Miss Whitaker." He bowed his head, pulled on the brim of his shako, and departed.

Sarah watched him ride away for a moment before turning her horse toward the other side of the property. She was glad for the visit. Not that she considered herself particularly lonely—work on the farm was far too busy for that—but still, there was something nice about having someone to talk to. Someone she didn't need to be on her guard constantly against.

Her thoughts continued to follow the sergeant as she wondered what he and Daniel Burton would talk about. Had Daniel's workers begun to build a house? Or did he live in a canvas tent or a bark hut like many of the early settlers? Were his sheep delivered? She wondered at the quality of their wool. If she'd been with him when he purchased the flock, she'd certainly have made sure Mr. Orton didn't sell him sheep that were too old or who'd been under stress. Such things would affect the fleece. Did Daniel know? Well from now on, he had Bill Hawkins to tell him these things. With an effort, she turned to the task at hand. The storage building. She kicked her horse into a gallop as she rode toward the homestead.

Her old friend Mr. Thackeray would arrive in the colony any day now, and she would make sure the hold of the *Coeur d'Alene* was filled with the very finest wool when it departed. She smiled as she thought of her old friend and dismounted to begin directing the workers.

Chapter 7

DANIEL GLANCED AROUND THE BALLROOM of the Government House as he stepped through the doorway. His first impression was one of surprise; he'd never seen a ball with so few women. It seemed to lack color. Oh, there were the bright regimental coats of officers that stood out here and there among the dark-clad gentlemen, but the scarcity of pastel ball gowns was all too apparent. The few ladies present were surrounded by clusters of men, vying for their attention. *Come lads, have a little dignity. Don't make yourselves appear desperate.* But Daniel realized that desperate was exactly how they felt. The bush was a lonely place; some of the outer settlements were more than a day's ride from the nearest town. And with the huge disparity in the ratio between the sexes, he could hardly blame the blokes for their efforts.

Music floated on the warm air, and for some reason it surprised him that the song was familiar. It was as if the British settlers—at least the wealthy ones—tried to make their surroundings as "English" as possible. When he'd walked up the pathway to the Government House, he'd seen a young wallaby hopping around the lawn and heard the laughing call of a kookaburra above. The inside of the house was decorated like any fine dwelling in London, and the contrast with the exotic world outside was a bit startling.

He watched two men attempting to capture the notice of a pretty lady, each speaking over the other's words and at times even maneuvering with their shoulders to push the other out of the way. Pitiful, he thought. But he wondered if, in time, he'd find himself acting the very same way. Thinking of his sister, Meg, and how happy she was with her husband, Rodrigo, brought a pang of jealousy into his chest. He'd felt the same when he'd seen Charrah's face glow as he introduced his little family.

As long as he could remember, Daniel had longed for that kind of relationship. Something more than passing fancy and instant attraction. Meg teased him for falling in love with a different young lady every week, and Daniel knew it to be true, but he was searching for something—for what she had and what the duke and Serena had. Knowing how much more difficult it would be to find it in this faraway place made his spirits heavy.

"Ye look like a man wantin' rum."

Daniel turned and found Conall grinning and holding two glasses.

He took the offered drink, his friend's good humor instantly raising his mood. "Exactly what I needed. Thank you."

"Strange to have a party with so few lassies." Conall tipped back his head, downing the drink in a gulp.

"It is strange," Daniel said. He quirked his mouth. "If you're brave enough to offer, perhaps one of the officers would agree to a dance. Although I'd make certain to ask a man you outrank."

Conall narrowed his eyes but could not hold the glower for long. He laughed heartily. "I'd get a split lip fer the effort."

"And is that any way to treat a man who's just hoping for a jig, I ask you?" Daniel grinned at his friend's good humor.

"They've no idea how fine a dancer I am, me friend. Boorish is what 'tis. Their poor attitudes—" Conall's words broke off, and he stood up straight as a group of three men approached.

Daniel recognized Captain Seymour from the *Bollerophon*, who was accompanied by an officer in a military coat. From the stripes on his sleeve, Daniel saw that he vastly outranked Conall. Apparently that was why his friend had turned into a stiff soldier as soon as he'd seen them drawing near. The third man was an older gentleman, probably above his fiftieth year. His dark hair was speckled with gray at the temples. Though his face was weathered and lined, his expression was friendly.

"At ease, Sergeant," the officer muttered. "We're at a party not the drilling grounds for heaven's sake."

Conall relaxed a bit. "Thank you, sir. This here's Mr. Daniel Burton, sir."

The man turned sharply toward Daniel. "Lieutenant Mason of the Seventy-Third. How do you do, Mr. Burton?"

"A pleasure, Lieutenant." The men exchanged bows.

"I'm glad to see you doing so well, Mr. Burton." Captain Seymour took a step forward and bowed his head. His bald pate shone in the candlelight. Daniel realized he had never seen the captain without a hat. "Heard you've a nice piece of land you're putting to good use."

"Yes, Captain. Thank you."

The man nodded, pleased. "Glad to hear it." He clapped Daniel on the shoulder in a friendly way. "And may I introduce an old friend?" He gestured toward the third man. "Captain Allan Thackeray of the *Coeur d'Alene*. Captain Thackeray's ship arrived just this morning."

"Welcome to Parramatta," Daniel said.

Captain Seymour spread his hand toward Conall. "And, Captain, this is Sergeant Conall Stewart, lately assigned to the *Bollerophon*."

Captain Thackeray smiled amiably at both men, and Daniel reaffirmed his initial assessment of the man. He seemed at ease and pleasant in their company. Daniel liked him immediately. "Well met, sirs," Captain Thackeray said. "Mr. Burton, I hear that you've taken the parcel of land next to Miss Sarah Whitaker."

Daniel couldn't keep his eyes from widening in surprise. How did the man know so much about him if he'd only arrived in New South Wales this very day?

As if he could hear Daniel's thoughts, Captain Thackeray explained, "I was given a ride to Parramatta in the carriage of a Mr. Pierce and his wife, and of course, they caught me up on the local gossip."

Daniel had met Mr. and Mrs. Pierce, and he thought he'd prefer walking the distance from Sydney to spending the hours in their company. He'd been forced to endure that experience when he accepted an invitation to take supper at their house the week before. The evening had been an exercise in patience. "Yes. You are quite right. I have taken the land—a fine property with good soil and a large pond." Daniel sipped his drink, hoping to sound offhanded. "And are you acquainted with my neighbor?"

The man's smile grew, and his eyes lit up. "Oh yes. She and I have been close friends for well on a decade." He shook his head fondly. "A dear girl— well, I should say a dear young woman now. Though I can hardly believe it. I've not seen her for more than two years, though she does write regularly." He accepted a drink from a passing servant and glanced around the room, using his glass to gesture to the assembly. "I hoped she'd be here tonight."

"She assured me she would, Captain," Conall said. "And you're right, she is a delightful lass."

Daniel looked at Conall but remained silent. The soldier had been quite charmed by Sarah Whitaker; however, "a delightful lass" wasn't the term he'd choose to describe a selfish employer who separates families and acts rudely to her neighbors. It bothered him that the others had been taken in by her. Perhaps it was her appearance that had duped them. She was quite pretty, and he had to admit he'd enjoyed the moment of banter when they'd met. He'd even felt a swell of attraction, but that reaction couldn't be trusted. He'd experienced it often upon meeting a new young lady. It would fade soon enough, once he knew her better. It always did. He pursed his lips together. And when he thought of Trudy being taken from her parents and sent to an orphanage, how could he ever consider Miss Sarah Whitaker to be anything but heartless?

After a moment, Lieutenant Mason and Captain Seymour excused themselves, but Captain Thackeray remained with Conall and Daniel.

Conall had somehow found another drink. He took a swallow. "And where did ya make the acquaintance o' our common friend, the lovely Miss Whitaker, Captain?"

Daniel felt a rumble of annoyance that the conversation should continue on this topic.

"We sailed to the colony together when she was just a young thing. I was first mate on the *Coeur d'Alene* then." He smiled and crossed his arms. "You've never seen such a plucky girl as that little Sarah. So trusting and happy. She enchanted all of the sailors with her charm. If I were a superstitious man, I'd say she had us all under a spell. Even the most hardened deckhand was smitten by her."

Daniel blinked at Captain Thackeray. This description of his neighbor was quite different than his own experience.

"You're surprised," the captain said.

"No, I—obviously, I don't know her as you do." Daniel scratched behind his ear, wishing he had schooled his expression quicker. "I only met her once, and she was . . . uh . . ."

Captain Thackeray's eyes turned cold, and he raised his brows, waiting. Daniel got the distinct impression that the man's protectiveness of Miss Whitaker was not to be trifled with.

"She was suspicious," Daniel finally said. "Wary. Of course, I was a stranger."

Conall laughed. "Wary? Tha's an understatement if I ever heard one. The lass came upon ye bathin' and held ye at gunpoint, demandin' to know why ye were on 'er property." He snorted.

Captain Thackeray laughed, pointing a finger at Daniel. His good humor had returned in full. "What did I tell you? Plucky as can be. You're lucky you escaped unscathed."

Daniel reluctantly allowed himself to smile at the memory as the other two enjoyed a good laugh at his expense.

Wiping his eyes, the captain brought his mirth under control. "Oh, that girl." He continued to smile, but his eyes dimmed. "She's had a difficult time of it. After her father's death, she refused to leave the colony. Convinced her aunt to remain, and those two women ran the farm alone." He blew out a sigh, and his eyes winced. "Learned some hard lessons, they did. You can imagine how two fine ladies, directly from England, were taken advantage of. And by people they should have been able to trust. Can't blame the girl for being wary—especially after the betrayal and, then such a tragedy—"

"Captain Thackeray, Mr. Burton." A voice interrupted the captain's words, and the men turned to see Mr. Pierce and his wife, Minerva, pushing through the crowded room toward them.

Daniel was frustrated, not only that the irritating couple had discovered him but because his interest had been piqued by the captain's story. What had happened to Sarah? She'd been betrayed? By whom? And he'd heard nothing of an aunt in his weeks in Parramatta, only that Sarah lived alone. Had the other woman left New South Wales? Had she died? His perception of Miss Whitaker's character felt like a soft piece of clay—every time he thought it was molded into one shape, something happened to change it. The contradicting information was confusing, and he didn't like the idea that he might have misjudged his neighbor without knowing the facts. It itched at him, bothering him, and made discovering the truth that much more important.

"How fortunate to find the two of you together." Mrs. Pierce squeezed into the tight corner of the room where the men had been speaking. She seemed extremely overdressed for the warm evening, and a sheen was visible on her cheeks and neck. "I was just telling Mr. Pierce that we should introduce Captain Thackeray and Mr. Burton, wasn't I, dear? And here you are. Already acquainted." She curtseyed then glanced at Conall, waving a retractable lacey fan in front of her flushed face. "And, Sergeant Stewart, you are here too. What a merry company."

The captain's smile looked rather forced. "Truly a delight to see you again so soon, Mrs. Pierce." He bowed. "And you, sir."

Mr. Pierce inclined his head. The man was a bit taller than his wife and every bit as plump. He supervised the government farm, and Daniel wondered, if his own fortune had been different, would he be working for the man? The thought made his lip curl. He disliked both the disapproving Mr. Pierce and his gossiping wife. He'd spent enough time with the couple to know he'd not escape anytime soon. He glanced toward the door, wishing he could think of an excuse to flee.

Conall greeted the pair graciously, and Daniel plastered on his own smile and followed suit, bracing himself for a windfall of idle gossip and complaining.

"And how do you find the ball, Mr. Burton?" Minerva said. Her elaborate headpiece teetered as she turned to him.

"Very nice," Daniel said. "A pleasant company." He kept his answers neutral, not wishing to encourage a drawn-out conversation.

"Hmph," she made a noise of displeasure. "If you ask me, the governor is becoming less discriminatory about who he invites to high-society functions. Many of the people here are former convicts." She spoke the last words in a loud whisper, as if she both wanted to appear to be sharing a secret and also wanted everyone nearby to hear it.

Daniel felt his face heat. She had no idea that the very person she was complaining to also fell into that category. He caught Conall's eye. His friend wrinkled his brow and shook his head slightly in a "do not let her words bother you" expression.

"You see that man there?" She indicated a tall, finely attired man with a patch over one eye. "Lord Ragsdale, the new lord inspector of the colony and Van Dieman's land. He was a wealthy earl in England before taking the post." She leaned in closer, lowering her voice. "And that young woman with him—his wife—is not only a former indentured servant but *Irish*." She spoke the word in a hiss as if it were too horrible to utter aloud.

Daniel studied the woman she indicated. The lady was attractive—he wouldn't say beautiful—but there was something about the countess that drew a person's eye. Her gaze moved around the room, giving the image of a perceptive mind, and she held herself confidently. He saw nothing in her bearing that would lead him to question her suitability as a nobleman's wife, but then again, he was American and that sort of thing was not as important to him as it was to the British.

Daniel could feel Conall standing stiffly beside him, and without looking, he knew his friend was irritated by the disdain in Mrs. Pierce's words. And when Daniel glanced at Captain Thackeray, he saw the man's face was also tight. The temperature in the room seemed to have risen. Could the Pierces not sense the group's discomfort?

"Those of us *honest* citizens are becoming fewer with each ticket-of-leave issued." Mr. Pierce glowered, a look that was made the more dramatic by his low-hanging jowls. "Soon the emancipists will expect to be included at every society function. There are already some former convict scum appointed to administrative positions in the colony. What next?"

"You are too right, my dear." Minerva nodded approvingly at her husband's snarling words.

Daniel's face grew hotter, and he searched his mind—both for an excuse to leave and a suitable reply to the insults.

Captain Thackeray frowned. "I'm convinced, in time, the *manner* of a person's arrival in the colony will no longer be important. Once terms are served and freed convicts start to own shops and manage farms, their children will be afforded the same opportunities as any other." He clasped his hands behind his back, keeping a pleasant expression as if simply sharing an observation, and rocked on his heels.

Minerva gasped and pressed her fingers to her lips. "Captain!"

"Outrageous," Mr. Pierce said.

"Not so outrageous." Captain Thackeray shrugged, his voice remaining agreeable. "It's the same in America, is it not, Mr. Burton?"

Daniel nodded, swallowing before he found his voice. "Yes. There are endless opportunities for people of all backgrounds. If New South Wales follows suit, in a few generations, a person's parents will be less important than what they've made of themselves." His opinion of Captain Thackeray had risen to new heights, and Daniel felt immense gratitude for the man's words, even though the man didn't realize the full extent of whom he was defending.

The couple stared at the men as if they'd been betrayed. Minerva's red face had darkened to the point that Daniel worried for her health. Perhaps he should offer her a seat. Mr. Pierce's scowl was so deep that his eyes were nearly invisible.

"Well," Mr. Pierce finally huffed. "If you'll excuse us, we . . . ah . . . yes." He glanced to the side then made a motion toward an imaginary person as if he'd been summoned. He pulled his wife away, and the two disappeared quickly into the crowd.

"Well, that was satisfying, don't you think?" Captain Thackeray's smile held a bit of mischief.

"Extremely," Daniel said.

"A fine answer ye gave, Captain." Conall raised his glass.

"I believe what I said." Captain Thackeray raised his own, returning the salute. "This is my sixth visit to the colony, and each time, I've seen more progress away from the class distinctions that existed before. Of course there will always be those who are unaccepting." He indicated toward a group on the far side of the ballroom with a jerk of his chin.

The women wore expensive jewelry and overly formal gowns, and the men with them were also excessively attired. They peered down their noses at those around them, giving no doubt as to their opinion of their own superiority. The Pierces joined the group, their disdainful expressions blending in perfectly with the others'.

"They call themselves *Exclusives*." Captain Thackeray didn't bother to hide the disapproval in his voice. "Rather ridiculous, don't you think? They avoid doing business with anyone not in their group, but as time goes on, I'm afraid they'll find completely avoiding emancipists to be increasingly difficult. I admire Governor Macquarie's efforts. Forward thinking, he is." He took a slow drink of his wine then rubbed his lip with the side of his thumb. "I wonder what life in the colony will be like in a few generations. Population's growing; more farms and shops are owned by freed convicts. Already the native-born children are taller and stronger than their parents. Seems working in the fresh air and having enough to eat is good for one's health—as opposed to starving in a London rookery."

Daniel listened with one ear as his gaze moved from the Exclusives and around the ballroom. His eyes snapped toward the entryway, and he drew in a breath when he saw Miss Sarah Whitaker standing there. He hadn't realized until he spotted her that he'd been searching for her, and he was not prepared for his reaction. His heart beat faster. She was enchanting.

Instead of trousers and a wide-rimmed hat, she wore a gauzy gown of light blue. Her dark hair was arranged in curls upon her head, and a single strand of pearls circled her neck. She stood alone, her bearing mostly confident, but a pinch in her brows betrayed the smallest hint of nervousness.

Daniel hadn't noticed before the fan of dark lashes that surrounded her eyes or that her figure was so . . . feminine. He flushed when their eyes met, and he realized she'd seen him staring with his mouth open. Could this possibly be the same woman he'd mistaken for a bushranger?

Sarah's gaze moved past him then stopped, her eyes widening in surprise. Her hands flew to her cheeks, and she opened her mouth, jerking in a startled expression that turned into a wide grin.

Daniel followed her line of sight and realized she was smiling at Captain Thackeray, who grinned back.

Sarah hurried across the room, abandoning any pretense of aloof elegance. She grasped the captain's arm. "Captain Thackeray! What a surprise. I didn't expect you for weeks yet."

The captain handed his glass to Conall. He pulled Sarah into an embrace, then stepped back, holding her shoulders as he studied her. "You've become a lovely young woman, my Little Minnow." He bent forward and kissed her forehead.

"I've missed you, Captain." Sarah's voice sounded brittle, as if she were holding in a wave of emotion.

Daniel couldn't reconcile the expression on Sarah's face with the person who had held him at gunpoint or dismissed him so curtly at their first meeting. This shining-eyed, smiling young lady could not possibly have selfishly kept her foreman from his family, could she? His mind was a mixture of questions as he watched the touching reunion.

Conall had the presence of mind to take Daniel's arm and lead him away, holding both glasses in his other hand. "Shall we give the old friends some time ta become reacquainted then?" He spoke in a pleasant voice, but Daniel heard more in his tone. Something along the lines of, "Yer makin' a fool o' yerself, lad. Stop starin'."

Daniel didn't know what had come over him. His emotions seemed to run the gamut from anger to compassion to . . . what? Something he couldn't explain. Was he envious of the look of adoration she gave the older man? Surely not. But Sarah Whitaker looked so *gentle*, fragile even. But why should that sight affect him so strongly? Was his reaction a result of months without any female interaction? Yes. That must be the case. That and the alcohol. What other explanation could there be?

"Yer lookin' a bit pale," Conall said, his brow raising.

Daniel pulled his thoughts together, shaking his head at his foolishness. "I could use some more rum."

Chapter 8

SARAH'S HEART FELT LIKE IT would burst; her fingers tingled with the excitement of seeing her old friend. *He had come!* She crammed down the resentment she'd felt at seeing *Daniel Burton* speaking with Captain Thackeray before Sarah herself even knew of his arrival in the colony. How did that man always manage to ruin things? To take over people and situations where he had no business? She glanced to the side, grateful to see Sergeant Stewart leading Mr. Burton away, and felt the smallest bit of shame that she'd wanted the entirety of the captain's attention to herself.

The feeling passed quickly, however, when she looked up and saw her old friend's kind smile that brought back a nearly overwhelming crush of memories. Though not related by blood, he was as close to a family as she had. With her aunt and father both dead, Captain Thackeray was the last link to her childhood, and the comfort his presence brought flowed over her, warm and pleasant.

"You look well, Sarah."

"Thank you, Captain." She gave a small curtsey. "As do you, sir."

He offered his arm, and she took it, walking through the ballroom doors to the governor's gardens, where they could speak without competing with the noise of the crowd and music.

As they stepped into the torchlight outside the doors, she glanced up at Captain Thackeray's profile. He had come to New South Wales to fill the hull of his merchant vessel with wool and other goods, not simply to visit her, but the knowledge did not dampen her happiness in the least. "The shearing won't be finished for at least two weeks. If I'd known you were to arrive early . . ."

"Not to worry." He patted her hand where it rested on his arm. "We were fortunate to have fine winds, and be assured my crew will be pleased for an extended shore leave until the wool is ready."

"And I am glad for it as well." She was delighted that his early arrival meant a longer visit.

They walked in silence for a moment until he indicated a garden bench, leading her toward it. Once Sarah was seated, he sat beside her.

The captain's eyes were familiar and comforting, though more heavily lined than they'd been when she'd first known him all those years ago. She'd also noticed a slowness to his gait that hadn't been there before. Her throat tightened at the realization that her dear Captain Thackeray was growing old.

"I have plenty to keep me busy in Sydney Towne while I wait for the wool," he said, his mouth pulling wide in a smile. "And I of course would love to see Sarah Hills once again. I've heard from multiple sources that you have been a fine manager. Not that I would have ever doubted you."

"Thank you. I do love the farm." His words brought a mixture of pride and embarrassment, and she felt her cheeks heat.

He looked thoughtful, his head tipped and his expression soft. "Sarah, you have endured such hardship in your young life but risen above your challenges splendidly. I could not be prouder of the fine woman you've become."

His words touched her, and she found it more difficult to swallow. She'd rarely been complimented so sincerely. She gave a smile, feeling shy.

His brows drew together the slightest bit, making a wrinkle between them. "And I should like to extend in person my most heartfelt condolences on the passing of your aunt. For her to die in such a way and for you to have to bear such a tragedy . . . I am so sorry, Sarah."

Sarah's stomach twisted at the reminder of that night. The fear, the anger, the guilt—it all erupted inside her, and she took a slow breath to calm herself from the blast of sensations. She nodded, not trusting herself to speak.

Squinting slightly, he studied her face. He opened his mouth then closed it, pushing out a breath. "The experience changed you, Little Minnow. The light's dimmed in your eyes."

Sarah didn't know how to respond. She knew her emotions were obvious on her face, and with Captain Thackeray, she couldn't hide them, even if she'd wanted to. The experience *had* changed her. Circumstances had forced her to take on adult responsibility much sooner than she'd have ever imagined. She'd learned a hard lesson and vowed never to be deceived again. "I suppose I've grown wiser," she offered as explanation.

He leaned forward, resting his forearms on his knees. She thought he must be quite exhausted after making landfall and riding all the way to Parramatta in one day. "You cannot think all men are evil."

"Not all men," she said, her voice soft but certain. "Just criminals."

He turned his head to the side to consider her. "Ah, but, Sarah, good people still exist. Even among the convicts." His voice sounded sad, as if he were disappointed with her caution. "People can change, and you mustn't let your dreadful experience define how you view everyone."

She rubbed her arms, uncomfortable with the course of the conversation. But she needed him, of all people, to understand. It had not been only one but a succession of dreadful experiences that culminated in betrayal and heartbreak she could have never imagined. "But allowing myself to be misled again would be foolish, would it not?" How could he think she would just forget the deception? If she'd only listened to her aunt's warnings. If she'd only been wary instead of so utterly gullible.

He nodded. "Aye, it's wise to be cautious, but don't lose your faith in human decency. Most people are inherently good. You believed this once."

"When I was a child. Before I knew the truth of how evil people could be."

His shoulders slumped. "If only I'd been there the night of the fire. I would have—"

"I'm glad you were safely away," Sarah interrupted him. The thought of Captain Thackeray being hurt as well made the breath catch in her throat. He would have no doubt tried to protect the women, and she could not have borne it, knowing that her poor decisions and misplaced trust had harmed yet another person she loved. *What if I'd lost him too?*

"You must promise me the girl who smiles and trusts still exists, Little Minnow."

She forced a smile, "Of course, Captain."

He seemed to consider for a moment then nodded, leaning back against the bench and breathing in cool air.

Sarah knew she was simply telling him what he wanted to hear. She'd learned a difficult lesson, but she was wiser now. She'd vowed that very night, two years earlier, never to allow herself to be duped again. No matter the captain's or the governor's good intentions, she'd never trust another criminal.

She rested back beside the captain, leaning her head on his shoulder. She felt so safe, so contented. She realized it was because she was relaxed instead of on her guard. She so rarely let her defenses down—how could she? The feeling was a relief. Constant suspicion was exhausting.

"I'll only be in Parramatta until tomorrow, then I have some business in Sydney Town," he said. "Merchandise to purchase, warehouses to visit, things of that nature. But I will come visit you soon."

"You know you are welcome anytime."

"I hope to return within a fortnight." He shifted. "Can you recommend an inn in town?"

She sat forward and turned toward him. "An inn? Why, you must stay at Sarah Hills as you always do."

He cleared his throat. "I . . ."

Realization dawned on her. She was a woman now, living alone. The captain could not lodge with her without causing a scandal. Her cheeks burned. He was simply acting as a gentleman, protecting her reputation, but knowing things would not be the same made her feel heavy inside. "Oh, yes, of course." She tried to smile. "Yorkshire Grey is a fine inn. The owner, Mr. Devon, will treat you well."

Captain Thackeray nodded. "You and I will still ride through the bush as we always have. I trust you've found new secrets to show me? And I sincerely hope your famous cook, Mrs. Tilbert, will make the lemon cake I am so fond of." His voice sounded as if he were trying to reassure them both that things had not changed so much, but Sarah knew the care he was taking in regards to propriety marked a distinct difference. A new distance existed between them now, and feeling it and knowing it would remain made her throat ache.

"Certainly," she said, forcing cheer into her voice. "And just wait until you see what I found in the forest last year."

"Splendid." The captain's strained tone mirrored her own.

Sarah sensed there was more the captain wanted to say. His manner rather than his words had seemed to indicate a silent "however." "What is it, Captain?" Sarah turned toward him, feeling a growing dread.

"This will be my last voyage, Little Minnow."

His words, though spoken softly, seemed to crash into her. "Captain?"

He let out a heavy breath. "I'm not a young man anymore, Sarah. My body's not as strong as it once was, and I've grandchildren that I've never even seen. I've saved enough funds to be able to leave the sea, and I'd like to spend the remainder of my life with my family in Liverpool."

But what about me? Sarah knew the thought was foolish. She was a friend but not Captain Thackeray's family. She was part of no one's family. She had acquaintances and even some she'd consider friends here in Parramatta, but none of them loved her the way she knew the captain did. The loneliness his words produced made her eyes burn, and she blinked to hold back the tears, not wanting to give him any reason to feel ashamed for his choice. It was a perfectly reasonable decision for a man to wish to be at home.

"And you know," he continued, "it is because of you and your wool prices that I'm able to leave the sea." He took her hand, squeezing her fingers affectionately. "You've done me a great kindness, Sarah Whitaker."

Her eyes continued to burn as she realized that he'd leave the colony in a matter of weeks, and she'd never see him again.

Just like her father.

Just like Aunt Hortensia.

Eventually, everyone she cared about went away. Her natural reaction was to firm up the resolve not to allow anyone close. Trust always led to pain.

Captain Thackeray leaned forward, tipping his head to catch her eye, and she realized she'd been quiet for too long. With an effort, she pushed away her self-pitying and squeezed his fingers in return. "I will miss you."

"And I you, Little Minnow. Of course, I hope you will still write to me." He looked worried. Naturally he would wonder how she would receive the announcement.

"Always." She compelled a smile to remain on her face and used a happy tone as she spoke. "Your family will be so glad to have you permanently at home. You must continue to write to me as well, and tell me all about life as a grandfather."

He smiled, looking relieved. He opened his mouth to say something further but, before he could, looked up, his gaze focusing on something behind her.

Sarah turned and saw Governor Macquarie and his wife, Elizabeth, approaching along the garden path. She stood, performed the proper curtsey and went through the motions of greetings and well wishes. She smiled when appropriate and participated halfheartedly in the conversation. All the while, she struggled to keep her roiling emotions in check and to calm her racing mind. She was counting down the moments until she could politely excuse herself. Her tears felt very close to the surface.

Once she'd made her farewell, promising Captain Thackeray she would speak to him before he returned to Sydney, she hurried back inside, hoping to . . . she did not know what. Perhaps lose herself in the crowd, find Dorthea and hear the gossip from town, or maybe calm herself with a drink—anything to distract herself from the rising emotions inside her. She felt like she had those months after her aunt's death. Like a ship without a rudder, being pushed at the whim of the winds and waves, completely unsure of how to manage the changes she was unable to control.

She glanced around the crowded ballroom. The heat from the throng and the surge of noise felt suffocating, and her breathing came in gasps. She fought to keep back her tears, realizing a crowded ballroom was the last place she wished to be. More than anything, she wanted to be alone to calm herself and sort through her thoughts. But she could not return to the garden.

Turning, she hurried toward another door, ignoring the greetings called after her. She rushed through the door into the passageway beyond, turning quickly and crashing headlong into—

The man gripped her elbows to steady her, and when she lifted her gaze, embarrassment turned to anger. Daniel Burton held her in an embrace.

"I did not realize my invitation for a dance would cause you to throw yourself into my arms." His brow arched, and a flirtatious smile spread over his lips as he looked down at her. "The offer *is* quite appealing, however . . ." his voice trailed off.

Finding herself in the arms of her enemy had the unfortunate effect of liberating her tears. They flowed out of her eyes accompanied by a humiliating and unattractive sob.

"Here now, what's this?" Mr. Burton's low voice lost its playful tone. He pulled a handkerchief from his jacket pocket and offered it to her.

Sarah snatched it from his hand. The concern in his expression made her tears come faster, and embarrassment caused her anger to flare. The sadness, hopelessness, and frustration stoked the flames, and she directed her wrath at the person who'd seemed to cause her nothing but misery since the moment they'd met. "I do *not* wish to dance with you, Mr. Burton. Not ever." At this point, small, dainty dabs of the handkerchief were doing no good. She wiped her nose, put her hands against his chest, and shoved, nearly losing her balance as she pushed herself from his grasp. His eyes were wide with surprise, but she did not care. "This is all your fault! *Everything* is your fault!"

Sarah whirled and ran through the hall and out the front door. A servant called out as she hurried down the path, but she ignored him. She reached the road and turned, moving away from the waiting carriages, not wanting to encounter anyone else until she had a hold on herself.

She knew her reaction had been utterly ridiculous, and now, atop the whole mess of unwelcome emotions, she could add humiliation at her latest encounter with Mr. Burton. She'd behaved like a child—lost her temper and thrown a tantrum. She couldn't have come across as less mature if she'd stomped her foot and broken her lollypop.

Sarah groaned at the memory. Ahead, she spotted a small building that she assumed to be a gardener's toolshed and moved toward it, leaning her hand against the wooden outer wall as she took deep breaths, calming her utterly absurd bout of weeping. She glanced down at the crumpled soggy mess that had, moments earlier, been a starched white handkerchief and let out a stuttering sigh. Of all the people in this colony, why was Mr. Daniel Burton the one to see her so completely come apart?

Chapter 9

Daniel stood in the passageway outside the ballroom, stunned. Miss Whitaker's words and behavior left him bewildered. Once the initial astonishment wore off, his first reaction was one of anger. She had accused him, blamed him, for—he knew not what. He'd certainly surprised her, caught her off guard, but her reaction was completely unexpected. His attempt to be charming had not only fallen flat but had seemed to enrage her. Both times they'd met, she'd acted with the utmost discourtesy, even though Daniel had been nothing but a gentleman. He had half a mind to spurn the woman all together.

He lifted his head, resolving to think of her no more, and took a step toward the ballroom, but he hesitated as an image flashed into his mind: the look of utter despair in Miss Whitaker's eyes, her tears, trembling lips, and the way her face had crumpled. She'd appeared not only distraught but . . . helpless. The memory tugged on something inside him, a part of him that didn't listen to reason. Tossing aside his good sense, he followed her.

A quick interrogation of the doorman directed him away from the house and along the moonlit street. He squinted, looking from side to side, then heard a sniffle and stopped, peering closer at the shadows of a small wooden building. Sarah stood there, facing away from him, her shoulders hunched and shaking. The sight made him feel heavy. He took a tentative step, unsure of what to say. He didn't understand what had caused her distress, but he felt a strange impulse to ease it. And he should have an opportunity to defend himself for . . . whatever it was that had upset her.

"Miss Whitaker? Are you all right?"

She straightened but did not turn.

At least she did not run away. "I am sorry," he said.

She tipped her head as if she'd not heard him correctly. "Why? What do you have to apologize for?"

Daniel scratched behind his ear. He wasn't sure, actually. But it had seemed like the right thing to say. "I am sorry our acquaintance started off poorly. I have only one neighbor, and I should have made a better attempt at being, ah . . . neighborly," he finished lamely.

Sarah turned. Even in the shadows, he could see her eyes were swollen and her cheeks shone with moisture. "You wish for us to be friends?" Her question sounded confused. No, not confused, incredulous.

"Yes." He vaguely wondered if he were going mad.

Sarah's chin rose as she studied him. She straightened her back, and her eyes hardened. "If you wished to start a friendship, Mr. Burton, then, perhaps you should not have pilfered my employee."

Daniel opened his mouth to form an angry retort, but a catch in her breathing stopped him. Though she acted strong, he could see she still fought to keep from weeping. "You are right," he said, realizing his mouth seemed to have an agenda completely independent of his.

Sarah blinked, and her eyes widened.

He understood her surprise. The words had surprised even him. "I should have spoken to you before offering a position to Mr. Hawkins, sought your approval."

Sarah's jaw tightened.

A bit of his anger returned at her expression. "But once I learned how the man was being prevented from living with his family, that his young daughter would soon be taken to an orphanage, I thought only of righting what I judged to be a cruel mistreatment."

She was quiet for a moment. "I felt the same once," she finally said. "It is difficult to understand. But you will learn the way of things soon enough."

"I doubt I will ever see the decency in hurting a family."

She took a step forward. "Mr. Burton, you cannot trust these people so easily. Mr. Hawkins is a nice man and a hard worker, but he is a convict, transported to the colony to serve a criminal sentence. He may *seem* to be honest, many do, but when you let down your guard—forget who they are and what they've done—" A flash of pain entered her eyes, and she swallowed. "They will betray you."

"Surely you cannot believe it to be true of all convicts." Daniel's insides felt cold at her words.

She lifted a shoulder in a shrug, turning down her gaze. "Once, I did not. I trusted as you do, thought people could change, took them at their word." She rubbed her arm and looked back to the lights of the governor's house. "Now I know better."

Daniel watched her, wondering what could have happened to hurt her so deeply, to harden her to the point that she was afraid to trust. Could she ever change her opinion about the criminals in the colony? If she knew the truth about him, how would she act? Looking at the firm set of her jaw, Daniel felt a wave of discouragement. She would despise him.

A part of him wondered why he should care. The loss of Sarah Whitaker's opinion hardly seemed worth troubling about. Based on their few dealings, she already thought poorly of him. Was he concerned because she had wept and seemed so vulnerable? Did he feel pity for her? Or was his worry made all the stronger because he found her so very pretty? Perhaps, like his sister so often said, he only wished for a lady's good opinion because she seemed to dislike him. Was it the thrill of the game? Trying to win the favor of a woman for the challenge of it? He didn't know, and the not knowing bothered him.

He glanced at her, trying to read her expression. For whatever reason, he wished for her favor, wished for Sarah Whitaker to think well of him, and the idea that she did not—would not—disturbed him, even though he could not for the life of him understand why.

He cleared his throat. "I do not know what upset you tonight, but I truly apologize if I was in any way to blame for your tears. To make a woman cry, such an act is inexcusable."

Sarah grimaced. "You are not to blame." She glanced at him and then away, twisting the handkerchief she held. "I heard some news that upset me, and you were the first person I encountered afterward. My emotions were raw, and you became the recipient of my outburst. It was very wrong of me."

"I understand."

She gave him a grateful smile.

Daniel offered his arm, tipping his head back toward the house "Come. Let me return you to the party. You will certainly be missed, especially by all the gentlemen wishing for a dance."

She darted her gaze to his, as if looking to see if there were more to his words than mere politeness. Even in the dim light, he saw color blossom on her cheeks. She looked unsure, and he found it difficult to believe he'd been at the receiving end of this woman's angry words.

Daniel hoped his expression looked simply friendly and open, and she must have seen he did not mean to slight her because finally she slipped her hand into the crease of his elbow.

Her fingers barely made contact with his arm as he led her back along the road toward the governor's house.

"Mr. Burton, I am sorry."

"What do you have to apologize for?" He imitated her words in an attempt to alleviate the nervousness in her voice.

"Aside from my churlish outburst, well, I've not been a good neighbor either."

"And do you wish to be friends?" He hoped for a light tone as he mimicked their earlier conversation with an air of humor, but he felt his gut tighten anxiously as he awaited her answer.

"Yes." Her fingers tightened the slightest bit on his arm, and the pressure made his heart skip. He realized how difficult the words had been for her and how little she permitted herself to trust. He felt ashamed that he'd spent the last weeks disliking his neighbor. He should have treated her better, at least not assumed the worst. She wasn't a tyrannical overseer who treated her workers poorly, but a young woman, alone and afraid. However, something told Daniel she would not be pleased if he were ever to voice the observation aloud.

"Miss Whitaker, would you do me the honor of joining me for luncheon? Perhaps Thursday next." He felt her fingers compress again and smiled, knowing his words had surprised her.

"I—"

"I know it is nearly two weeks away, but I should have a roof by then and, if we're lucky, even a table."

From the corner of his eye, he saw her shake her head. "I do not think it would be appropriate, sir."

"Ah." He should have known she would have been concerned with propriety, even though they lived miles from any sort of civilization. "Is there a guardian to whom I should speak first?"

"No. I have no guardian." She spoke softly, and he could not tell whether it was out of embarrassment or uncertainty. "My aunt died two years ago, you see. And I suppose there was no one to assume that responsibility."

They turned up the path toward the brightly lit house.

"If you'd like, Mrs. Hawkins would happily join us."

She darted a look at him. "I don't know."

"Or surely your lady's maid would accompany you?"

She seemed to consider the idea. "I suppose that would be acceptable."

Daniel stopped, turning toward her in the lantern light of the governor's porch. "I would like it very much if you would come, Miss Whitaker. I want to show you my farm, and I should like your advice on the management of my flock. I want us to behave as neighbors." He waited for her to lift her gaze, then he held it. "Please consider it."

Her eyes were still red. Between her brows was the same pinch he'd seen earlier, betraying her nervousness. She glanced toward the servant who stood with a hand on the door, ready to admit them back into the party, then back to Daniel. "I would be delighted, Mr. Burton."

He scratched behind his ear. "I'm afraid I have no carriage to send for you."

"I prefer to ride if you don't mind. The path over the hills is much faster than the road. And if we have no rains before then, the creek will be low enough to cross."

"If that is your pleasure."

Sarah looked as if she would say more then thought better of it. "Thursday next." She curtsied quickly then nodded to the servant, sweeping into the house before Daniel could even offer a bow.

For the second time in an hour, Daniel stood watching her go and wondering why spending more time with Miss Whitaker actually *decreased* his ability to understand the woman.

Chapter 10

SARAH GLANCED TO THE SIDE, taking stock of her two new workers. The supervisor that delivered the men earlier that morning had assured her they would be quick learners, but the two seemed uninterested and sullen. She'd gathered from the few questions she'd asked that both had arrived in the colony merely days earlier. Their fair skin and stiff movements spoke to the months they'd spent chained in a prison hull.

Frustration rose inside her. She'd specifically petitioned for seasoned workers, preferably with some farm experience, and these men were practically the opposite of that description. She was not surprised, however. Farming was seen by most in the colony as "a man's profession," and over the past ten years, she and Aunt Hortensia had been continually stymied in their efforts to succeed. They'd been assigned the least competent workers, sold the scrawniest sheep, and dealt substandard feed.

She remembered one particular day when they'd found an entire flock infected with "the scab" from their newly purchased and deceptively unhealthy rams. The discouragement had felt like too much to bear. She and her aunt had discussed selling the farm and returning to England. That morning they'd had a purchase offer, but even a young girl could tell it was insultingly low.

"We have made a good effort here, but it is simply not enough," Aunt Hortensia had said. Her eyes were tired, and Sarah saw her typically ramrod straight back was slumped against the sofa.

Sarah pushed through the gloom that hung heavy over them. "But we cannot leave. This farm was Papá's dream. Surely there is something we can do."

"Four years is a long time, Sarah. I have tried; we both have. But it is not enough."

"We cannot let them beat us." Sarah's words had been nearly a shout. She slammed her hand down on the table with all the strength and passion of a fourteen-year old. "I will not give up and sell my Papa's farm. These colonial men think to intimidate us, but we can do it, Aunt Hortensia. We've learned so much already." She took her aunt's hand. "We are clever and stronger than the silly women in town, and I do not give one fig if they think we are blue-stockings."

The older woman had regarded her for a long moment until something hardened behind her eyes. She straightened her head and lifted her shoulders, tightening her fingers around Sarah's. Her lips pressed together in a straight line, an expression Sarah recognized as an indication of her aunt's resolve. She gave a brisk nod then rose and moved to the desk, opening a book of ledgers. "They can think what they want, but it will take more than a few sick sheep to defeat us."

Sarah's throat constricted as she remembered her aunt—ill-tempered, complaining. Yet she'd been the person to support Sarah, to understand her, to give all she could to growing this farm, and why? Because, despite her haughty demeanor, she loved her niece. And Aunt Hortensia was another reason Sarah would not let the colonial administration intimidate her.

She led the men over the hills toward the flock she planned to assign to them. Since neither had any experience on horseback, they walked while Sarah led her horse. She wore a holstered pistol on her hip and kept an eye on the men. She didn't know them and wouldn't allow them to walk behind her.

The trek took nearly an hour, even with the occasional rest. The men's muscles were obviously flaccid from months of disuse, so Sarah did not reprimand them for their complaining. She hoped within a few days, they'd regain their strength. It would return faster with hard work and sunshine than lazing about.

They stopped on a rise overlooking the flock. "Three hundred ewes." Sarah spread her hand to indicate the white animals grazing below. "In the next weeks, most will have lambed." She motioned for them to accompany her down the hill, waving in acknowledgement to the two shepherds approaching. "Typically, two workers are assigned to each flock, but the new lambs are the most vulnerable, and I prefer to have more men—not only to help with the lambing but to protect them from predators."

"What predators, my lady?" One of the men, Jack Smythe glanced around nervously.

Sarah realized how foreign this world must seem to him, a young man from the streets and rookeries of London. She briefly wondered what his crime had been—it wouldn't have been anything violent or he would have been hanged instead of transported. Likely he was a pickpocket or perhaps a house burglar. She kept her hand near her weapon regardless. "Wild dogs, primarily. There are no tigers or bears, Mr. Smythe." She noticed his glance at her pistol. "You'll need a big stick, and keep a pile of rocks handy, especially at night. The four of you will scare a pack away easily enough."

"A pack?"

"In ten years, I've not lost a worker to dogs. You will be quite safe. However, a newborn lamb is simply too tempting to dingoes." She didn't tell him that wild dogs were the least of his worries in the bush. Poisonous snakes, quicksand, venomous spiders, even the large flightless birds with their sharp beaks and deadly claws were dangerous to humans.

She greeted the seasoned workers once the group reached them.

"Quite a few lambs today, my lady," Marcus Payne said, speaking through his thick beard. He had been assigned to Sarah Hills since before she'd arrived, ten years earlier, and Sarah liked knowing that her father had worked alongside him. She nodded.

She introduced the newcomers to the experienced tenders, then studied the flock. Many were yearlings, ready to birth their first lambs. Some would need help.

The noise of their bleating—some high pitched, some low—sounded soothing to her ears, like a familiar song. "Mr. Smythe and Mr. Hammond, you'll need to keep an eye on the new lambs. Make sure their mothers don't reject them, or we'll need to bottle feed them or find a surrogate until they're old enough to wean."

Both men looked at her with confusion.

"It's simple enough," Marcus said. "Make sure every lamb's drinkin' its ma's milk."

"The rains will come soon, so keep the sheep away from the creek. The water rises fast." She lifted her chin toward the trees. "Not only is there danger of drowning, but you don't want their hooves to remain wet, or they'll develop foot rot. The disease is highly contagious and can devastate a flock. But it's preventable if they remain dry."

The newcomers continued to stare at her with blank looks.

Sarah sighed and moved through the flock, assessing the sheep ready to give birth and those who tended their new lambs.

They came upon a yearling ewe laboring hard. It lay on the grassy earth, sides heaving. Occasionally, it let out a pained bleat. Sarah knelt, tugging on the legs protruding from the posterior of the sheep. She looked up, motioning to Jack Smythe, whose face was pulled in a grimace.

"Look here, you see? Three hooves. Twins, tangled inside." Sarah rolled up her sleeves as she spoke. "She'll not be able to get them out without our assistance. Hold her hind legs so she doesn't kick." Her words trailed off as she noticed a rider headed in their direction. It took only a moment for her to realize who it was. Daniel Burton raised a hand, and a wide grin shone in the shade beneath his hat.

Sarah's cheeks flushed as she remembered their last meeting. What must he think of her? And why had he come?

Daniel reached them and dismounted, bowing to Sarah. "Good morning, neighbor."

She nodded to him then returned her attention to the ewe. She plunged her hand into the sheep, there was no time for chitchat, not with an animal in distress and three lives at stake. She felt along the foreleg of one lamb until she reached the shoulder, then she twisted it around to untangle the animal from its sibling. She pushed on the sheep's side with one hand and tugged with the other, pulling out the lamb in a whoosh of fluid.

Jack Smythe cursed, moving back to avoid the spray.

Sarah ignored his reaction. "Return to your position. I do not wish to be kicked."

He did so, but she could tell the action was done grudgingly.

Sarah dragged her hand firmly over the lamb's wet face, pulling the liquid from its nose and mouth and checking that it breathed before laying it on the ground and reaching back inside for the other. With just a bit of maneuvering, she pulled, and it came free with the same rush of liquid.

"The trick is to pull downward; let gravity help you," she said to Jack Smythe and the other men.

"I ain't puttin' my arm in 'ere," he muttered.

Sarah made certain both animals were breathing and their faces cleared of mucous, then she twisted around to face her new worker. She still knelt with a hand on the ewe. "Mr. Smythe, I've been told working as a sheep tender is preferable to laboring on a government farm or a chain gang." She held his eyes until he dropped his gaze.

He muttered an apology and, at Marcus's bidding, followed the others as the older man continued to give instruction about the flock.

Sarah patted the sheep and stood, moving out of the way to allow the mother sheep to tend to its lambs. She looked up at Daniel and saw that his face was pale.

"I did not expect to see that."

Sarah glanced down at her arms, covered in animal bodily fluids. She recognized Daniel's wrinkled nose and grimace and had to repress a laugh as she walked toward the creek to wash. Why were men so squeamish when it came to these matters?

Daniel followed, leading their horses, and stood near the creek as she crouched down to splash water on her arms, cleaning them as well as she could, and then rolled down her sleeves.

She stepped up the bank and joined him, smiling, knowing a curtsey would look silly while she wore trousers. "Have I confused my calendar—is it Thursday already?"

He shook his head. "No. I simply saw you from my field and thought I'd pop over to say hello."

Sarah glanced over the tree-lined creek at the hills of his property then back at him. "As you can see, I was not expecting a visit." She swept her hands down, indicating her clothing. She wondered what he must think of her attire. Men she'd known, and some who had courted her, had often commented disapprovingly on her choice of attire. But she hardly thought there was a better choice, not with the work she did.

"I apologize for not giving you more notice. I didn't intend to pay a formal visit." He smiled, and she noticed, as she had the first time they'd met, how very charming his crooked smile was. She felt disconcerted as the sight sent a shiver through her middle. "You were upset last time we talked. I thought to ask after your health or I suppose your, ah, emotional well-being." He smiled again, and she couldn't help but smile back at his teasing.

"I am very well. I've new workers today, being trained to be tenders."

The sides of his mouth lowered, and he nodded slowly. "Do you mind if I join you? I could make use of some training myself."

"Very well." She tipped her head toward the flock.

He tied the horses' reins to a branch and lifted his arm with a bow, motioning for her to lead the way.

Sarah glanced at him as they walked. She clasped her hands behind her back, unsure of what to make of Mr. Burton and the way he acted as though the two were old friends. She had to admit, she enjoyed his company in this informal way. It was so much easier than an awkward visit in a drawing room. Here, she could be herself. She felt anxious, wondering if seeing her where she felt comfortable would cause Daniel to scorn her. Her nerves wound tightly as she led him into the flock, unsure of what the man expected. Why had he come? Had he an ulterior motive? She couldn't help her suspicion; it was in her nature.

Perhaps he was simply not able to think of an adequate excuse for a quick departure. Was he worried she would start crying and yelling at him again? Her insides tightened at the memory. Or was he genuinely interested in being her friend? She figured he'd already seen her covered in sheep after-birth, and yet he remained. Perhaps that was a good sign.

Daniel walked beside her in silence. They stopped as two lambs bounded past, kicking their legs awkwardly as they romped, then at the sound of their mother's bleat, they returned quickly to rejoin her.

He laughed, and Sarah felt pleased that he found amusement in the animals' antics. Over the next weeks, as the lambs grew more coordinated, the meadow would be filled with their frolicking. She could not think of anything that could bring more joy than watching the sight.

"Mr. Hawkins tells me some of my own ewes will deliver soon," Daniel said.

"Ah, so you're shearing then."

He lifted a shoulder in a shrug. "I thought it would be easier to wait until after the lambs are born. The ewes won't be so large then."

Sarah shook her head. "You don't want to lamb in the wool."

"Pardon?" He cocked his head, regarding her with a furrowed brow.

"The ewes giving birth when they are unshorn. Some do it that way, but I would recommend shearing first." She pointed beneath a sheep. "Drinking is more difficult for the lambs when their mothers are covered with heavy wool. And of course the wool becomes distressed when the animal is pregnant. You want to shear when the distressed fibers are at the end of the wool not in the middle."

"So apparently, I need to shear, as well as, learn how to, uh, do what you did." He pointed toward where Sarah had delivered the lambs, his nose wrinkling.

She huffed a small laugh at his grimace. *Honestly.* "I thought you said your grandfather was a farmer."

"He is what you would call a 'gentleman farmer,' I suppose. He owned the land, but workers performed the actual labor. My grandfather supervised. I did sometimes give handfuls of straw to the horses, I'll have you know." He smiled and rolled his eyes good-naturedly.

Sarah found it refreshing to hear the man admit that he was inexperienced. He seemed willing to learn—and even more surprising, willing to learn from a *woman*. Her former assessment of him was changing, and she was starting to believe Daniel Burton to be sincere.

He broke off a tall blade of grass, swishing it as they walked. "I foolishly considered myself more than capable to this task, but until a few weeks ago, I had no true idea of how little I understood what I had undertaken nor how difficult the work was."

"And you dislike the work?" Sarah felt a twinge of disappointment at his words.

"No, exactly the opposite. I enjoy it, quite a lot actually. There is a very real satisfaction that comes from laboring with one's own hands and seeing the results of those efforts." He whipped the blade of grass. "But in all honestly, I do not know what I'm doing."

"Perhaps you need Mr. Hawkins more than I do." She said the words without thinking then darted a look at him, wondering if he'd think she intended them rudely. She was surprised to realize she hadn't. She gave him a smile that she hoped appeared reassuring. "You'll figure out the way of it soon enough. And you've plenty of people willing to assist in the meantime."

"Thank you."

His words made Sarah uncomfortably shy. No, not his words, his tone, and even more, the soft-eyed expression he directed to her. She looked around for something to change the topic and pointed toward a sheep laboring. Immediately she chided herself, remembering the discomfort on his face earlier. *The man is not interested in the more unpleasant aspects of animal husbandry.* But Daniel stopped walking and studied the ewe.

The animal continued chewing on a mouthful of weeds and seemed not to notice what was happening behind, even as its sides heaved and strained. After a moment, a lamb dropped out. The mother spun to tend to her new baby.

Sarah had always thought this a miracle. The way the animal knew exactly what to do, even though seconds earlier, it had seemed unconcerned with what was happening. It set to work immediately, carefully cleaning off the newborn, then nosing it up until the lamb rose on wobbly legs and stumbled around, finally finding her milk. She glanced up at Daniel, studying his face as he watched the scene.

A small smile touched his lips as he turned to her. "You must never get tired of this."

She nodded. Even though she'd seen a similar sight thousands of times, each new birth brought a warmth to her heart and made her eyes teary. "It's true. I don't think anyone could observe a birth and not feel as though they were witnessing something close to a miracle." Her face flushed as she said the words. She'd given him an insight into herself that she'd shared with few others. Typically with the workers, she maintained a businesslike manner. She kept her gaze on the animals.

They stood side-by-side and watched a few moments longer, then Daniel patted her shoulder. A simple act. Friendly, even brotherly, if she were to be honest. But the touch made Sarah's heart flip over. Her breath caught.

He moved away, clearing his throat. "Apparently I have shearing to do."

She nodded, finally raising her eyes to his once she was certain her reaction didn't show on her face. She was being silly, but she figured living alone for so long made one rather unused to social interactions.

"And do I purchase shearing equipment at the dry goods store in town?"

"There's a chance you could find some there—shearing scissors are what you'll need." Miraculously, her voice sounded normal. "But you can't depend on the store having a consistent inventory. You'd do better to place an order with the blacksmith, but tools typically require a few weeks." She tapped a finger on her lip, glancing across the flock to where the other men were still talking. "I'll happily lend mine to you once my own shearing is finished, and I will see if I can locate some this week when I am in Parramatta."

Daniel scratched behind his ear, squinting as he gazed over the field. "Or perhaps I might accompany you?"

"Oh." She felt heat bloom on her cheeks and wished for a fan or a parasol, something for her hands to do aside from fidgeting. She clasped them behind her back, trying to look as if his suggestion did not catch her unaware.

"Unless you are tending to clandestine matters, of course, and do not wish for company." He sounded as though he was speaking offhanded, but something in his voice made her think he was anxious for her reply. She'd remained silent too long.

"I should be grateful for your companionship, Mr. Burton." She was rewarded with his crooked smile again. "I thought to go on Wednesday. Early, of course. I shall need to take the wagon. We've supplies and a repaired plow blade to bring back to the farm." She didn't mention that she also planned to meet with the dressmaker to order a gown for her luncheon with him the following Thursday. She'd have to find time alone to attend to that.

"Splendid. I will meet you at the fork in the road."

"I should like that." Sarah gave a small smile.

Daniel reached for her hand, bowing over it in farewell. His gaze held hers. "As should I, neighbor."

Chapter 11

DANIEL'S SADDLE CREAKED BENEATH HIM when he shifted his position. He rubbed his neck, rolling his shoulders as he waited at the fork in the road for Sarah Whitaker's wagon. She'd said they would be leaving for Parramatta early but hadn't specified a time. Had he missed her? He didn't think so. She wouldn't have left before dawn, he was nearly certain. He leaned forward, stretching his back and idly wondering if he should dismount, perhaps give the horse a rest before their journey.

His visit to Sarah Hills had been two days earlier, and he'd thought of little since. What was it about the woman that occupied such a disproportionate amount of his thoughts? He supposed most of the work on his farm was rather mundane and left his mind plenty of time to wander. But it seemed when he allowed it the liberty, it meandered across the creek and always settled on his dark-eyelashed neighbor.

She managed to surprise him with each meeting. Typically, he got the measure of a person within merely a few minutes, but this particular woman seemed to be comprised of contradiction. A young lady who walked gracefully into a ball, wearing an elegant gown, seemed, by all reasoning, to be the reverse of the woman who plunged her arm nearly to the shoulder into a sheep to pull out a slippery lamb. The same woman who commanded her workers without hesitation and spoke confidently of matters such as shearing and farm management had fled sobbing from a ballroom.

He dismounted, tied his horse to a low branch, and stretched his legs as he paced, knowing he'd spend the next few hours in the saddle.

Maybe he was so fascinated with Sarah Whitaker because she was a puzzle. Maybe because he'd always fancied himself able to understand people, to compartmentalize them, and for some reason, this lady didn't fit into any mold. She was a paradox, and he wanted to know why. What had happened to change her from the carefree, trusting girl Captain Thackeray had described into a woman who kept a hand near her pistol as she instructed her employees? Why did she mistrust felons so deeply, and more importantly, would her view ever change?

That must be it, he thought. *I'm hoping to prove her wrong on that.* This was no doubt why he felt compelled toward Miss Whitaker. But the more he considered it, the idea didn't seem to explain fully his motivation.

The sun continued to rise, and finally Daniel saw a cloud of dust on the road. He waved as a wagon approached. The rough conveyance rode on large wooden-spoked wheels with metal rims. A pair of muscular, cream-colored bullocks yoked at the neck plodded along, kicking up dust in their wake. The wagon and its occupants drew near, accompanied by a man walking alongside, a long stick-handled whip resting on his shoulder.

Daniel lifted his hat and bent forward. "Lovely morning, is it not, Miss Whitaker?"

Sarah smiled and inclined her head. "We had a bit of a slow start today. I hope you did not wait long, Mr. Burton." She wore a gauzy white dress trimmed with blue ribbons and upon her head was a chipboard bonnet. A few strands of hair escaped, brushing over her cheeks and neck. If he didn't look at the rustic wagon or the wild country surrounding them, he could imagine her sitting prettily on the bench of a fine carriage in Hyde Park. Sarah shifted, and he immediately amended his assessment when he saw the pistol she held on her lap. *She is a paradox indeed.*

"Not at all," he said. Now that the wagon had stopped, he allowed his eyes to travel over the occupants. Sarah sat beside a man on the wooden bench. A younger woman with freckled cheeks sat on a sort of stool fastened behind the bench facing the empty wagon bed.

"These are my workers, Tom Gilbert and Martin Boyd." Sarah gestured toward the men and then twisted in the seat. "And Molly Green, my lady's maid."

"A pleasure, gentlemen, and Miss Green."

"And I should like to introduce Mr. Daniel Burton of—" Sarah cut off her words, raising her brows slightly and pinching them together. "Oh dear, Mr. Burton, I do not know the name of your farm."

"Not to worry, I have still not hit upon the perfect nomenclature for the property. Perhaps you could help me with the task on today's outing."

She gave a small smile, the very one he'd hoped to elicit. Her lips did not stretch thin as did most people's when forming the expression, but they curled just at the ends, pushing against the apples of her cheeks, and making her eyes brighten. He wondered if she practiced the effect in the looking glass, but he immediately decided against it. The expression seemed too genuine to be contrived. And Miss Whitaker did not strike him as the sort of woman to give too much effort to that kind of thing.

The man with the whip raised his hat, which Daniel noticed was made from some sort of leaves. "Uh, good day, Mr. Burton." The man looked between Daniel and Sarah, apparently unsure if his response was appropriate since their introduction had been interrupted. Tom and Molly followed his cue and greeted Daniel as well.

"Shall we be off then?" Sarah asked, situating herself back into the seat.

"Mr. Gilbert?" Daniel asked.

"Tom, sir."

"Tom." Daniel nodded. "If you don't mind, I would appreciate it very much if you'd ride my horse." Daniel retrieved the reins from where he'd tied them on a branch. "Miss Whitaker and I have a matter to discuss, you see, and it would be much more convenient if we were to ride together."

He heard Martin make a snorting sound and tried not to smile.

Tom chewed on his lip as he studied the horse. The man could not be pleased with the idea of riding on the hard wooden bench for hours, and making the journey on Daniel's fine stallion was surely tempting. He turned to Sarah. "My lady?"

Daniel didn't wait for a reply. He handed the reins to Tom and then climbed onto the wagon.

Tom scooted off the bench, hopping to the ground to make room.

"I appreciate it, Tom." Daniel sat beside Sarah, giving her a grin. He searched the bench and then looked toward the oxen. "And, ah, the leads . . . ?"

"Leads?" Sarah tipped her head.

"The reins. So I might pilot this contraption."

Sarah's brows shot up, then a smile grew on her face, culminating in a laugh. "Mr. Burton, one does not drive a dray from within it. Usually, the wagon is only used to transport goods, but it seemed silly to bring both the wagon and the carriage. That is why we are late. The men fastened this bench and stool onto the wagon so Molly and I did not have to sit in the bed." She pointed to the man with the whip standing to the side of the large beasts. "Martin is a Bullocky. He'll drive the animals."

"Oh." Daniel sat back, feeling rather foolish. He'd assumed bullocks behaved much like a team of horses, but over the next few moments, he saw how mistaken he'd been. Martin spoke, and the oxen responded immediately. With a jolt, the cart began to move. The bullocky didn't use his whip but called out in a firm voice what Daniel realized were the animal's names, Lou and Wally, when adjustments were needed.

"He's very skilled, isn't he?" Daniel watched, amazed by the man's calm as he controlled the huge oxen.

"Extremely," Sarah said. She nodded toward Martin. "One of the best you'll see. He's trained these two since they were calves, tying them together until they got used to constantly being side by side. Now they work as a team."

Daniel wondered if he'd ever get used to the strange world of New South Wales. He glanced to the side, watching Tom manage his spirited horse. The man was very capable as well.

Tom glanced up and met his eye. He smiled, showing dark holes where his teeth were missing. "A fine mount, sir."

"You ride very well."

Tom's smile widened. "Thank you, sir."

Daniel turned and saw Sarah watching him. Her eyes squinted slightly as if she were unable to make a determination.

"You seem to be confused, Miss Whitaker. I hope it is not the result of my company." He grabbed onto the brim of his hat as the cart rode over a rock. The wagon could use some springs, he thought.

Sarah held tightly with one gloved hand to the bench beside her. "Not yourself, sir, but your actions. I am afraid I do not understand you at all."

He thought her perplexed expression to be quite endearing. "Could I clarify in some way?"

"Why would you sit in this horribly uncomfortable dray instead of riding your horse? Heaven knows I only endure the jarring miles on this hard bench and bumpy road because I need to appear a respectable lady when I arrive in town." Her distasteful expression showed exactly how she felt about the situation.

"And do you think your actions are any less confusing?" Daniel asked.

"I explained the reasoning behind mine, Mr. Burton. They are not of my choosing, but yours on the other hand . . ."

"And I told you my reasoning as well." He shifted his weight onto one hip, thinking it might ease the impact on his backside. "I need your assistance to choose a name for my farm." Another bounce convinced him to shift back, resigning himself to sitting flat on the hard board. "As Sarah Hills is already taken, I'm afraid I'll need to come up with another." He smiled at the roll of her eyes and twisted around. "And I'd appreciate your input too, Miss Green."

Molly turned from watching the landscape.

"Very well," Sarah said. She looked back at Molly and nodded her permission for the maid to participate in the conversation. "Let me see. Obviously, you will want a name that is easy to pronounce and one that you like quite a lot since you will say it and write it often." She squinted and looked up at the trees passing slowly beside them. "Personally, I think it should be a name important to you. It should mean something. My father named his property after me, since I was his only family. Perhaps there is someone dear to you." She turned back to him. "Your mother? What is her name?"

"Harriet, but she is usually called Hattie."

"Hattie Hills?" Molly suggested.

Daniel smiled but shook his head. The name sounded silly, and it didn't feel right to him. He thought of what Sarah had said. He wanted the name to mean something, to be important, and while he loved his mother, he didn't want to name his farm Hattie Hills.

"A sister?" Sarah asked.

"My sisters are called Meg and Rosalind."

"Ooh, I like Rosalind Acres." Molly clapped her hands.

Daniel shook his head again. This was going to be more difficult than he'd anticipated.

"Some people name their farm after a feature of the land," Sarah continued. "The pond, perhaps? Or you have a fine forest along the west side."

"Burton Pond?" Molly offered.

Daniel shook his head, feeling like the motion was so far his only contribution to the conversation. "I don't wish to name the land after myself."

"Hmmm." Molly pursed her face into a look of concentration.

Sarah just watched him, and he winced, hoping she didn't think his statement was meant as a barb. Her expression remained thoughtful, and he decided that she'd not taken offense.

He pondered the options. Should he name the land after the Duke of Southampton? He was, after all, the reason Daniel was master of the property, the person who'd provided him with the opportunity for a new life. Would it honor the man or seem presumptuous to give his humble acreage such a lofty title? Or he could name it for Charleston, the city where he'd been raised. He didn't feel as though that was the correct answer either. Daniel scratched behind his ear.

The trio rode in silence, and the creak of the wheels, the bouncing of the wagon, and the plodding of the oxen became louder to his ears. He looked up at the trees above, hoping to spot a koala bear among their bark-less branches. In the month since his arrival, he'd only seen one of the shy animals with its flat oval-shaped nose. Somewhere above, he heard a Kookaburra's laughing call, and from the corner of his eye, he glimpsed a speckled monitor lizard's tail flick as it scuttled away from the road.

"Maybe a name that's important to you from literature or the Bible." Sarah's voice pulled him back from his mind's wanderings. "A person whose story inspires you or one that you relate to?"

Her words brought a name to mind. "St. Francis," he said slowly.

"St. Francis of Assisi?" Sarah continued to watch him.

He considered what he knew of the man. Francis had been known in his youth for drinking and revelry. He was imprisoned, and once he was free, he changed his ways, becoming an honorable person. As Daniel thought through Francis's life, he felt a connection to the saint. He grinned. This was the one. He'd hit upon the perfect name for his property. "Yes, Francis."

"Francis Park," Molly said.

"Francis Park." Daniel dipped his head in a firm nod.

Sarah smiled. "I like it."

Daniel said the words again in his mind and felt even stronger surety about the name. He hadn't realized how closely his life paralleled St. Francis's—well, up to this point anyway. He thought it was a fine reminder of his own transformation not to mention the workers on his property. St. Francis's story seemed to him the essence of this land. A place where men and women who had made mistakes were given a second chance to live an admirable life.

He glanced back into the trees, scanning the branches further for the elusive koala. The women probably assumed he had chosen the name because he appreciated the wild and domesticated animals on his farm. He smiled to himself, liking the idea of a name that was significant to only himself unless he chose to share its true meaning.

"You ladies have been extremely helpful," Daniel said, gripping the bench and leaning as the wagon thumped down into another dip on one side. "The exercise didn't take nearly as long as I'd expected; we still have quite a journey ahead. What shall we talk about?"

Sarah kept her eyes on the oxen ahead of them. "I think you should choose the topic, sir. You are, after all, the guest on this bullock dray."

He studied her profile and could see nervousness in her expression. The pinch of her brows gave her away. Despite her light-toned response, he could see she was uncertain. Daniel wondered again why she spoke so confidently about some topics but turned shy when the conversation threatened toward a more personal course. He considered making an observation about the weather or inquiring about a mutual acquaintance but felt inexplicably bold. "Then I choose to talk about . . . you."

Sarah's eyes widened and her lips parted, but she did not look at him.

"Will you tell me about your family? How did you come to live on a farm in the Australian countryside? And why are you such an expert on sheep farming?"

Sarah turned toward him. She was quiet for a moment, and he wondered if she would answer. When she raised her eyes, he saw something in them. Her expression seemed to firm up, resolved. "My mother died three days after I was born, and from what I've been told, her death was difficult for my father. So much so, that he left me in the care of an aunt in Crawley and journeyed here to New South Wales, perhaps thinking to be as far away from his memories as possible."

"So you grew up in Sussex?"

"Yes." Her gaze moved from his.

Though she seemed shy, Daniel amended his earlier thought. She was not nervous but wary. Sarah did not like to reveal too much of herself.

"Papá visited England, and he would tell me tales of the magical land where he raised sheep. Where the seasons were reversed, and Christmas is in summer. Of animals that stood straight like a man and bounded on their hind legs; dark-skinned people with clay-painted bodies, who hunted with bent sticks; and exotic birds that burst from trees in an eruption of color. He did love the birds." She smiled softly, her eyes far away as she spoke. "I begged him each time to take me back with him." Her voice trailed off but only for an instant, then her gaze focused once again.

"Finally he did send for me. Aunt Hortensia and I made the journey aboard the *Coeur d'Alene*. When we arrived, we learned Papá was dead."

"You and your aunt took on the management of the farm then?"

She nodded.

Daniel tried to imagine a lady and her young charge, accustomed to life in an English town, undertaking the responsibilities of a farm in a foreign land. He could not begin to guess how difficult it must have been.

"I know what you're thinking." Sarah looked to the side and breathed out heavily. "You're wondering why we didn't just return home to England."

"I admit, the thought did occur to me."

She nodded. "My aunt was determined to do just that, but when I saw the farm, walked through the halls of the house, and sat at my papá's desk . . . I could not do it. Selling the farm, leaving, it made it feel like Papá never existed." She lifted her shoulder in a shrug. "Those notions might simply be the product of a young girl's understanding, but staying and continuing Papá's dream seemed the most important thing to me. So I convinced my aunt to remain."

"Ah, yes, your aunt. You mentioned that she had passed away. How long ago was that?" Daniel asked.

Sarah's brows pulled together. "She died two years ago. A fire."

"I am sorry."

Her shoulders sagged as if telling the story had wearied her. "And now you know." She tipped her head as if trying to read his reaction to what she'd said.

He didn't allow anything but approval to show in his expression. He felt strongly that was what she sought when she looked at him so closely. The story she told was vastly incomplete, but he got the notion that he'd learned more than she felt comfortable sharing. He felt as though he'd scored a victory, that perhaps she was testing him, deciding, based on his reaction, whether or not to trust.

After a moment, she looked down, brushing her thumb over the design on the metal barrel of the pistol. "And now you should tell me about yourself, Mr. Burton." Her lips quirked. "Who is my new neighbor? What brought you from the distant states of America to the wild outback of New South Wales?"

He smiled. "My story is rather dull compared with your own." He grabbed onto the edge of the bench again to keep from sliding off when the dray bounced over an uneven stretch of road. His gloves caught on the rough wood; if he were not wearing them, he would likely have splinters all over his hands. "My younger sister, Meg, and I journeyed to London a few years ago as guests of a relative—the Duke of Southampton. I quite fell in love with the society in England, and she quite fell in love with a Spanish man named Rodrigo. And once they married, I felt rather lost."

He thought of how to tell the remainder of the story without divulging the whole truth of his past. He shifted on the bench, wishing there were a more comfortable way to sit—an armrest, or a chair back or something to lean against—but knew he was simply stalling, and so he took a breath and continued. "While my cousin treated me very well, I spent too much time on frivolities. I was happy for the chance to set out on my own, become my own man, you know."

Sarah nodded. "Why didn't you return to America?"

"The war between Britain and the States prevented me from going back across the Atlantic, so my future had to lie elsewhere. And, here I am."

His story was every bit as incomplete as hers had been—more so, since he left out the most important parts—but he wasn't ready to tell her yet. He thought if he could win her trust, then he could let out the less savory details a bit at a time. And perhaps she'd tell him more of herself than the extremely brief summary she'd given.

They rode for a time in a companionable silence. Daniel thinking over the small snippets he'd learned about the woman beside him, and Sarah watching the landscape at the side of the road. The creaking wheels and the monotonous plodding of the oxen lulled him into a sort of trance. He closed his eyes briefly and breathed in. The air was not as humid as it was in Charleston, although that might change as they moved into summer. And it smelled clean and crisp, so unlike the streets of London. He wondered how he'd lived so long in that enormous crowded city with buildings all around. The thought now seemed suffocating as he stared at the vast open space and the lush foliage. The trees had silvery feathering leaves that shimmered in the breeze, and their trunks were sometimes reddish or pink, and other times, he could have sworn they had a bluish hue. The land was strange and wonderful and, in an untamed way, beautiful. He was feeling more and more attached to Australia with each passing day.

Eventually, Sarah shifted, and he glanced at her. She turned and looked ahead, pointing. He followed her gaze, seeing in the distance, the few buildings that marked the outskirts of the small town of Parramatta.

"I am glad you did," Sarah said.

He turned toward her, thinking back to where their conversation had left off. "I beg your pardon?"

"I am glad you came to the colony, Mr. Burton." She didn't meet his eyes, and her cheeks reddened.

The words settled on him pleasantly, making his chest warm. He was disappointed their ride was nearly at an end, but he could not wait to get off this horrible bench. He would be feeling its effects for weeks.

But he'd feel the much more pleasant effects of Sarah Whitaker's shy declaration for some time as well.

Chapter 12

SARAH TOOK DANIEL'S HAND AS she stepped—or rather jumped—down from the wagon in front of the dry goods store. She did not think it would be possible to put into words how completely she despised riding in the horrible conveyance. If she'd traveled by horse, she would have arrived in a fourth of the time and not been bounced around for hours on a hard slab of wood, wearing a gown, of all things. Why did practicality and basic comfort have to be so opposite to ladylike decorum?

Daniel touched her lower back to steady her, and heat flared over her skin. She turned her face to hide the fierce blush she could feel on her cheeks. Perhaps the ride hadn't been completely terrible after all. Mr. Burton had been a pleasant distraction, and the journey had not seemed as tedious as it typically did.

She pushed the pistol into her reticule. The long-barreled weapon stretched the satin awkwardly as it hung from her wrist.

While Mr. Burton tended to his horse, she gave Martin and Tom instructions and set a meeting place. It wasn't as though she wouldn't be able to find the large wagon in a town with only a few roads, but if she allowed the men too much freedom, they'd spend the day in the pub and lose track of time. Two hours should be sufficient for them to gather supplies and the repaired plow blade and still have a chance for some socialization with the townsfolk. And she would certainly be finished with her errands by then.

Mr. Burton opened the door to the dry goods store, and Sarah entered, followed by Molly.

"Good day, Miss Whitaker." Alvin Grimes waved from the far side of the store, where he was arranging jars on a shelf. He was a tall, slender man with a beakish nose and a mass of dark curls that he attempted to keep under control with some sort of grease. When she was younger, Sarah had thought the effect was rather like looking at a heap of shiny black worms. "You've come for your monthly order?"

"Yes. Tom and Martin will be around shortly." She stepped farther into the store, squinting as her eyes adjusted to being inside. The dry goods store was the most popular place to purchase goods in the town. As a convict, Mr. Grimes worked under license and wasn't permitted to adjust his prices. Sarah was a little surprised to see the store empty.

Daniel closed the door behind them. "Mr. Grimes, have you met my neighbor?" She turned to the side, motioning toward Daniel. "Mr. Burton of Francis Park?"

Daniel met her gaze, and the right side of his mouth rose in his crooked smile. He gave a small wink, then turned to the shopkeeper. "Yes, we've met a few times. Good day, Mr. Grimes."

"How can I assist you today, sir?" Alvin wiped his hands on his apron as he moved toward the counter at the front of the store.

Sarah half listened as the men discussed shearing scissors. She moved away and perused a shelf but didn't actually pay attention to anything upon it. Daniel's wink and that uneven smile—though she knew the implication had been nothing more than a friendly acknowledgement of her use of his farm's new name—left her flustered. There was no reason his silly gesture should cause such a stir within her, and the feeling was disconcerting. Just like his simple action two days earlier. Honestly, he'd only patted her shoulder. Why must she remember such an inconsequential thing? And why did a rush of goose pimples accompany the memory? She picked up a jar and pretended to look at the label.

Realizing Molly was speaking, she turned. "Pardon?"

"Might I wait outside, my lady?"

"Oh, yes, of course." Sarah glanced toward the men.

Daniel leaned with his elbow on the counter and shrugged when he saw her looking toward him. "Miss Whitaker, sadly, you were correct. There are no shearing scissors to be found in this fine establishment; although, Mr. Grimes assures me there is a distinct possibility some will arrive within a few months." The side of his mouth twitched as if he were holding back a smile.

"Indeed I apologize, sir," Mr. Grimes said. "One never knows what products will arrive in the colony, and it is even less certain which items will make it to the outer towns. But I will send a specific request for farming shears in your name to Sydney."

"I appreciate it."

The door opened, and Mr. Grimes moved to greet another customer.

Sarah joined Daniel at the front of the store. "Our shearing will be finished soon. For a while anyway," she said. "So do not make yourself overly worried, Mr. Burton. I'll happily lend you shears."

Daniel opened his mouth to speak but then closed it, his head tipping slightly as he looked at her. Instead of the grin or witty remark she expected, his eyes grew soft, and deep within, they darkened. His gaze darted from her eyes to her lips and back.

Sarah stood, frozen beneath his gaze, and the air between them grew hot. He stood so very close. She drew in a shaky breath, heart pounding as she fought both the compulsion to step forward and to pull back. For that moment nothing existed outside of the two of them.

"Can I be of assistance, Miss Whitaker?" Mr. Grimes appeared behind the counter.

Sarah jumped. "Oh." She turned fully toward the shopkeeper. Her legs were shaking. "No, thank you. My men will be by presently for the order. Good day." She felt Daniel watching her, rattling her mind. She needed to escape. Without looking at either man, she dipped in a curtsey and started toward the door.

"Miss Whitaker?"

At the shopkeeper's words, she spun back around.

"Would you like to purchase that item as well?"

Sarah looked at Mr. Grimes blankly for a moment, before she realized he was indicating the jar she held. She walked back, placing it on the counter. "Yes. Please add this"—for the first time, she looked closely at the jar—"ah . . . pickles to my order."

Mr. Grimes's brow ticked upward, but he just nodded. "Very well."

Sarah snatched the pickle jar from the counter and hurried out.

Once outside, she closed her eyes, taking in a deep breath as she willed her heartbeat to calm. What on earth had happened? She'd felt something. Something that she couldn't begin to describe in words, but it had stolen the very breath from her lungs.

Hearing the door open behind her, she started. She couldn't face Mr. Burton right now. She spotted Molly on the other side of the road, speaking with a man. Sarah hurried across.

The couple stopped talking when they saw her.

Sarah nodded, acknowledging the stranger but not speaking to him. She judged him to be in his midtwenties; his tanned face and duck-cloth uniform told her he was a government man. She glanced at his wrists and saw the scars of manacles.

Molly curtseyed to her mistress. "Shall I carry your purchase, my lady?"

Sarah glanced down, for the second time realizing she held a jar of pickles. She *hated* pickles. Handing them to her lady's maid, she glanced back and saw Mr. Burton walking toward them.

The stranger excused himself, but Sarah hardly noticed as she pushed down her shoulders, hoping she didn't look as rattled as she felt.

Daniel tipped his hat to Molly's friend as they passed, then smiled when he neared the women. "Well, that was disappointing, but I suppose it wasn't a complete waste of time. Something good did come of the visit."

Sarah looked up at him, her skin prickling in anticipation of what he might say. He *had* felt something in the dry goods store.

But his expression remained casually friendly as he lifted his chin toward Molly. "Pickles."

She felt her insides wilt but kept her head up and put on an equally pleasant expression. "Yes. We were very fortunate indeed." She switched the heavy reticule to her other wrist as she spoke. "I suppose this is where we part, sir. I have another errand, and you are headed to the smithy?"

He nodded, glancing up the road to where the blacksmith's forge bellowed out smoke.

She inclined her head in farewell, not wanting to meet his gaze. "Thank you for the company, Mr. Burton, and I wish you a pleasant return journey. Come, Molly." She started away.

"Miss Whitaker?" Daniel called.

Having no other alternative than to face him, she turned back, looking up.

"I hoped we might meet for luncheon before we start back. It's a long ride on that bench, and I would very much prefer to undertake it with a full stomach."

His words took her by surprise. "I . . . but wouldn't you prefer to make the return journey on horseback? Your horse is here, and you will arrive in a fraction of the time."

He pulled down the sides of his mouth and tapped his chin, looking upward as if he were considering. "No, I don't believe I would, Miss

Whitaker." When he looked back at her, the right side of his mouth rose, and in his eyes, there was a trace of what she'd seen before. Somehow, his gaze had grown more intense and gentler at the same time.

Sarah's heart stuttered.

"Shall we say Freemason's Arms in an hour?"

She nodded dumbly, and he tipped his hat, bowing before he turned away. Sarah stared after him for a moment before shaking her head, lifting her chin, and walking purposefully in the other direction.

Fifteen minutes later, she sat on a wooden chair, looking at fashion plates and running her fingers over the bolts of fabric Mrs. Wright, the dressmaker, had in her inventory. Aunt Hortensia would have complained that the styles in the drawings were years out of fashion and the fabric patterns horribly outdated, but Sarah knew they were lucky to have a dressmaker in town at all.

Sarah studied Mrs. Wright. She was young and pretty, a shy woman who'd married a sergeant in the Royal Marine Corps a few years earlier, causing quite a scandal. She wore her hair pulled back tidily beneath a mob cap, and her gingham dress, though simple, was made in a modern style with sleeves that reached nearly to her elbows. She carried herself with elegance, Sarah thought.

Sarah knew her story—everyone in town did. As a young girl, Mrs. Wright had worked as a seamstress for a prestigious modiste in London but had been caught stealing lace, resulting in her transportation to the colony. Her term served, she had started a small business in her home, and ladies came from as far away as Sydney Town to enlist her services.

"With your coloring, Miss Whitaker, this lilac silk would be lovely." Mrs. Wright unrolled the fabric from its bolt, draping it over the table.

Sarah slipped off her gloves and ran her fingers over the beautiful material. Within the fabric, small white flowers had been embroidered, dotting the lavender background. The effect was breathtaking, and a part of her she didn't listen too very often longed to wear a stunning dress made from the soft material. The more practical side of her wondered if it were too fine to wear to a simple luncheon at her neighbor's farm. She decided to ask Mrs. Wright for something a bit less extravagant.

She turned back to a bolt she'd been looking at earlier, a simpler green cotton, but stopped as the image of Mr. Burton's bewildering expression appeared in her mind. Simply the memory was enough to bring back the blush to her cheeks.

She could not for the life of her understand what had changed between the two of them. What had led up to the moment in the dry goods store? Perhaps she had simply misinterpreted his intent or even imagined it. Had she allowed her neighbor's handsome face and playful smile to color her interpretation of his friendliness? Over her short lifetime, she had so few interactions with gentlemen that she feared she was reading more into the incident than had actually taken place. She'd felt so curious, so off-balance. Perhaps her mind had jumped to erroneous conclusions. Could the heat be to blame? Or the long ride in the sun? Maybe she was simply hungry.

Her hand hovered between the fabrics, and suddenly the choice felt too great, as if deciding on a material for her dress would confirm or refute the reality of a connection with Mr. Burton. She rubbed her eyes, wishing she had someone to give her advice or with whom to discuss this turn of events, whether it was real or not.

Her mind turned to Dorthea Iverson. But though they were friends, she didn't feel as if she could confide something like this to Dorthea. And besides, she lived nearly two hours in the opposite direction from Sarah Hills.

The backs of her eyes itched, and more than anything, Sarah wished her aunt were here. She would have decided on a dress and been out the door and off to the next task with hardly a thought. Sarah slumped back in the chair, letting out a sigh. "I just don't know." Her voice cracked, and she was completely humiliated that the two women should see her come apart like this.

"Both would favor you, my lady," Molly said tentatively.

"No need to decide today, Miss Whitaker." Mrs. Wright spoke in a kind voice and patted Sarah's hand where it rested on the table. "Perhaps you would like some tea?"

"Yes, thank you."

The dressmaker moved into her other room.

Sarah closed her eyes and held her head in her palms, resting her elbows on the table in a very unladylike fashion. She didn't know why she felt so overwhelmed by something that, an hour ago, would have been no more than a simple decision. She'd placed too much significance on this gown and next Thursday's luncheon, just as she'd placed too much significance on the moment in Mr. Grimes's shop.

Hearing Mrs. Wright return, Sarah twisted her head around, stretching her neck and sitting up straight. Enough wallowing. She accepted the tea gratefully, blowing over it as she sorted through the pictures with a new determination. She found two dress fashions, one with the elbow-length sleeves like Mrs. Wright's and another with a much fancier neckline and gathered sleeves.

"I would like both." She used her most decisive voice. "This dress in the silk, and the other in green." She set down the teacup, allowed Mrs. Wright to take some measurements, then discussed embellishments, lace borders, and complementary headpieces.

Ten minutes later, once delivery arrangements were made, she bid Mrs. Wright farewell and led Molly toward the Freemason's Arms with renewed purpose. It was time she remembered that she was the mistress of one of the most profitable farms in the colony. She would not let a crooked smile and a pair of deep brown eyes turn her into a ninny.

Chapter 13

DANIEL LEANED BACK IN HIS chair in the Freemason's Arms dining room. He took a drink and without thinking glanced again to the door then chided himself for his distraction. He twisted in his seat, crossing one leg over the other as he focused back on his companion.

Mr. Gregory Blaxland seemed to be a young man, but Daniel thought his roundish face was deceiving. He wore his thick, brown hair short with long sideburns. After speaking with Blaxland for some time, Daniel decided the man was probably in his midthirties.

After a quick visit to the smithy, where Daniel had again failed to procure shearing scissors, he'd spent the better part of an hour sipping rum from the government brewery and listening to Mr. Blaxland describe his expedition across the Blue Mountains, the resulting road, and the land beyond.

"And how long is the journey to Bathurst?" Daniel asked.

"Now that the road's complete, you can make it on horseback in five or six days, and that's taking a leisurely pace." He tipped back his head, finishing off his drink, then motioned to a server to refill the glass. "You've never seen a lovelier plain. A wide flowing river and stretching out before you, untouched land thick with vegetation and chock full of wildlife."

"Sounds like a fine sight." Daniel drummed his fingers on the table until he realized what he was doing. He took another drink, letting his eyes wander toward the door before snapping them back. He was acting ridiculous. Of course she was coming. It was perfectly reasonable for a lady to be—he glanced at the clock on the wall—*two minutes late*. He could maintain a conversation with this gentleman without letting himself get distracted every few seconds.

Mr. Blaxland moved his newly filled glass beneath his nose, sniffing before he took a drink. "There's money to be made in the west, Mr. Burton. A man can purchase an enormous amount of very fertile land for a pittance." He leaned closer, lowering his voice. "And I've even heard rumors of gold."

Three minutes late.

Daniel scratched behind his ear. "It sounds very nice, but I'm quite taken with my farm."

"Bah, you could sell that place and buy ten times the acreage with your profit. I know of a certain female sheep rancher who'd give ya top dollar for it."

And with that, Daniel's best efforts to keep his mind off Miss Sarah Whitaker were defeated. He could not hold back the memory of that moment, even if he'd wanted to. What had come over him in the shop? He'd been enjoying the day, feeling rather happy, despite the soreness in his posterior region. Then she'd stepped up beside him at the dry goods counter, and the world had changed.

In that brief moment, Sarah had looked up at him through her dark lashes. The light from the window had caught her eyes just right, making them shine. Her skin had seemed to glow, and when she smiled at him, his wits had fled. He'd only just been able to restrain himself from touching her cheek.

Mr. Blaxland cleared his throat, nodding with a pleased expression. "I see you're considering the idea."

Daniel tried to push the thoughts away, along with the flood of questions and emotions they brought with them. They were making him anxious, and his eyes itched to look toward the door. "It is a fine idea, sir, and I thank you for your suggestion, but at the present time, I'm not inclined to sell."

"You're making a mistake. Those horses you talked about breeding, they'd thrive in the wide open land of the plains. There's more opportunity out west than a man can . . ." Mr. Blaxland's words trailed off as his gaze flipped upward over Daniel's shoulder. He stood.

Daniel turned and saw Sarah had approached without his notice. She'd removed her bonnet, and her hair curled in wisps around her cheeks. Her eyes squinted slightly as she studied him, and he wondered if she'd overheard any of the conversation. "Miss Whitaker." He rose, smiling and bending forward as he took her hand. "And Miss Green," he said to the maid, who stood behind her.

"Mr. Burton, I thank you for waiting for me again. It seems I'm destined to be tardy today." Sarah curtsied. "And, Mr. Blaxland, a pleasure. It's been some time since I've seen you in Parramatta."

He took her hand and bowed. "Always nice to see you, Miss Whitaker."

Daniel pulled back a chair, motioning for Sarah to be seated, then did the same for Molly.

"Are you joining us for luncheon, Mr. Blaxland?" Sarah asked.

"I'm afraid not. I just stopped in for a quick drink before leaving town."

"I am sorry to hear it." She folded her hands in her lap, and Daniel wondered how she could look so calm after—

His gut grew heavy. Perhaps the reaction had only been on his part. Of course, it was just as his sister always told him, he found himself in love with a different pretty young lady nearly every week. He felt irritated with himself for the silly notion that this time it was somehow different.

Daniel shook the man's hand. "Thank you for the drink and the interesting conversation."

"I hope you will consider what I told you." Mr. Blaxland raised his brows and leaned forward in a knowing look.

Daniel nodded. "I shall, thank you."

"And I will certainly see the both of you at the Hawkesbury races next month."

Daniel's stomach tightened. He smiled, but knew his expression looked forced.

"I look forward to it, sir," Sarah said. "And will any of your horses be racing?"

He shrugged. "I have a few slated to run, but you know, I never miss an opportunity to see the most superb horseflesh in the colony."

Daniel wiped off his forehead while the two talked. He pocketed his handkerchief and clasped his hands behind his back, pushing out a few breaths until his heart stopped pommeling his chest.

"And you will come, as well, won't you, Mr. Burton?" Sarah said. Her brows pinched together when she looked at him, but other than that, her expression didn't change.

"Perhaps, but as you are well aware, I have quite a bit of shearing to do." He grimaced then smiled.

Mr. Blaxland shook his head. "You'll not want to miss this, and surely you've sufficient workers to give you one day's respite. The finest society in all of the colony will be represented."

"I will keep it in mind, sir."

Mr. Blaxland took his leave, and Daniel sat into his chair more heavily than he'd intended.

"You have grown quite pale, Mr. Burton." Sarah pushed his drink toward him.

"Just hungry, I think." He took a drink then waved over a server and placed an order for their meal.

When he turned back to the table, Sarah still studied him. "I think you will enjoy the races quite a lot. Especially since you have such an interest in horses."

Had the room suddenly become stifling? And his cravat must have grown tighter by several inches in the past few moments.

Luckily, the inn's owner chose that moment to approach. "Miss Whitaker, how fortuitous to find you here."

"Mr. Steadman." She smiled and allowed him to take her hand.

"I was just now passing through the dining room on my way to seek out a messenger." He handed her an envelope. "This came for you this morning."

"Thank you." She turned over the letter, a smile lighting her face.

Mr. Steadman excused himself.

"It is from Captain Thackeray," Sarah told Daniel. "Do you mind?"

"Not at all." Daniel motioned with a wave of his fingers. He was grateful for any distraction that would keep them from revisiting the topic of the horse races.

Sarah broke the seal and slid out a folded sheet of paper. She turned it over and read. "Oh, Captain Thackeray is coming back to Parramatta sooner than he planned." She glanced up at him then continued reading, a smile growing on her face. Daniel's throat felt sour, and he realized he felt jealous of her delight at the captain's letter. He chided himself for the petty reaction.

Plates of food were set in front of them, and when Daniel inhaled, he realized he was ravenous. He'd not eaten since before sunrise, and the hour was well after noon.

"He will be here on Sunday and hopes for a visit." She folded the paper and set it on the table. "Of course he shall come for dinner."

Daniel offered a basket of rolls to the ladies. "I spoke with the captain on the night of the governor's assembly."

Sarah bit into a roll, nodding as she chewed, then swallowed. "He is my oldest friend—well, not my oldest, but I have known him longer than any other person. I sailed to the colony on his ship when I was a girl."

Daniel nodded. "Yes, he told me."

She turned to him, a question in her gaze, and he realized he'd let it slip that they'd been discussing her before she arrived at the party. "He inquired about you, hoped you'd be attending," he said by way of explanation.

Sarah nodded. "And you liked him?"

"He seemed to me a very sincere person. Quite likeable." Daniel took a bite, making a note to purchase some beef for Winnie to cook. He'd grown rather tired of bat, fowl, and kangaroo.

Sarah looked at him, and he saw the pinch of her brows that he'd learned to mean she felt uncertain. "Should you like to come as well, Mr. Burton? I think Captain Thackeray would enjoy your company. As would I." She said these last words in a softer voice that had a curious effect on his heartbeat.

"Sunday?"

Sarah nodded.

"All of these events arising between now and next Thursday are quite ruining the impact of my luncheon, you know." He smiled and winked to let her know he was teasing.

"I promise I am not trying to subvert your party planning."

"I suppose the earlier occasions will just serve to whet your appetite for the grand festivities."

She laughed. "I hope I do not die from the anticipation."

After their meal, Sarah left a reply for Captain Thackeray with the inn's owner. Then they climbed into the dray and began the long ride back.

The conversation for the return journey remained on easy topics. They were quiet for long stretches, but Daniel did not feel as if the silence was awkward. He took the opportunity to consider the woman beside him. There was still so much he didn't know about her. For example, he didn't understand her intense mistrust. Captain Thackeray had hinted at a reason behind it, but Daniel would not press her. He didn't feel as though she was ready to divulge more about herself, not today anyway. And he understood. He wasn't ready either.

As the time passed, he experimented with various positions, but there were only so many ways to sit on a backless wooden bench. For a while, he rested an elbow on his knee and his chin on his hand—until a jolt made him smack his own jaw and bite his tongue. He folded his arms but found, after dozing off and nearly sliding off the side, that he needed to keep a grip on the seat.

A loud noise gave him a start. He heard it again and recognized it as a snore. When he twisted, looking into the bed of the wagon, he saw Molly had dropped from her stool and lay sprawled on bags of beans, sugar, and flour. She snored again, and he grinned, thinking how comfortable her makeshift bed must be. He looked at Sarah, wondering if she'd chastise her lady's maid for her bad manners, but her head hung forward, bobbing with the movement of the wagon. She still held on to the seat, propping herself up with one arm, and the other hand held her gun in her lap.

Daniel knew, caught unawares, one good bump could send her off the edge. Should he wake her? He decided against it and leaned closer, gripping the bench behind her to be ready if she should slide.

Sarah's head continued to bounce, and a few times, she bumped into his shoulder. He held her arm, gently, just to steady her. *Vanilla*, he thought. *She smells like vanilla.*

They neared the fork in the road as the sun dropped nearly to the horizon.

Daniel motioned for the men to continue onward. He knew from Conall Stewart that the road to Sarah Hills would curve around the hills for another hour, at least. And, well, he didn't want to wake her until he absolutely had to. He liked feeling as though he was taking care of her. Even if she didn't actually need it and didn't really want him to.

The road started to rise, and ahead Daniel could see lights. He realized he hadn't ever seen Sarah's house; as they approached, he squinted to get a better look. By the glow of the setting sun, he saw a white stone structure with pillars beside the front entrance, holding up a second-story balcony. The house was built in the style of a country manor house though not nearly as grand. But for the colony, he thought it every bit as majestic as any structure he'd seen, excepting perhaps the Government House.

The gardens were bathed in shadow, but he could smell flowers, herbs, and the scent of orange blossoms.

"Miss Whitaker," he said in a quiet voice, patting her arm softly. "Wake up. You are home now."

Sarah sat up, blinking. She rubbed her eyes, an expression of confusion moving across her face. "Oh, Mr. Burton." She turned, looking toward her house then back to him, tipping her head. "You rode the entire way. Why did—?" Her brow softened. "It is because I was asleep, isn't it?"

"I couldn't have you falling off the bench," he said.

The wagon stopped, and he stepped down, groaning as he rubbed his lower back. He reached to help Sarah down.

"Thank you. You really didn't have to do that."

"It was my pleasure."

"That, Mr. Burton, is a completely untrue statement." She winced and rubbed her neck.

"Not untrue, perhaps exaggerated." He smiled and leaned to the side, stretching with another groan.

Tom approached, leading his mount. "If ya please, sir. I'll water your horse and fetch another so as I can accompany you to the creek."

"I'd appreciate it, Tom. I fear I'd wander in the dark until morning, and even then, I'm not sure I'd know the way."

Workers came from the house, unloading the dry goods and taking them inside. Sarah watched them then turned toward him, frowning. "This entire trip was a waste for you, wasn't it?" She lifted her chin toward the wagon. "I accomplished all of my errands, and you spent the entire day riding on a hard wooden bench with nothing to show for it."

"Not a waste of time at all. I quite enjoyed our time together, didn't you?"

She studied his face, perhaps trying to decide whether he was teasing. Finally, she gave a small smile. "Yes. I did enjoy it."

"I almost forgot." He reached inside his jacket and pulled out a paper sack. He unrolled it, took out a peppermint stick, then put the sack back in his pocket. He planned to save the other for Trudy. "This is for you."

Sarah took it, her confused expression returning.

"My mother always gave me a sweet if I kept out of mischief on an outing. And I must say, Miss Whitaker, you behaved very nicely." He winked.

She looked at the peppermint stick then up at him, and instead of her confused expression or the smile he'd been hoping for, her eyes were damp. She looked utterly overwhelmed at the gesture. "I don't remember the last time anyone bought me a sweet. Perhaps my father or Mr. Thackeray when I was small, but . . ." She swallowed. "Thank you, Mr. Burton. This was very thoughtful." Her voice was so quiet, he almost couldn't make out her words. She looked up at him, holding a sweet in one hand and a pistol in the other in a perfect display of the contradicting woman he was coming to be fond of.

He heard hoofbeats and turned to see Tom carrying a lantern and leading two horses.

"Good night, Mr. Burton." Sarah curtseyed and executed a smile that was perfection, before she hurried into the house.

The memory of the expression lingered in his mind for the entire ride home. *Not a waste of time at all.*

Chapter 14

Two days after the trip into town, Sarah sat atop her horse, pausing on a rise near the creek. She'd argued with herself since she'd awoken about whether or not she should take the shears to Francis Park herself. It was certainly not proper for a young lady to call upon a gentleman. But this was a matter of business, was it not? Surely that made it acceptable. She rolled her eyes as she went back over her line of reasoning. Should she have brought along a servant? She wasn't calling on him, not really. Just making a delivery. A delivery that any of her workers could make without going against propriety.

She nearly turned back around, but the fact of the matter was she *did* wish to see Mr. Burton, and the shearing scissors were simply an excuse. Her face burned at the admission. Well, at least she was honest with herself. She'd visited this section of her fields so many times over the past two days, the workers must be on edge with her constant presence. She used the excuse of wanting to check on the lambs, but it was flimsy, and she knew it.

Apparently Mr. Burton had no need to ride on this side of his property lately—at least not when she'd been in the field. She was behaving exactly like the hoydens Aunt Hortensia had warned her about, and she had a reputation to consider.

She turned the horse, following the creek toward the foothills of the mountains, scanning the slopes to make sure the sheep weren't too close to the water. She blew out a breath, wiping a bead of sweat from her cheek. She looked up. It was still morning, and the day promised to be a hot one.

She adjusted the heavy leather pouch that hung over her shoulder and made the decision. She would go. Mr. Burton needed the shearing scissors, and perhaps she'd find him in the fields with his sheep, and it would not be a "visit" after all.

Kicking her horse forward before she changed her mind again, she splashed through the low creek, emerging onto Francis Park. She rode over a grassy hill and down into the flat area of land, seeing no one but noticing the fields were planted. She nodded approvingly as her eyes traveled over the orderly rows and ditches that brought water from the creek. This is precisely how she would have arranged the crops.

She rode around the edge of the plot so as not to trample the seedlings, and presently, she came to a cart path. She stopped, examining it. One direction would lead to the road, and she estimated that the other led to the pond. She turned toward the pond, wondering if she was headed the correct way. She realized she had no idea where Mr. Burton's house was.

Looking ahead, she saw green hills, growing higher as they neared the mountains. To the side was a thick forest that came near to the pond and continued, up into the mountains, bordering her own property. She continued along the path, and her worry resumed. What would Mr. Burton say when he saw her? Would he be pleased that she'd brought the shears? Or disapproving that she'd come alone? She didn't think he was overly concerned with etiquette. He *was* an American after all.

The path led around the pond, and on the far side, she saw it. She reined in and studied the structure from a distance. The building was unfinished, with only a partial roof. The outer walls were constructed of stone. The building was situated in the space between two rounded, tree-covered hills. Sarah thought the location was charming.

Her own house was built on a high rise, visible from much of the property, and Sarah thought it was meant to be imposing. But this spot, surrounded with the pond and tall trees with a large yard on each side, was snug and inviting. In a way, she could see Daniel's hand in the place. His house seemed to reflect his cheerful nature. As she neared, she could see movement around the yard. The sounds of hammering and the voices of men sounded from somewhere inside. A man atop a ladder called to another, who handed up a bucket.

Other workers moved around the area, cutting wood, carrying boards, going about their business with an air of cheerfulness. Looking past the house, she noticed workers' huts and what looked to be the beginning of a barn. Farther ahead, sheep dotted the grassy slopes, but she could not tell from this distance whether any of the men among them were Mr. Burton, and she didn't want to give the shearing scissors to just anyone.

She dismounted, tying the reins to a branch, then walked toward the house. The more she saw of Mr. Burton's farm, the more she liked it. He'd chosen the location well. It was far enough away should the pond overflow its banks, and the hills and trees would offer some protection from the wind. She imagined he would plant flowers and shrubs, some fruit trees, and maybe in the rear, an herb garden. At least that is what she would do.

Men tipped their hats as she approached the door. She felt foolish now that she had no servant or calling card, but this was not a social visit, she reminded herself.

Before she had a chance to knock, the door opened and a woman stepped out.

Sarah recognized her right away. She'd seen the woman at church with Bill Hawkins. A short woman with a turned up nose and reddish hair pulled back beneath a cap. This must be his wife. A young child with wispy blonde curls peeked out from behind Mrs. Hawkins's skirts.

Sarah felt a twist in her stomach, remembering what Daniel had said at the governor's assembly. He'd thought her cruel for keeping this family apart. She hated that he'd thought ill of her, but he didn't understand how things were in the colony. Mrs. Hawkins was serving a sentence for a crime, child or no, and just because a person seemed pleasant and good didn't mean they weren't simply waiting for a chance to betray.

The woman curtseyed. "Yes, my lady? How may I help you?"

"I am looking for Mr. Burton. Is he at home?"

"I'm afraid not. He's gone hunting. Left quite early. I expect his return any time now. Would you like to wait?" She stepped aside, lifting her hand toward the open doorway.

"No. Thank you." She patted the leather bag, trying to decide what to do. She didn't want to leave the shears with Mrs. Hawkins, but perhaps it was the best course. "I will just—"

"Mr. Burt!" The little girl's scream cut off Sarah's words. The child darted past her, down the path.

When Sarah turned, she saw Daniel emerging from the forest. He carried a bulging sack over his shoulder and a rifle, but when he saw the child, he dropped both to the ground, squatting to catch her and lift her into his arms.

The little girl patted his cheeks, and Daniel laughed.

Sarah's chest grew warm at the sight. And she felt something else, a wistfulness that she didn't understand. She didn't examine the feeling too closely, afraid of what it might mean. Daniel's actions seemed so natural.

He set the girl back onto the ground and watched her run back to the house. When his gaze met Sarah's, he opened his eyes wide, then grinned, raising a hand. "Miss Whitaker!" He started toward her. "To what do I owe the pleasure? It isn't Thursday yet, you know." He winked.

Sarah walked toward him, unable to keep a smile from her face. His words and pleased grin dispelled the last bits of worry she'd had about paying a visit. She should have known he'd be nothing but happy to see her. It was his nature.

She lifted the leather purse from her shoulder. "I brought—" The words caught in her throat when another man stepped from the woods. An aboriginal man. He carried a rifle and, over his shoulder, the carcass of a 'roo. He carefully leaned the weapon against the sack Daniel had dropped.

Sarah's mouth went dry.

Daniel turned to see what had stopped her. He said something she didn't understand. Sarah stared at him. Was he speaking in the man's language?

"Miss Whitaker, allow me to introduce my friend Charrah."

The man dropped the carcass to the ground and joined them. He wore only a short apron in the indigenous style. Lines of white clay marked his chest and arms, and his hair and beard were unruly and coated in a sort of wax. He grinned, showing a missing tooth. "Miss Wita-ka," he said carefully, reaching out a hand.

Sarah stumbled back. "Mr. Burton. That is . . ." She shook her head against the image that crashed into her mind—an image that was not a memory, she knew, but a child's fabrication. Though she could hardly remember her papá's face, she'd imagined him often enough as the adults had described him when they thought she wasn't listening: lying in the dirt, his mouth and eyes wide, and a wooden spear through his chest. Even after all these years, it haunted her, and she still awoke crying with the image in her mind.

"Miss Whitaker? What is wrong?" Mr. Burton touched her arm.

She couldn't make herself speak. She whirled and hurried to her horse.

"Miss Whitaker?" Daniel called, but she didn't turn back. She pulled the reins from the branch and flung them over the horse's head, blinking away the maddening tears that swelled in her eyes.

"Sarah."

The sound of her given name made her pause.

He put a hand over hers, loosening her grip on the reins and turning her toward him. He pushed up her chin. "What is wrong?" She willed her tears not to spill over, feeling foolish. But he must understand. "Mr. Burton, he—" She pulled his hand from her chin and darted a look toward the native. "That man is an aborigine." Over her years in the colony, she'd successfully avoided the native people, prohibiting her workers from associating with them and not allowing them on her property. The man's sudden appearance was a shock.

Daniel blinked and his brows lifted. "Yes. I . . . well, I did know that."

She shook her head and blew out a frustrated huff through her nose. "You cannot befriend them."

"It is actually not as difficult as you might suppose."

His teasing expression fell away when Sarah's tears leaked onto her cheeks.

"Sarah, tell me."

It was the second time he'd used her name, and instead of feeling indignant at his boldness, she held the sound of it in her mind. It was familiar of him, yes, but in a way that made her feel cherished. Daniel stood close, his hand on the horse behind her. She was practically in his embrace.

Her stomach flipped, and her skin tingled with nervous energy. But she also felt warm and . . . safe. She dragged her hands over her cheeks, tears soaking into her gloves. "They killed my papá." The image rose back into her mind as she spoke. "He was found with a spear in his chest." Her voice hitched, and she swallowed. "You mustn't trust them, Mr. Burton."

"I am sorry." He pressed his lips together and glanced to the side. "Truly I am, but Charrah would not do something like that. He's my friend. I trust him."

Sarah clenched her teeth together, wanting to scream. She balled her hands. The earlier feelings of warmth and comfort were swallowed up by a surge of frustration. How could he not understand?

She turned, her shoulder brushing into his chest as she took the reins from his hand. Her body felt like a wound spring, and she could feel the tears clogging her throat and prickling her eyes—angry tears brought on by the frustration that she could not convince him. She lifted her foot into the stirrup, and Daniel stepped back as she swung up into the saddle.

"I am sorry. I don't know . . ." He scratched behind his ear. "I wish I'd not upset you."

Her shoulders slumped, and she felt suddenly tired. "You trust too easily." She glanced to where the man still stood, watching them. "You must understand. The aborigines, the felons—they are not your friends. They will hurt you if you let your guard down. They are just waiting for the opportunity."

Daniel looked up at her. The lines around his eyes seemed deeper, and his expression was sorrowful. "I hope that is not true. I must believe people can change." He spoke in a soft voice, and the sound pushed Sarah's tears free.

She moved to turn the horse and felt something bump her hip. She pulled the leather purse from her shoulder and handed it down to him. "The shearing scissors," she said then tugged on the reins and rode down the path at a clip, leaving Francis Park and Daniel Burton behind.

She took the longer route, out along the main road, letting her tears fall and feeling foolish for even going to Francis Park in the first place. What must Mr. Burton think of her? Would he describe her to his friends as the woman who leaves every interaction in tears?

She tried to sort through her extreme swings of temperament. Obviously the sight of the aboriginal man had upset her, but as she peeled away layers of her raw emotions, she found there was more beneath her weeping than she liked to acknowledge.

Seeing Daniel's farm, hearing the child's squeal and Daniel's laughter had stirred a feeling inside her. She knew a bit of it was jealousy, though she wasn't proud of the admission. Not only envy of Daniel's interaction with the girl specifically, but she felt as if she'd intruded on a place where people were friendly and cared about one another. A place she didn't quite understand. It produced a longing she hadn't been prepared for. As if it was something she'd been missing but didn't know until she'd stumbled upon it.

Francis Park felt like a *home*, she realized. Daniel had created a place where people worked together happily. *A family.* At the thought, her tears returned again in full force. She pressed a hand to her mouth, though no one was around to hear.

She reined in, wiping her eyes, and studied her house from a distance, just as she'd studied Daniel's a few hours earlier. The building was impressive with expansive grounds, elegant gardens, and beautifully furnished rooms.

But when she entered, only a butler would greet her. She ate her meals alone on a large, imported dining table surrounded by silk-covered walls, then read or perused ledgers in the evening. The servants moved about quietly, tending to their duties. There was no laughter, and she did not know if there ever had been.

Sarah gasped as the ache of loneliness grew so strong she feared her heart would crumple.

Chapter 15

TWO HOURS LATER, DANIEL HESITATED as he approached the far edge of the field behind the house at Sarah Hills. At his inquiry, the butler had directed him toward the grove of trees where he would find a small cemetery. But when he actually arrived and saw Sarah sitting on a stone bench, her shoulders dropped, his heart grew heavy, and he was tempted to turn back. He was in over his head.

He'd acted impulsively following after her the night of the governor's party, and it had turned out well. He'd expected this to be the same. The circumstance was similar. She'd left sobbing, and he'd stood like a halfwit, watching her go and having no idea what to do about it. At least now, he had a bit of a notion as to what had upset her. But this time, he also knew he had to tread lightly. He felt as though much more were at stake.

Walking closer, he noticed her hat, gloves, and coat on the ground beside the bench. Her hair was still tied in a braid, but strands had fallen free, and the light breeze blew them across her face and neck.

Her gaze was turned toward the trees, and he saw she was watching an animal snuffling along in the leaves of the forest floor. It was roughly the size of a well-fed cat, but he had never seen a creature such as this one. Long spikes covered its body except for its head, which was furry and small and ended in a spiky beak-like nose. When the animal heard Daniel's steps, it curled into a ball.

Sarah glanced up, but she didn't rise. Her eyes were red.

Daniel sat beside her. "What on earth is it?"

She turned back to watch the animal. "An echidna," she said. "I caught one once when I was younger." She gave a small smile. "I wanted to keep it as a pet. My plan was to show it to Captain Thackeray when his ship returned, but it escaped within only a few hours, burrowing out of the pen I'd made."

The animal unrolled and glanced their way before continuing along at its unhurried pace. A long tongue darted out from time to time, and Daniel thought it must be eating ants or other insects.

"He was a birder." Sarah glanced at him then back. "My father. He would make sketches of the different species then write pages of notes about their habits and songs. I heard the overseer tell my aunt that Papá was discovered that day in the forest with his notebook and field glasses. No weapons. He'd just been looking at birds."

"I'm so sorry, Sarah."

"No, I am sorry." Sarah spoke in a small voice.

"You've no need to apologize."

"But I do." She let out a breath and turned toward him. He noticed she held a delicate handkerchief. Her trousers and thick leather boots presented a sharp contrast to the lacy white cloth, and he smiled at another unique juxtaposition. "I should not have insulted your friend at your home. It was impolite. I apologize for behaving so rudely." She turned her gaze back toward the animal. "I should not have gone to Francis Park," she said quietly.

"Nonsense. I was pleased that you came. You are always welcome." He leaned to the side, bumping her shoulder softly with his. "And I consider *you* to be a friend as well."

Sarah sighed. "I know why you're here."

"You do?"

"You've come to convince me that I do not understand people, that I shouldn't be so suspicious, that I should trust. It bothers you that I do not."

Had he been so obvious? "I came because you left my house in tears, and I was worried."

She shook her head back and forth slowly. "I do not know what has come over me lately. I am not typically prone to bouts of weeping."

"I must bring out the best in you, Sarah."

She turned fully toward him, blinking and opening her eyes wide. Her brows rose, crinkling her forehead. "You are very presumptuous, sir. That is not the first time you've used my Christian name."

Daniel shrugged. "I thought I'd try it out. Seemed a pity to waste it."

Her lips twisted as if she were attempting to hold back a smile. "And? What is your verdict?"

"I quite enjoy calling you Sarah. A beautiful name suits you much better than a formal title."

Pink bloomed in her cheeks, and she looked back to where the echidna had nearly disappeared into the trees. She remained quiet for a moment. "I am not cruel, Mr. Burton." She spread out the handkerchief on her lap, folding it into fourths. "There was a time when I thought like you. I believed everyone deserved a chance. That people could change, and that we should all forgive as it says in the Bible."

"And now you feel differently? Why?"

"I learned the truth."

He could hear an ache in her voice that made his heart grow heavy. "Which is?"

She twisted, facing him. "People *don't* change."

Daniel slipped his hand beneath hers, holding her palm against his. "I can't believe that is true. I refuse to believe it." The heaviness in his chest grew. He must convince her of this. He had to. "Not all aboriginal people are murderers just as not all white men are criminals."

"I do not think every white man is a criminal," Sarah said. "Just . . . the criminals. Once a person has started down that path, they do not alter course."

"You must see that isn't true, Sarah." He could hear pleading enter his voice and tried to keep his tone even. Her words hurt, making him desperate to convince her otherwise. Convincing himself had been difficult enough.

"It has happened again and again. Maids and housekeepers that have stolen silver, a tender who sold away lambs right out from under us."

Daniel shook his head. "Look at Bill Hawkins. There are good people, Sarah, even among convicts. Some truly do penance for their misdeed and change their lives. Every person has made a mistake, and we should not be defined by it."

"A mistake?" Sarah did not pull away her hand, but he felt her grow tense. She raised her chin toward the two graves. "These were the only family I ever knew, and both were killed by people that, by your reasoning, should have been trusted, given another chance." Sarah's lip shook, but her eyes were hard. She managed to look both defensive and vulnerable at the same time.

"Your aunt? I thought she died in a fire."

"A fire created by a person I convinced her had changed his ways. Oliver Winchell. Our steward."

Daniel stayed quiet, waiting for her to continue and bracing himself for what she'd say.

"Mr. Winchell was transported for document forgery, but when we met him, he was so friendly, his eyes so kind, I knew he was a changed man. I was certain. And I convinced Aunt Hortensia he would serve as an honorable steward.

"He managed the ledgers and all of the farm's finances. He was such a pleasant person. He had a smile and a friendly word for everyone." Sarah's voice was bitter. "But Aunt Hortensia was convinced something wasn't right. She studied the ledgers and found discrepancies. Mr. Winchell had been stealing from the farm every week. Not enough to be noticed unless one looked closely. She confronted him about it, and he, of course, denied any wrongdoing. She sent for the convict supervisor, but soon after, we found the ledgers aflame." Sarah drew in a jagged breath, but her jaw was set. Her face relaxed slowly as her expression moved from anger to sorrow to resignation.

"Aunt Hortensia sent me to fetch the workers to put out the fire, and from what we could tell, she tried to save the books, but the door to the library was barred behind her, and she could not escape. He killed her. Over seventy pounds." Sarah spoke slowly, holding his gaze, as if to ensure that he understood.

Daniel watched her, saddened to realize the hurt she felt—and the guilt. "It is not your fault." He clasped her fingers tighter.

Sarah glanced down at their joined hands. "*I* convinced her to trust him. *I* was the one taken in by him. But it will not happen again. I told you. I learned my lesson. Trusting someone gives them the ability to hurt you."

Daniel scratched behind his ear, feeling a wave of nausea twist around in his stomach. If she were ever to find out his secret . . . He averted his gaze, swallowing through a tight throat. He wished he knew what to say, how to convince her, but it was hopeless. She must never find out the truth, he decided. Only a few people in the colony knew about his past, and none were likely to make it known. Sarah would probably never cross paths with most of them. Could he keep a secret of this magnitude? He was torn between wanting her trust and knowing that he had to mislead her to keep it.

Perhaps she's right about criminals, he thought. *We are liars.* But how could he do otherwise?

He shifted on the hard bench, stretching one leg straight and shifting his weight to the other. "We do find the most uncomfortable places for our conversations." His attempt to change the topic felt like another deception, but he put on a teasing expression anyway.

"This bench is an improvement, I would say, since it's not moving."

This time, seeing her shy smile, Daniel didn't have to pretend. He winked. "A very true observation."

They remained silent for a time, each lost in thought. Sarah held on to his hand and leaned closer, brushing against his shoulder. He smelled vanilla when the wind blew her wisps of hair.

Daniel's nausea grew along with the ache in his chest as he came to a realization—one that he'd known all along but would not let himself admit. He'd not paid for his crime. And it was becoming increasingly clear that, to do so, to fully become the man he wished to be, to serve his penance, would mean losing this woman whose every word and expression imbedded her deeper into his heart. His throat was so tight he found it difficult to breathe.

Sarah Whitaker was not like the other women he'd spent his adult life finding himself smitten with, then, upon learning more of them, losing interest. He'd thought he was destined to fall in and out of love forever, but he realized what he'd taken for love had merely been infatuation. He'd not *loved* any of those women—until now. With each new discovery, each perfect smile, each touch, and each moment, he was losing his heart to the complicated paradox that was Sarah Whitaker.

"I trust *you*, Daniel."

Her shy declaration and the tentative way she said his name was almost his undoing. He closed his eyes, feeling moisture there. Of all people, she trusted the person who was this very instant deceiving her.

"Why?" he whispered.

"You are different. You would never hurt me."

Daniel winced against the pain her words caused. If he'd known his heart would be the price of redemption, he'd have chosen to stay in Newgate.

Chapter 16

SARAH FOLDED HER HANDS IN her lap, wishing she'd thought to bring a fan. The doors and windows were closed, making the building stuffy. The air felt thick. Every convict was required by law to attend church each Sunday, and since the law also forbade anyone from performing manual labor on the Sabbath, most of the free settlers in the surrounding areas came regularly to the Sunday service in Parramatta as well as their servants. It made for a crowded church. Around her, she heard coughs and fidgeting and felt certain the heat was to blame for the restlessness of the congregation.

Sarah very carefully glanced at the man sitting beside her. Daniel leaned forward slightly, his expression thoughtful as he listened to the sermon. He didn't seem bothered by the lack of ventilation despite the fact that he wore a coat and a vest. She smiled. He was such a good man, a God-fearing man, and even though church was not the appropriate place for such ponderings, she had to admit Daniel Burton was exceptionally handsome as well. His ginger-colored curls and coffee-brown eyes were the type that made ladies swoon. He held his hat upon his lap, his full attention on the words of the Reverend Samuel Marsden.

Sarah could not help but feel pleased that Daniel had joined her on the pew. She kept herself from glancing up at him again. It was not strange for acquaintances to sit beside one another during the service, but she didn't want the rest of the congregation to see her staring or the blush that resulted with every glance.

Against her wishes, that very blush stole up her neck as she remembered their conversation at her father's graveside. Daniel had come after her, worried about her. He'd listened. He'd cared. At the memory of his touch, her palm grew warm, as did her cheeks. *I must learn to control this blushing if I plan to spend time with Mr. Daniel Burton.*

Her heart flipped as she realized she *did* intend to spend time with him. Although the words weren't spoken aloud, they had parted with an understanding that they would see each other more often, perhaps regularly. He was to come to a dinner party that evening with Captain Thackeray, and then, of course, she'd go to his house the Thursday following. And after that—

The organ began to play, and she startled, realizing she'd not listened to any of the sermon. Sarah stood, and her gaze found Daniel's. He smiled, and she thought there was just a hint of tension around his eyes. She hadn't noticed it earlier, but she hadn't looked. The time before the service was typically quiet, reserved for prayer and personal reflection. Visiting would have been improper. She studied his face for a moment. There was surely something there. As if he carried a burden. Did it have something to do with the sermon? She should have listened instead of allowing herself to indulge in daydreams.

"Are you well, Mr. Burton?"

"Very well, thank you." The sparkle returned to his eyes as he smiled, though she felt as if it were a bit dimmer. Perhaps he was tired or hungry or hot. He offered his arm, and she took it, ignoring the curious glances they drew as they walked down the center aisle toward the doors.

When they stepped outside, she inhaled the fresh air gratefully, knowing that within a few weeks, the summer heat would be as stifling outside as it had been in the church.

She nodded and greeted acquaintances until her attention was drawn to a man in a red coat making his way across the churchyard toward them. Sarah slipped her hand from Daniel's arm and offered it to Conall Stewart in greeting. "Good day, Sergeant Stewart."

Conall grinned as he looked between them, and she didn't miss the tick of his brow when his gaze met Daniel's. "'Tis a fine day indeed, Miss Whitaker," he said. He shook Daniel's hand, smacking him on the shoulder. "And lovely 'tis to see the two o' ye."

"How nice that you are back in Parramatta," Sarah said, pretending she didn't hear the insinuation in his voice. "Will you be in town long?"

"A week a' the least. I'd hoped to call on ye."

"If you've no plans this evening, I'd be very happy if you'd join us for dinner. Dan—Mr. Burton will be there, as well as my old friend, Captain Thackeray." She glanced around at the people exiting the church. "I didn't see the captain at the service, but I expect him to arrive in Parramatta at any time. Perhaps he is even now at the inn."

"I'd not want to impose, miss," Conall said. He glanced at Daniel, perhaps wondering if his presence would be an intrusion.

Daniel smiled, and she thought he looked pleased with the idea of his friend joining them. The earlier tension seemed to have lessened, even if it was not completely gone.

"Nonsense," Sarah said. "If I'd known you were in town, I'd have invited you already."

He pressed his palm to his chest. "In tha' case, how could I refuse?"

She smiled and inclined her head. Conall was a cheerful person and a close friend to Daniel. She thought his addition to the dinner party would be a welcome one.

Movement caught her eye, and she turned to see Dorthea waving from the other side of the street. Sarah excused herself, leaving the men to their conversation.

She heard Conall's voice as she walked away. "So 'Dan—Mr. Burton,' is it?" he teased. "Ya look well, friend . . ." Sarah couldn't help but smile as she moved out of earshot.

When she reached Dorthea, the woman took both her hands. "It has been quite some time since I've seen you, Sarah."

"The farm keeps me quite busy in the spring," Sarah said. She squeezed Dorthea's hands, pleased to see her friend.

"I see." Dorthea glanced across the road behind Sarah. "And perhaps your new neighbor occupies some of your time as well."

At her words, the wretched blush returned, spreading over Sarah's skin like liquid heat. It must have been quite noticeable because the reaction elicited the largest grin she'd ever seen on Dorthea's face.

Sarah shrugged, giving a small smile. "I suppose a bit."

Dorthea laughed, releasing her hands. "I am very happy that you've found such a pleasant—"

The sound of raised voices broke off her words, and Sarah turned, wondering what was happening. Among them, she heard Daniel, sounding angry. Without taking her leave, she hurried back to the churchyard.

It wasn't difficult to discern the source of the commotion. The remainder of the Sunday worshippers had moved away, giving the arguers a wide berth. She could feel the tension in the air as she approached. It seemed as though even the birds had stopped their singing.

Sarah reached the edge of the cleared space and saw that Daniel and Mr. Pierce stood, facing one another on the packed dirt of the churchyard.

Daniel's arms were folded, his jaw tight. His legs were planted in a wide stance, and he stood protectively in front of Bill Hawkins and his family. Sarah realized this was the first time she'd seen him angry. His manner was controlled, but based on the hard look in his eyes, he was furious.

Mr. Pierce, on the other hand, looked close to apoplectic. His round face was beet-red, and veins bulged from his neck and forehead. His wife waved a fan in front of her face wildly, pressing a hand to her forehead as if she would succumb to hysterics. Mr. Pierce was pointing an accusing finger at Mrs. Hawkins, spittle flying from his mouth as he raged. ". . . living in sin. You are an indecent and despicable woman."

The woman looked terrified. She cowered behind her husband, holding her child. The little girl was crying against her shoulder.

Daniel shifted to the side, blocking the man's view of his housekeeper. "I'll thank you not to speak to my servant in such a manner, sir."

His voice was calm, but Sarah heard the clipped tones and felt a shiver at the sound of his restrained fury. Conall Stewart stood near Daniel, and when she met his gaze, she saw worry there.

Mr. Pierce turned his glower to Daniel. "And you harbor this wickedness under your roof?" He stepped to the side, pointing at Mrs. Hawkins. "Woman, you are a concubine, and your child is—"

"Enough." Daniel's voice was like a crack, making Mr. Pierce take a startled step back.

"We are legally married, if you please, sir." Bill spoke in a soft but sure voice. He put an arm around his wife.

"In a *Catholic* ceremony." Mr. Pierce snorted. "You know what Reverend Marsden says. Such a marriage does not hold in New South Wales. You are considered in the eyes of the church to be sinners."

"Are you speaking of the same reverend, who, not twenty minutes ago, delivered a sermon about Jesus Christ's admonition to love our neighbors, care for the poor, and forgive our enemies?" Daniel took a step closer to the round man. Though he did not raise his voice, his words rang clear in the silence. "Perhaps you attended a different service today? Or it is possible you did not understand the lesson, Mr. Pierce?"

Mr. Pierce's jowls shook as he opened and closed his mouth, apparently unsure of how to answer. Beads of sweat stood out on his forehead.

Minerva took her husband's arm. Her expression was tight. "Mr. Burton, why do you defend these . . . criminals?"

"Madam, I know these people. I work with them every day and see how they treat their family and others." He turned toward her husband. "And in all honesty, I find them to be much more decent than many of the free settlers in the colony." His lip curled, leaving no doubt as to whom his words signified.

"Well, really." Mr. Pierce glanced around, his eyes wide and apprehensive. His gaze landed on Sarah, and a look of relief relaxed his features. "Miss Whitaker." He stepped toward her, taking her hand and pulling her forward. "Surely you agree with me. You, of all people, know the evil nature of felons. You must convince Mr. Burton of his error."

Sarah stood frozen as Daniel's gaze locked onto hers.

His expression was no longer angry but sorrowful. His eyes seemed to wince when she looked at him, as if he were resigned to the fact that her words would go against his. She was surprised to realize it would not only upset him but actually cause him pain. He felt more strongly about this than she would have believed. She knew she could not hurt him. Not when he was trying to do what he considered to be honorable.

She looked at the Pierces, angry that the couple had put her in a situation where she would either hurt this man that she cared for or go against her own convictions. This issue already stood unresolved between Daniel and her—one they'd tentatively agreed to disagree on. She balled her hands into fists, resenting the spiteful couple and her own predicament.

She drew in a breath, steeling her resolve. "Mr. Burton is an excellent judge of character, sir," she said. "And he certainly has no reason to answer to anyone but the convict supervisor concerning either his treatment of his workers or their personal lives." She did not look at Daniel but tried to read his body language from the corner of her eye. He hadn't moved. "And since you asked for my opinion, I will give it to you." She paused. "Passing judgment on the legitimacy of a marriage is neither my duty or yours, and the location and timing of your condemnation is utterly inappropriate." She could feel the eyes of the entire crowd on her. "I would suggest taking up the matter with the appropriate authority. Or, since the issue does not affect you directly, I recommend attending to your own affairs."

Minerva gasped, and her husband's face changed from bright red to a rather mottled-looking hue. "Young lady, I never . . ." He motioned toward his carriage driver. "I cannot believe you would speak to your elders in this rude manner."

"If you please, it was you who drew me into the conversation with the expectation that I would answer bluntly." She curtseyed. "I do hope you have a pleasant Sunday."

Sarah felt a swell of satisfaction as she watched the Pierces storm away, darting back rude glances and whispering as they went. Once the moment passed, however, her stomach twisted. She'd never spoken so impolitely to someone she should have treated with respect. The Pierces were not the type of people one wanted as enemies. Perhaps this was the reason for Sergeant Stewart's worried expression. The ill feeling grew.

She looked at where Daniel stood. Conall whispered something to him, patting him on the back as if to reassure him. When Daniel looked back at Sarah and smiled, her worries evaporated. He spoke quietly to the Hawkins family, lifting the young girl from her mother's arms, leaving Bill to comfort his wife.

Daniel turned and closed the space between him and Sarah with a few strides. "I don't think I've introduced you to Trudy." He shifted the small girl in his arms. "Trudy, this is my very good friend, Miss Whitaker." As he spoke, his gaze held Sarah's, and she could read volumes in the way he said the words.

Trudy rubbed her eyes and looked up shyly.

Daniel adjusted his hold, turning her to face outward. "Now you must be a polite young lady and say, 'How do you do, Miss Whitaker?'"

"How do you do, Miss Witter?"

Sarah smiled at the girl's endearing manner. "Pleased to meet you, Trudy."

Trudy turned her face back against Daniel's vest.

He shifted, patting her back, but his eyes did not leave Sarah's. "Thank you," he said.

The way he spoke, his voice low and earnest, made Sarah's insides feel like melted chocolate. Her thoughts filled with endless things she wanted to say to him, but none sounded right. She wanted to tell him that she admired the honorable way he defended his beliefs, that it warmed her heart to see him tenderly holding the child, that he was a fine man and should not care one jot what the Pierces said. But none of the thoughts seemed just right, so she simply returned his smile, hoping he understood what she could not express in words.

Daniel's eyes were warm.

The crowd around them dispersed, going about their regular Sunday visiting, and the commotion shook her back into awareness. She grinned and Daniel winked, then he returned to the Hawkins with Trudy, and Sarah crossed the space to join Conall.

"Yer a right spitfire, aren't ye?" He winked, nodding approvingly.

"Hardly, Sergeant." She turned away to hide her own smile. "I simply think people oughtn't meddle in matters not of their concern."

He barked out a laugh. "Och, and ya told 'em off smartly, miss."

They watched Daniel return Trudy to her mother once the woman looked to be calmed. He placed a hand on Mrs. Hawkins's shoulder, speaking quietly, then bid the family farewell.

Sarah folded her arms and glanced to the side at Conall. "It was unfair for them to confront Mr. Burton in such a way."

"'Twas at that. He's a lucky man tae have such a defender."

Daniels watched his servants leave then joined Sarah and Conall, all boldness gone from his bearing. His stance, typically straight and tall, seemed to sag under a weight.

Sarah touched his arm. "You look pale, sir. I'm off to inquire after Captain Thackeray. Perhaps you'd join me for tea at the Yorkshire Grey?" She'd nearly forgotten about Captain Thackeray's arrival in all the fuss.

"Needs somethin' stronger than tha', if ya ask me." Conall caught Daniel's eyes. His broad smile disappeared, turning his face remarkably serious, and he gave Daniel a tight nod of approval. Then he cuffed his friend's shoulder.

It seemed men found expressing their feelings to be every bit as difficult as women did, Sarah thought. She moved between the two, smiling at both as she took their arms. "Shall we then?" The trio crossed the bridge and strode toward the inn.

Chapter 17

Being Sunday, the dining room in the inn was deserted, and for this, Daniel was grateful. His confrontation with Mr. Pierce had left him feeling exhausted and unsettled. He didn't think he could muster the energy to smile and make pleasant conversation with strangers. Fortunately, Sarah and Conall seemed to understand how he felt and kept their discussion easy, touching on casual topics such as the weather and Conall's military duties.

They chose a table where they could watch the door—Daniel smiled, remembering the last time he'd sat in a similar spot anxiously awaiting Sarah's arrival. Less than a week had passed since that day, but so much had changed between the two of them. The thought was not an unpleasant one.

Sarah ordered tea and sandwiches, and insisted Daniel eat. She watched him with pinched brows but did not voice her concern. She seemed to understand that he didn't wish to discuss the incident.

Captain Thackeray arrived within an hour, and soon after, Sarah departed in her carriage to prepare for the dinner. She'd requested they come for an early supper, claiming she had something to show the group afterward, but she remained silent on exactly what it was.

Though he would have liked her to remain or perhaps to have ridden back with her, Daniel was glad for the time alone with the men. They must have sensed his strain. He felt close to the breaking point—a fraying rope. It took only a little prompting on their parts to convince him to talk. And once he started, he disclosed everything.

Conall, of course, knew the majority of the story. His contribution to the exchange consisted mostly of cursing at Daniel's mention of the Pierces, reassurances about Sarah's affection, and ordering another round when their drinks got low.

Captain Thackeray, on the other hand, listened with hardly a word save to ask an occasional clarifying question. Daniel had not sensed any judgment on the man's part. No censure, and for that he was excessively thankful. It had felt like unburdening himself of a heavy load, once he revealed the whole of it—everything from the moment he'd left Charleston nearly two years earlier, through his unrestrained lifestyle in London and the resulting incarceration. He told of his attempt to change, his resolution aboard the ship to make a new life for himself, of his concern for his workers and their families, his resolve to forego wagering, and his growing fondness for Sarah and the hope that she'd see past his mistakes and forgive.

Daniel thought Captain Thackeray was the nearest Sarah had to a father or a guardian, and he asked for the man's blessing before moving forward with the relationship—as well as his advice.

When he'd finished speaking, Daniel heaved a sigh. He sank back into his seat, took a long drink, and awaited the older man's response. Captain Thackeray twirled his glass on the wooden table, watching it move between his fingers. He seemed to be considering.

Daniel tried not to squirm. He scratched behind his ear, glancing at Conall, who gave a reassuring nod.

After a moment, the captain raised his eyes. "I love that girl—that young lady—like my own daughter, I do. I worry about her. Ever since we arrived in Sydney ten years ago and I held her as she sobbed for hours upon learning her father was dead. I've tried to do what I could for her and her aunt, but of course, I have been irregularly in and out of her life."

Daniel nodded. "Your friendship has been quite dear to her."

"Yet, I feel as though it is not enough. I wish I could have done more." He tipped back his head and squinted, studying Daniel. "I hoped Sarah would meet a good man—not someone to take care of her." He chuckled. "Heaven knows she can take care of herself." He pointed a finger as he spoke. "She needs a person who will love her. Her young life has been sadly lacking in that area."

Daniel felt a swell of sorrow at the words. He could think of no response and only nodded his head.

"Poor lass," Conall muttered.

"I've fretted about her," Captain Thackeray said. "It's been a great worry, knowing I'll not be returning to the colony. Feels as though I'm deserting her. I've long hoped for someone to step in, someone I could trust." The captain raised his eyes, locking his gaze with Daniel's. "Mr. Burton, in this, I could not ask for a finer man than yourself."

Daniel was taken aback by the man's words. He felt touched and a little intimidated. "Thank you, sir."

Captain Thackeray nodded once then gulped down the remainder of his drink.

Conall grinned. "I'll drink to tha'." He raised his glass, downed the contents, then motioned to a server to refill their drinks.

"Captain," Daniel said, nodding a thanks to the server, "do you think I do the right thing by revealing to her my . . . history?"

"Of course honesty is always the correct answer." He answered rather hastily then seemed to consider. "And she would surely learn it eventually." The captain scowled, then his faced relaxed as if he'd come to a conclusion. "Better to hear it from you, I say."

Daniel's worry returned. The answer wasn't reassuring. "Do you think . . . How will she respond?"

"I do not know, my friend." He blew out a slow breath. "Though I don't agree with her strong opinions on the topic, I do understand the reasons behind them." He smiled and rested his arms on the table. "Take heart."

Late that afternoon, Daniel sat at the elegant oak table in Sarah Whitaker's dining room, feeling as near to utterly contented as he had in a long while. He could attribute a portion of the sensation to the delicious food, but he would be a fool if he did not give the credit to the mistress of the house.

Sarah looked radiant in a light blue gown, her hair pulled back softly. She was an elegant hostess, greeting the men warmly and maintaining a pleasant conversation. They'd visited for only a moment before the butler announced supper was ready and Sarah led them to the dining room.

As the party ate and socialized, he let his gaze travel around the space. He'd not seen an elegant room such as this since his arrival in the colony. The silks on the walls were striped in green and gold, and paintings of landscapes and exotic birds were displayed throughout. A spectacular chandelier hung over the table, casting prisms of colored light, and he wondered exactly how Sarah's father had managed to arrange passage for the fine furnishings, as well as keep them from damage aboard a ship.

Daniel took another bite of the delicious lamb chops and regarded the members of the dinner party. Sarah sat at the head of the table and to her right, Captain Thackeray. Daniel was seated on her other side and next to him, Molly, the lady's maid. Conall sat beside the captain. In his cheery manner, the Scotsman was recounting the humorous tale of an unlucky hunting party in Iceland. His descriptions of the marines being chased by an angry walrus had the entire table erupting with laughter.

Daniel smiled and laughed at the appropriate times but couldn't quite dispel the melancholy that hung over him like a dark cloud, a result of the earlier confrontation in the churchyard. He felt physically ill when he remembered Mr. Pierce's cruel words and saw them directed at the young mother. He closed his eyes, pushing away the thoughts. He was at a party after all. But the sensation wouldn't fully leave.

He'd felt anxious ever since his conversation with Sarah in the cemetery days earlier—when he'd made the decision to reveal the truth about what had brought him to the colony. And try as he might to distract himself, the apprehension continued to prickle, leaving him unsettled. He wished he could be certain of her reaction. *Come, man,* he chided himself, trying to shake away the uninvited reflections. *This is a dinner party.*

Daniel pulled his thoughts to the present and glanced around the table. He realized the room had gone silent, and everyone watched him, as if waiting for an answer to a question he hadn't heard.

He grimaced. "I beg your pardon. My mind was wandering."

Sarah smiled, but he saw her brows pinch together as if to ask if something was bothering him.

Daniel smiled and winked to reassure her that he was well.

She gave a small nod, though her eyes were still narrowed, not completely convinced. "I was telling the party that the cook has packed dessert for us to bring along." Her mouth twisted, and she raised her brows high as if she had a secret. "If all of you are agreeable to an adventure—I do not want to be encumbered by the faint of heart."

He heard Molly's quick intake of breath and turned toward her. The maid looked worried. "We'll not be facin' any real danger, will we, my lady?"

Sarah shrugged, the teasing look still in her eyes. "One never knows."

"Nay to fear, miss," Conall said. "Plenty o' us to protect ya."

Daniel glanced at Captain Thackeray and saw the man studying him thoughtfully. He gave Daniel an encouraging look, cuffing his shoulder as the party left the dining room and walked to the entry hall, where a maid waited with their hats and gloves.

Sarah excused herself then returned a moment later, wearing thick leather boots beneath the gown.

Daniel smiled.

The group moved outside and down the steps to where horses awaited on the packed dirt of the pathway before the house. Servants held the reins. Daniel noticed lanterns, thick blankets, and a basket attached behind various saddles. Those horses, he thought, must belong to the grooms. He also saw that two of the horses wore ladies' saddles. Of course Sarah will ride like a lady. *We are off for an adventure after all.* He'd not expected the contradicting woman to behave characteristically. He reckoned she would always manage to surprise him.

Sarah mounted her horse, then she gestured for the others to do likewise. She settled into the sidesaddle, led her horse a few paces ahead, and turned in front of the company, looking over them with a critical eye. Her attitude reminded Daniel of a general inspecting her troops. Apparently, all met with her approval, and she nodded. "Shall we, then?" She grinned at Captain Thackeray.

As they'd ridden to Sarah Hills earlier that day, the captain told Daniel and Conall about the adventures Sarah had devised for them when he'd visited the farm. She'd always managed to find something new and interesting to show him, even as a young girl. Daniel smiled, thinking of the bright-eyed young girl leading the older man around and devising escapades.

Sarah led the group northwest, following the path that wound to the main road access. She reined in atop a hill and waited until the rest of the group joined her. "The new storage barn, Captain." She pointed to a large stone building with a wooden roof that sat next to a large paddock farther down the road.

"Very nice." The sides of his mouth turned down as he nodded, studying the structure.

"And the shearing is all finished," Sarah said. "Some fleece has already been sent to the warehouse in Sydney Town, but I am sending the remainder into Parramatta this weekend to be delivered to your ship by barge."

"I cannot thank you enough for what you've done for me, Sarah," Captain Thackeray said.

"You are my oldest friend, sir." Sarah's voice grew thick. She waved a hand in the air. "But this is talk for another time. Business is hardly the purpose of our expedition." She turned, speaking to the entirety of the group. "Here we'll leave the road and continue over the hills." Her gaze caught Daniel's, and she gave a playful smile. It thrilled him to see her so excited about the outing.

She led them across grassy meadows and rocky hills toward the forest on the far side of the property. The land looked much wilder close to the mountains. Daniel glanced back over his shoulder, judging their location. He realized it was the same forest on the far edge of his property that rounded Francis Park and followed the creek along the foothills of the mountains.

When the group reached the tree line, they rode parallel to it for a time until they came to a cloth tied to a low branch, marking something that only their leader comprehended. Sarah halted, glancing up at the lowering sun. "We need to hurry if we're to arrive by dusk," she said, sliding off her horse. She removed the pistol from her saddlebag then slid it into a satchel she slung over her shoulder.

They left the horses in the care of grooms. As per Sarah's instructions, the gentlemen carried the lanterns, and the two women carried the folded blankets. Conall hung the handle of the picnic basket over one arm.

She started toward the marked tree then glanced around, locating a batch of long sticks. When she handed one to Daniel, he hefted it. The stick was straight, nearly as tall as he. The wood was not heavy, and he couldn't imagine what good it would do. It wasn't strong enough to be a good walking stick. Perhaps it was part of the custom she and Captain Thackeray had started.

"And am I to defend all o' ye with this twig?" Conall said, giving it a swish.

Sarah shook her head. "It's for webs along the path. You'll not want to walk into any. The spider bites can be deadly." She distributed the other sticks. "And, of course quicksand. Our destination is a bit marshy. Best to be cautious."

Daniel blinked. He studied her face, trying to tell whether she was teasing. Deadly spiders, he knew about. They were one of the first warnings he'd gotten upon disembarking onto the colony, along with caution about venomous snakes. But *quicksand?*

Molly gasped. She held the stick with both hands in a white-knuckled grip. Daniel didn't think many women in the colony—convict or free— had spent as much time in the untamed areas of the outback as had Sarah.

Sarah started off through the trees, Captain Thackeray following then Daniel. Conall and Molly brought up the rear of the company.

Beneath the canopy of the trees, the birds seemed louder, and the air felt dense and cool. Daniel inhaled the smell of eucalyptus and noticed a dampness to the scent. They followed a trail Sarah herself had apparently made by tying cloth to trees. After a few hundred yards, the path became mud.

Sarah led them around the thicker patches of swampland, using her stick to test out the ground ahead when it appeared boggy.

Daniel thought it ridiculous that three adult men should walk behind as a smallish young woman carried a weapon, swept the air for deadly spiders, and tested the stability of the path.

Once, as she stopped, indicating for them to wait while she used her stick to poke the ground ahead, Captain Thackeray turned to Daniel, grinning. "What did I tell ya? Plucky as she can be."

"I'm starting to doubt my merit as a gentleman." Daniel spoke in a low voice. He moved the lantern to his other arm and scratched behind his ear. "I don't enjoy following behind while she assumes the risks."

"Aye. But she'd not thank ya for pointing it out." The captain glanced at Sarah. "Shoving ahead and protecting her, telling her she's not capable just because she was born a female would only raise her ire." He turned, watching Sarah as he spoke. "But, aye, it's difficult to hold back, when ya just wish to keep her safe."

Sarah turned back, motioning them forward.

Captain Thackeray started to follow then turned. "One thing I've learned, my friend, is every person you meet has different needs, and when we wish to be a valuable part of the person's life, we must learn them." His mouth quirked in a wry grin. "I suppose that's the trick, isn't it? Caring for a person in the way they require, even when it's not how we'd wish to." He gave a smile and turned, continuing forward.

Daniel considered the man's words and realized the truth contained in them. He related it to his earlier conversation with Sarah. Trust. It always seemed to come down to trust. Just as he wanted her to trust him in spite of his mistakes, he needed to do the same.

The boggy area grew into a muddy pond. Sarah pointed to where one bank was a bit higher. Mr. Thackeray held her arm as she stepped up, and at her direction, they spread the blankets on a dry-looking patch of grass.

Sarah settled herself onto a blanket, smoothing her skirts and sitting with her knees to the side.

Captain Thackeray sat beside her, looking near to bursting with anticipation. "What do you have in store for us, Sarah, my girl?"

Sarah simply patted his arm. "You will have to wait and see." She shifted, moving her legs in front of her. "Mr. Burton?"

When Daniel met her gaze, she patted the blanket on her other side, indicating with a smile for him to sit.

He did so, stretching out his legs and trying to keep his muddy boots away from her gown.

Molly and Conall sat on the other blanket.

"How did you ever find this spot, Miss Whitaker?" Daniel asked.

"You'd be surprised where sheep can get lost." Sarah shrugged. "Although, I'll admit I'd never actually seen this particular pond until last spring."

"Surely you didn't come here alone?" Daniel reminded himself of Captain Thackeray's admonition. Sarah didn't need to be taken care of, but blast it if he didn't want to keep her safe.

"Not the first time. Mr. Hawkins was with me. But I have returned on my own since." She grinned, looking at each member of the party. "You will see why in just a moment."

Daniel glanced around the marshy area, wondering what could possibly draw her to this foul-smelling place.

"Molly, would you serve our dessert?" Sarah said.

The maid opened the basket and took out napkins and small pastries, passing them to the group.

Once they had all been served, Sarah sat back. She held a pastry in one hand and smoothed a napkin over her skirts with the other. "Now we must be quiet, or it will not emerge from its den." She pointed to a grassy clump of earth.

"What, my lady?" Molly's voice trembled.

"Not to worry," Sarah said. "You are in no danger."

Captain Thackeray sat back, looking relaxed, though the ground was far from comfortable. Daniel thought the captain was the type of person to be happy in any situation.

Daniel looked closer at the clump of ground. It was a bit up the hill, far enough away that it wouldn't flood if the pond swelled. He thought he could see a hole, but it could have just been a patch of upturned earth. He squinted, trying to imagine what was going to emerge from the burrow.

Conall crossed his ankles and rested back on his hands. "Seems just the place fer a kelpie to lure an unsuspectin' traveler."

"Sergeant Stewart, you're frightening me," Molly whispered.

"Jes don' follow any ghost-like horses," he whispered back.

"Shhh," Sarah hissed.

Daniel bit into a pastry and wanted to moan in pleasure. It had been quite a while since he'd eaten fancy desserts. He wiped the corners of his mouth with the napkin, his eyes moving between the clump of ground and the woman beside him. If it were up to him, he'd watch Sarah.

She stared at the burrow, and moments passed. Daniel's legs were starting to ache from maintaining his position. He shifted, bending a knee and resting his forearm on it. He wished he could stretch his back. Why did every encounter with Sarah include prolonged sitting on an uncomfortable surface?

Sarah started and leaned forward, squinting. She put a hand on his arm and squeezed. "There," she whispered.

He peered closer and saw an animal emerging. The creature was brown, covered with shiny fur. It didn't have ears like a fox or a raccoon, and when it started scuttling across the ground toward the pond, he saw it had a bill protruding from its face. Its tail was flat and shaped like a paddle.

"Well, I'll be," Captain Thackeray said in a soft voice. "After all these years, all these trips to the colony, I finally get to see one."

"What is that?" Molly asked in a whisper.

"A water mole," Sarah responded.

Daniel noticed the creature had duck-like flippers instead of feet. He also noticed that Sarah's hand was still on his arm, and he remained motionless in hopes that she wouldn't realize and pull it away.

"George Shaw of the Royal Society calls it a *Platypus Anatinus*," the captain said. They watched the animal reach the water's edge and plunge into the pond. It swam about making hardly a ripple in the muddy water.

"I wonder if we could catch it. A sweet thing, isn't it?" Molly said.

"Looks sweet," Captain Thackeray replied. "But they've poison spurs on their hind feet. Best not to bother the creature."

"We'll hardly be able to see it any longer," Sarah said. She moved away her hand from Daniel's arm then stood to look over the bank. "It swims long into the night."

Daniel frowned as he realized her statement meant she'd been out here in this boggy forest well past dark. He could think of a hundred threats that could have befallen a young woman alone, each scenario more menacing than the last.

The others stood with her.

"I could not have asked for a more perfect adventure, Sarah," Captain Thackeray said. "I've read of the platypus, and of course seen stuffed specimens at curiosity shops, but to witness the animal in its natural habitat"—he grinned, his eyes twinkling in the fading light—"a perfect adventure indeed."

Sarah smiled back. "I knew you would like it."

"'Twas a fine outin', Miss Whitaker," Conall said, and Molly agreed.

Sarah's smile grew, and even in the fading daylight, Daniel saw color on her cheeks. She picked up her stick and used it to point in the direction from whence they'd arrived. "We should hurry back before it becomes too dark."

Within a moment, blankets were folded, lanterns lit, and the group started their return journey. The forest seemed much different in the dark. The lantern flames cast strange shadows over the trees as they passed, and the noises around them took on an ominous feel. A rustle in the undergrowth drew his attention, and Daniel stopped, raising his lantern for a better view.

"The animals grow more active in the dark. No need for concern."

The sound of Sarah's voice startled him, and Daniel jumped. "I'm not . . . concerned," he said, feeling foolish. "Just, well, I heard a noise."

Her hand slipped into his. She gave a small tug, and they continued following behind the others. Daniel was relieved that Conall and Captain Thackeray were ahead, testing for quicksand instead of Sarah.

Molly stayed close to the sergeant, likely assuming he was the best choice of a protector, should trouble arise. Daniel chuckled to himself. He'd put his money on the woman beside him.

"You've been quiet tonight," Sarah said. "I hope you're not still worried about the Pierces. Their favor is not worth troubling yourself."

"I apologize if my company was lacking today. I suppose my mind has been rather occupied."

"Occupied with good things?"

He smiled, thinking how the simple act of holding a lovely lady's hand could transform a dark forest from a perilous wilderness into a pleasant nocturnal woodland. "Some are good. Some less good. Others, well, let's just call them *hopeful*."

Even though they both wore gloves, Sarah's hand warmed his. The warmth spread throughout his entirety, giving him the assurance he sought. He was glad she didn't pry. She must understand that he needed support but that he wanted to work out his decisions on his own.

It appeared she already knew the lesson Captain Thackeray had told him earlier. All people needed to be loved in their own way. He glanced to the side as the thought struck him. Did Sarah love him? The light from his lantern made her eyes shine, even though her face was shadowed by her bonnet. She felt affection for him, of that he could be sure.

Her actions today, the way she'd defended his position to the Pierces—surely those were an indication of something more. Daniel dropped his tense shoulders, feeling resolved. Thursday was only four days away. With their repeated teasing about the date, the engagement seemed to have taken on some sort of significance. He'd do it then. His heart jolted at the thought, but he was decided. He would tell Sarah about his past, explain how he'd changed, and make his feelings known.

The plan was simple enough in theory. *So is shearing a sheep*, he thought, rolling his eyes at memories of his pitiful attempts these last days. He tightened his hand around Sarah's and figured he had four days to contemplate the various scenarios and ways it could all go wrong. For now, he'd enjoy walking hand in hand with the woman who held his heart.

Chapter 18

S ARAH FELT LIKE HER STOMACH was flipping end over end as she stood in her bedchamber studying her reflection. Thursday had come at last. She ran her hand over the lavender silk gown, admiring the drape of the soft fabric and the embellishments of lace and ribbons around the neck and waistline. She turned her head from side to side to inspect the curls Molly had formed and fastened into place with a multitude of pins. She was pleased—and a little embarrassed at her vanity.

She pressed a hand against her waist, trying to calm the building anticipation, sighing as her thoughts returned to Sunday evening. Walking hand in hand through the forest had seemed like a moment from a dream. And when Daniel had bid her farewell, reminding her of their engagement, she'd seen something deepen in his eyes. Thursday held more significance to their association than just a luncheon. Sarah had felt it in his gaze, and her stomach flipped at the memory.

At the sound of a knock on her bedchamber door, she turned.

Molly pushed open the door. "My lady, the horses are ready."

"Thank you."

Molly stepped to the side, and Sarah started past her but paused as her gaze alighted upon the woman. Her maid wore one of Sarah's older gowns, and Sarah was taken aback by the effect of the well-made dress. She hadn't before considered that Molly was close to her own age. And with round cheeks and honey-colored curls, she was, well, pretty. A memory moved into Sarah's mind. When they were in town last week, Molly had been talking to a man. Was he her beau? She hadn't thought to ask.

Molly's face scrunched with worry. "Is something wrong?"

Sarah shook her head. "Not at all. You look very nice, Molly."

The maid's cheeks turned the brightest red Sarah had seen on any person. She smiled, eyes bright. "Thank you, my lady."

Sarah gave a nod and continued on. What was she doing? She was Molly's supervisor not her friend. *Daniel Whitaker's soft spot for the criminals must be influencing my judgment.* The woman was a convict felon for heaven's sake, a prisoner of the Crown, and her personal life was none of Sarah's affair as long as it didn't impact her ability to perform her duties. Sarah needed to tighten her guard against inclinations to the contrary.

In the entry hall, she carefully pulled on a straw hat, trying not to smash her hair, then slid on her gloves.

With a groom's help, she mounted her horse, settling into the sidesaddle so as to only minimally wrinkle her skirts. She hated riding this way, especially over rough terrain, but her other choices were an hour long ride in a stuffy carriage or rumpled silk. She opted for the shorter path.

Molly rode beside her, and the two started off across the meadows for Francis Park. Sarah set a slow pace, not wishing to arrive looking too disheveled.

"If ya don't mind my sayin' so, miss, those slippers are the very thing to match your gown." Molly was looking at Sarah's feet—which were inappropriately showing, along with quite a bit of her calves, but a riding cloak this time of year would be stifling. Sarah had decided they'd be off their horses before anyone saw them making such an immodest exhibition.

"I agree." She glanced fondly at the slippers Captain Thackeray had brought her from India. The Bengal leather was beautiful and surprisingly comfortable, hand-tooled with intricate designs. She loved how the toe came to a point and curled slightly upward. "The captain is good to me." Captain Thackeray had returned to Sydney a day earlier to prepare for his departure in two weeks, once the remainder of the wool was safely secured in the hull of his ship and the other provisions were purchased and ready.

Sarah planned to travel to the harbor to see him off. It was with a bit of surprise that she realized she hadn't fretted all day about the captain's departure. It had, in fact, only crossed her mind a very few times lately. Her thoughts had been occupied with her contemplations about her neighbor.

Sarah heard a distant rumble and looked up. Dark clouds spread along the horizon like the soft fleece of a black sheep. The clouds were still a distance away, but she was nearly certain they meant rain within the next few hours. Perhaps when she arrived at Francis Park, she'd send a servant to fetch her carriage for the return trip.

She glanced upward toward the mountains, making sure the sheep were well away from the lower ground where the creek might flood. She looked closer, seeing the flock with the new lambs in the distance. Those she could see were safely out of the flooding zone, but there seemed to be fewer animals than there should be. Could the others be down among the trees near the creek? From this far away, it was difficult to be sure. She squinted, blocking the sun with her hand, but still the count appeared lacking. And where were the tenders? There were three assigned to this flock.

Looking back at the sky, she gritted her teeth, trying to think of a way to get word to Tom or one of the other workers, but riding back would take as much time as checking on the sheep herself. Continuing to Francis Park and sending back word with a servant would risk the men arriving after the rain had already begun. She watched for a moment more, hoping to see the shepherds or come up with another plan, one that didn't involve interrupting her luncheon. But she couldn't think of anything.

It had to be her. Sarah could see no other choice, and as it was accustomed to do, her mind switched from uncertain deliberations to decisive planning. If she rode fast, she could reach the foothills, locate the shepherds, determine the condition of the flock, then hurry back to Francis Park, arriving only a few moments late for luncheon.

Sarah turned to her companion. "Molly, ride ahead and give Mr. Burton my apologies. I'm afraid I'll be a bit tardy." She turned her horse and pointed with her chin toward the tree line separating the meadows from the mountains. "It appears part of the flock is missing, and I need to investigate. I shouldn't be long."

"Yes, my lady." Molly looked nervous at continuing alone, but there was nothing to be done for that now.

Sarah worried that her hurried ride would ruin the hairstyle Molly had worked so hard for, but, she reasoned to herself, if she rode too slowly, she'd be caught in the rain and that would do even more damage. She used her riding crop on one side and her foot on the other, urging her horse faster and wishing for a decent saddle. Riding astride was not only more comfortable, but now that she was used to it, she felt off-balanced perched in a lady's saddle.

Once she reached the high ground, her apprehension grew. The tenders were nowhere in sight, and she estimated a full third of the flock was missing. Were they simply beyond the next hill? She didn't think so.

Sheep didn't often stray unless they were somehow separated deliberately from their herd. She continued through the meadow and to the hill beyond, but the missing animals weren't there either. Her nerves tingling, she opened the leather flap of a saddlebag and removed her pistol.

The temperature started to drop as the heavy clouds drew closer. Sarah decided to check the other side of the creek. Perhaps some of the sheep had wandered across the low water and into the foothills.

Sarah ducked as the horse entered the screen of gum trees and acacia then crossed the stream. On the other side, she reined in, listening. In the distance she could hear the rumble of thunder and the calls of birds, but there was something else. She closed her eyes, straining her ears, and heard it. The sound of bleating came from farther up. She pushed onward, emerging from the trees into the rocky foothills. The area was a maze of gorges, walls, and large boulders. The horse skidded on the loose gravel, and Sarah slowed the pace. After a few more skids, she tied the horse to a tree and continued on foot. From the corner of her eye, she saw a flash of lightning. She had to hurry.

She picked her way through broken branches, over red rocks, and down into stone gaps. The sound of the bleating gradually got louder. After nearly an hour of searching through the craggy rocks, reaching dead ends, and turning back for easier paths, she climbed up onto a rocky knoll, her leather slippers sliding as she scaled the hard surface.

Looking down onto the slopes below, she saw them. The flock grazed happily on the low salt bush and spiny spiniflex that grew among the rocks.

Sarah's nerves felt tight. Her skin tingled. Something was wrong. The sheep's strange location was so far away from the meadow—and she sensed that she was in danger. Keeping her head down and her finger on the pistol's trigger, she studied the area. The canyon wound like a twisting furrow through the hills, but the area where the sheep grazed was open and relatively flat, gently sloping upward with rocky hills surrounding it on three sides. She waited, wondering if someone would emerge from the shadows or come out from beneath an outcropping, but, as before, the tenders were nowhere to be seen.

The rumble of thunder sounded closer, and Sarah considered her options. She didn't imagine the sheep had gotten here on their own, and if the person, or people, that brought them here spotted her, she could be in peril. She liked to think herself a good shot, but she was only one person. Even if there was no one to confront, she was certain she couldn't lead the whole herd out of the canyon and back to the meadow by herself, not before the rain came. The flock was safer here than if they were caught crossing the stream when the storm hit, especially the small lambs. And if hail followed the rain, as it often did in the colony, the rocks would provide the animals cover. They were better off where they were. She gave one last sweeping glance over the area then climbed carefully down the knoll and started back to where she'd left her horse.

Branches caught on her skirts, snagging the delicate fabric, and she grimaced. Could she really arrive at Francis Park looking like this? Another flash of lightning, this one much closer, made her start. She needed to get off this mountain and find shelter.

Disappointment stung her throat. The luncheon plans, the gown, they were all ruined.

More lightning, a crash of thunder—and this time Sarah smelled smoke. The bolt must have hit a tree. She couldn't see the source of the smoke, but it appeared to be coming from beyond the trees, perhaps along the creek.

Now her disappointment over a luncheon and a dress seemed silly. She prayed that the rain that had threatened to ruin her outing would hurry and douse any blazes that might light the grass of the meadows. Dread swelled in her middle, spreading outward. She needed to get help.

She heard a bleat and stopped to listen. The sound was faint, but she thought she could guess the direction. The bleat came again, and she could hear urgency in the sound. It wasn't the casual noise of a contented sheep but of an animal in danger. Had a lamb become lost?

She hurried toward the noise, no longer caring about her dress. The smell of burning grew stronger, but with the darkening clouds, it was difficult to spot the source of the smoke. The air took on a haze. The sheep's bleating led her down a steep slope. Sarah had to slide part of the way over the loose gravel on her backside. Once she reached the bottom, she continued onward, skirting around boulders and through gaps.

She continued downward into a gulley, thinking this was precisely the sort of place to avoid during a spring storm. A flash flood could easily wash down the narrow chasm once the rain started. The lamb was in danger.

When she came around a bend and found the source of the noise, Sarah froze.

An aboriginal woman lay on the rocks where she must have fallen. Sarah watched for a moment and saw the movement of her chest, indicating that she was breathing. Her body was in an awkward position, twisted and hunched to the side. With the darkening skies and the hazy air, it was difficult for Sarah to see what she held. A sack of some sort? Had she been picking berries in the mountain and slipped?

Sarah didn't approach. Her dislike of the native people had, over time, become so definite that she could feel nothing but loathing. She scowled. *If it weren't for your kind, I would still have a father.*

The woman's eyes were closed, but at the sound of Sarah's skirts rustling, she twisted, a look of fear flashed on her face as her gaze locked on the pistol. She hunched further, and what Sarah had taken for a part of the woman's body squirmed. Sarah felt her eyes go wide when she realized wasn't a lamb's bleating that she'd heard but a baby's cries. The aboriginal woman pressed the child against her protectively, wincing as she moved her position. She was hurt.

Sarah glanced around, wondering if there were more of her people, spears in hand, lying in wait, but they would not have left an injured woman and baby in the canyon with a storm approaching.

She turned back, and seeing the terror on the woman's face, she realized she was aiming a gun at them. "I'm not going to hurt you." She didn't use compassion in her voice as she lowered the weapon. The tone could be more accurately described as exasperation. A crack of thunder sounded directly overhead, and she glanced back the way she'd come. The smell of smoke grew stronger. She needed to get out of this canyon before the rains started.

The woman said something, which Sarah couldn't understand. She repeated herself, speaking more slowly, as if that might help.

Sarah folded her arms. "Of course I don't know what you're saying."

The woman spoke again, pointing to the overhang above her head. She made a sliding motion with her hand then pointed at her ankle.

Craning her neck, Sarah looked closer. She didn't need to be a surgeon to know the woman's ankle bone was broken. Her foot bent unnaturally to the side, and the ankle was at least double the size it should have been.

The woman held the baby toward her. She lifted her brows and nodded, signaling that she wanted Sarah to take the baby, then she lifted her chin, pointing to the slope behind. Her meaning was obvious.

No, I can't. Sarah took a step backward.

The woman's expression changed to one of desperation. Her tone was pleading. She cradled the baby against her then held it toward Sarah again.

Tears fell from her wide eyes, leaving shiny lines through the dust on her dark cheeks. She spoke the same word over and over, and Sarah didn't need to understand the language to know the woman was asking *please*.

Sarah's own feelings had become an odd mixture that she couldn't understand. The sight of the woman had at first been abhorrent to her. The image of her father, pierced by a crudely made spear, swam in her mind. But then something changed. The woman's face, her pleading, her willingness to give her baby to a stranger—potentially an enemy—for a chance at the child's survival. The action was so selfless, so admirable. Sarah knew nothing of a mother's love. She'd never known her own mother and had only interacted with families in passing. She'd been touched by a ewe's care for her lambs, but that was the extent of her experience.

Without understanding why, Sarah reached forward and took the child.

The mother nodded gratefully, then pressed her fist to her mouth, holding back a sob.

Sarah examined the baby at arm's length as she tried to decide the best way to hold it. The child was naked except for a scrap of 'roo leather wound around it. Gray clay had dried over its skin, caked in the folds beneath its neck and on the insides of its elbows. She took in its small toes, chubby apendages, and tuft of dark hair. When she cradled it in one arm, the baby put a fist into its mouth, seeming content.

She looked at the mother, surprised that she hadn't thought of the woman that way before. She'd only considered her to be an enemy, but now . . . what was she? Sarah's stomach soured with guilt. She'd been willing to risk her life climbing into the slot canyon to find a lamb but so easily could have left the injured woman to her own devices. How could she have faced Daniel if she'd acted on her impulse? How could she have faced herself? She wasn't cruel. Isn't that what she'd told him that day at her father's grave? Would she really doom a child to a life without a mother? She made a decision.

Stepping forward, she knelt down, looking more closely at the woman's ankle. "Is this your only injury?"

The woman, of course, didn't respond to the question. She gestured toward the slope.

"Yes, yes," Sarah muttered. She looked over the woman but saw no other wounds. She could very well have internal damage, but Sarah couldn't do anything about that. She held the woman's gaze. "I will go, but you're coming with me." She glanced down at the baby and smiled. "With us."

She handed the baby back to its mother, ignoring the woman's protests as she pulled off her gloves and bunched up her skirt, exposing the layers of petticoats. Using a sharp rock, she poked a hole in the fabric then tore it into a long, thick strip.

Glancing up, she saw the woman regarded her strangely. The urgency hadn't fully left her expression, but her eyes squinted curiously as she watched. Sarah folded the long strip of material in two, then wrapped it around herself. She lifted the baby, settling it inside the crease, and pulled the sling tight, the baby held before her.

The mother realized what she was doing and leaned forward, helping to tie the ends together. Once the baby was secure, the woman raised her brows as if to ask what Sarah had planned next.

"You won't like this," Sarah said, though she knew her companion didn't understand. "I'm not a bone-smith, but we need to hold your foot into place until you can get to a doctor." She tore more strips from her petticoats then stood and searched the area for sticks. She held the baby against her with one hand as she bent over, pulling out a thick piece of scrub brush. Stripping off the smaller twigs, she ended up with two relatively straight pieces of wood. They would have to do. Another crack of thunder made her jolt. The baby started to cry. She patted its back and hummed a tune.

"Hush, little one," she said in a low singsong voice as they hurried back to the mother. The woman sat up now and watched with cautious eyes as Sarah laid the sticks on either side of her leg.

"It will hurt; I'm sorry." She pulled the strips tight, tying them to the sticks and securing the ankle with a splint.

The woman's face paled beneath her dark skin, and she gasped. She looked as if she'd be sick. Sarah knew firsthand how badly a broken bone hurt. She'd once slipped on a skating pond and landed on her wrist. When the surgeon had set the break, she'd fallen unconscious. She shivered as she remembered the pain.

She took the woman's hand and slid an arm around her back. "Put your weight on me," she muttered, as the woman struggled to her feet.

Without warning, the clouds burst open and rain poured down on them. Within an instant, Sarah was drenched. She held her hand over the baby's head, wishing she could keep its face dry.

The mother leaned heavily against Sarah's shoulder, and Sarah kept an arm around the woman's waist. Now that they were moving, her sense of urgency returned. She needed to get them out of the canyon and find the baby some shelter, especially if the rain turned to hail.

They moved slowly, the rain coming down so heavily it was almost painful, pushing down on them. Her leather soles were slippery, and she placed her feet carefully on the rocks, grateful that the shoes were somewhat sturdy. True, they weren't her work boots, but at least she hadn't chosen satin dancing slippers.

Sarah maneuvered her group as well as she could toward higher ground, but soon they'd have to climb to get out of the gully, and she didn't know how the woman would manage. Trickles ran between the rocks. Sarah had hoped for a gentler slope, but they hadn't the luxury to continue until they found one. Water could come rushing down the canyon at any moment. If she were alone, Sarah could have scrambled out of the gulley in a few quick minutes, and she felt frustrated that she couldn't get herself and her companions out easily.

She pointed toward the sloping wall of the gorge and led the woman to it, pulling herself up to a rock with a flat top a few feet above. Water ran down the rocks making them slippery under Sarah's fingers. She turned, leaned down—hand cradling the baby—and pulled on the woman's arm.

Her companion grasped onto a scraggly bush with her other hand, obviously trying to keep from pulling Sarah off balance. She got a knee onto the ledge, and Sarah heaved, pulling her the rest of the way. They had only climbed a few feet, but they both panted, exhausted from the effort. Sarah leaned over the baby, wishing her hat provided more of a shield against the water pouring over the child. She cradled its head, holding the baby against her for a moment, then started for the next rock.

They repeated the process three more times. With each climb the woman was weakening. Her arms shook as they bore the brunt of her weight. Try as she might, she could not keep her broken leg from bumping into the rocks, and Sarah heard her soft moans of pain. She wished for a better plan, but for now, the best thing was to get to high ground and find shelter. They were nearly to the top.

One more climb, and Sarah knelt on the rocky ground, looking down the slope. Wiping rain out of her eyes, she turned, reaching back.

The woman knelt on the ledge beneath. She leaned forward, her hands and forehead pressed against the rocks. Her shoulders sagged.

"Come on!" Sarah called. "You're nearly there."

The woman raised her face, rain flowing over her cheeks and pooling in her eyes. She blinked but seemed to lack the energy to even wipe the water away.

Sarah pointed to a rock a bit to the side then another rock. "Step there then there. You are so close."

The woman glanced to the spots she indicated but shook her head. She lifted an arm in a slow motion that appeared to take great effort then pointed, flicking her hand in a gesture for Sarah to continue.

"I will not." Sarah felt a surge of frustration, but she knew it didn't come from anger but from worry. She turned around, holding onto the baby as she slid back down next to the woman. She took the woman's arm, helping her to stand and placing her hand on a higher rock. "We go together," she said.

Water streamed from an overhanging branch, splashing down onto her face, but Sarah ignored it. She put an arm around the woman, pushing a shoulder into her side and bracing herself to hold the woman's weight as she stepped up onto the rock.

Sarah's knees nearly buckled, but she pushed, making sure the mother was stable on the next footing, then shifted closer, preparing for another push. The woman grasped a rock, and Sarah shoved, holding her weight until she found a foothold. One more shove and the woman was at the top. She turned, reaching down, and the two shared a smile as their positions were perfectly reversed from moments earlier.

Climbing with the help of her companion, Sarah pulled herself out of the gully. She panted, holding the baby against her, and glanced down. The hill was relatively steep but not impossibly so. And they had only climbed around ten feet. From the aching in her shoulders and the fatigue in her muscles, she felt like she had just scaled a hundred-foot cliff.

The woman remained lying on her front, her hands beneath her forehead. She breathed heavily as rain showered down on her. The baby had fallen asleep, and Sarah could not believe the child managed to sleep while water poured over its head.

She glanced around, hand over her eyes, looking for an overhang or anything that would provide shelter, but the rain made it difficult to see very far. *Well, we can't remain here.* She patted the woman's arm. "Come, you can rest soon."

The woman allowed Sarah to help her stand, letting out a hiss when her foot bumped a rock.

Sarah winced at the sound. She put an arm around the woman's waist, taking as much of her weight as possible. A moment later, Sarah found a spot beneath a rocky shelf. The ground was muddy, but mud was preferable to the constant rain. She helped the woman beneath and scooted next to her, leaning her head back against the rock and closing her eyes.

The day had certainly *not* turned out as she'd planned, she thought. She should be, this very moment, sitting in Daniel Burton's dining room in her lovely new dress. What did he think when she still hadn't arrived? Was he disappointed? Worried? Were he and Molly eating without her?

The baby shifted, making a sweet noise in its sleep. She glanced to the mother, who had apparently fallen asleep. Sarah held the baby close, leaning her cheek on the pillowy hair.

Chapter 19

Daniel paced before the hearth in his sitting room. He figured this was the very reason hearths were invented: a spot for a man to pace. Heaven knows he didn't need the thing for warmth. Bill and Winnie had tried to convince him that burning dung would keep mosquitoes away, but he'd not agreed to the practice. They assured him he'd change his mind in a few weeks when the insects were out in full force, but he didn't imagine he would ever wish for his home to smell like cooking manure. He turned and paced in the other direction, the dung-in-the-hearth train of thought terminated, and he cast about, trying to think of something else to occupy his mind. Pacing was one thing, but he was very close to *brooding*.

He glanced at Molly, who sat primly on his new sofa. The maid had arrived nearly an hour earlier, and Daniel made small talk for a little while, but there are only so many topics a man and his neighbor's lady's maid can converse comfortably about. They'd exhausted the list rather quickly.

Daniel leaned his forearms on the mantle. He'd expected by now to be free, unburdened of the secret he'd harbored from Sarah. But instead, it remained, pressing down on his shoulders like a sack of stone. He rubbed his forehead. And what was keeping her?

A rumble of thunder drew his eyes to the window. Molly had said Sarah rode toward the mountains, worried that some of her flock had gone missing. Should it take this long? He pulled out his pocket watch. More than an hour? Or had something gone amiss?

What should he do? He thought of Captain Thackeray's words. If he rode out searching for her, Sarah would be indignant, assuming that he didn't think her capable of tending to her own affairs. But how long should he wait? When was it acceptable to offer assistance? What if . . .

Pounding sounded on the door.

Daniel's shoulders relaxed as his worries melted away. She was here.

He turned, smiling, expecting Winnie to enter the room and announce his guest. But instead, he heard raised voices coming from the entryway. *Is that Charrah?*

Daniel and Molly shared a curious look, then he followed the sound. She trailed right behind.

The housekeeper stood in the doorway with one hand on the knob, the other, she held, palm out, toward the aboriginal man. "Mr. Burton has company right now."

Charrah looked past her. "Dan-yah!" His eyes were frantic.

"It's all right, Mrs. Hawkins."

The woman moved out of the doorway, and Charrah ran toward him. "*Guwiyang!*"

"Charrah, what is it?" He laid a hand on the man's shoulder, hoping to calm him.

"Guwiyang!" He spoke urgently. Seeing Daniel's blank look, Charrah grabbed his arm, pulling him outside. He pointed over the trees toward Sarah Hills. "Guwiyang!"

Daniel's heart rose into his throat. In the distance he saw a trail of black smoke. Fire! Guwiyang. And it appeared to be in the trees at the base of the mountains. Exactly where Sarah had gone.

Charrah turned Daniel toward him. His breathing was rapid and his brow furrowed. The man looked as if he were having a difficult time keeping his wits about him. "Dan-yah, guwiyang. *Kiturra.*" He spoke the last word with fear in his voice.

Daniel gave a quick nod, understanding immediately what his friend was trying to tell him. Kiturra was in the mountain. "We will go after her—them." He spun, calling to his workers to saddle two horses and to bring Molly's mount for her.

"Mrs. Hawkins, fetch a pair of trousers for Charrah."

When Molly's horse arrived, Daniel helped her into the saddle, handing her the reins. "Go to Sarah Hills. If Miss Whitaker has not returned, send as many men as you can."

"I will, sir."

He knew it was possible that Sarah was safely back at the house, but his gut told him otherwise. She would have either come here as she'd promised or gone to investigate the fire. He swallowed against his rising worry. And if that was the case, who knew what had befallen her.

Daniel gave Charrah the trousers. He didn't think his friend would be comfortable riding on a leather saddle with just a bit of 'roo skin around his waist. The man raised a brow but didn't object. He pulled them on, struggling for a moment to figure out the buttons at the waist.

When the horses were brought out, Charrah's lips pulled into a tight line. He appeared nervous, but he followed Daniel's lead and climbed on. They both knew the fastest way to the fire was on horseback. Another rumble of thunder followed by a flash of lightning. This one sounded close.

Using sign language, Daniel gave a quick riding lesson, then once he thought Charrah could at least stay seated, he set off, trusting the other horse to follow despite its inexperienced rider. When he reached the creek, he glanced back, relieved to see Charrah was right behind. His eyes were tight, but he held his shoulders straight. Daniel could not help but admire his determination.

They splashed through the water to Sarah Hills. Thunder rumbled again, and the temperature dropped further. Daniel could see the herd up on the hill, just as Molly had said. He urged his horse forward.

The dark clouds were drawing over the sky like a blanket. The smoke was growing thicker, haze darkening his vision, but it didn't come from the forest in the mountains as they'd assumed. The source was closer to the road.

They rode through the meadow toward the flock. Once they reached the sheep, Daniel scanned the hills for Sarah or the tenders, but he saw neither. Was part of the flock missing? There certainly seemed to be fewer sheep, but perhaps it was because they were more spread out. He couldn't be sure.

He halted his horse and waited for Charrah. The aboriginal man's gaze was focused on the rocky hills beyond the screen of trees that ran along the creek. Daniel looked toward the fire, thinking that was surely where they'd find Sarah.

Charrah turned in the direction of the fire. "Miss Wita-ka?"

Daniel nodded.

His friend looked toward the mountains, his brow furrowed. Then he seemed to come to a conclusion. "Guwiyang." He spoke in a purposeful voice, pointing toward the dark cloud of smoke. He must have thought the fire presented the greatest danger if either woman were near it. Daniel nodded, and they continued on.

Cresting a hill, they reined in. Daniel saw the source of the fire, and his stomach turned to stone. *Oh no.* The fleece-filled storage building was ablaze. Flames from the wooden window frames licked the stone. Thick smoke billowed from the burning roof.

Men stood a distance away watching the fire, knowing there was nothing to be done. The building and its contents were a complete loss.

Daniel scanned the gathering, looking for Sarah, but he didn't see her. He and Charrah rode closer.

A thunderclap sounded directly over their heads, spooking the horses. Daniel held tight to the reins, keeping his horse under control. He glanced to the side and saw Charrah imitating his actions. The man clung to the reins, concentration making his face tight.

Once his horse was calm, Charrah gave a curt nod, and they continued forward.

Daniel recognized Tom, Sarah's foreman. He raised his hand in greeting as they approached. Tom's face was in shadow, the fire behind casting a red glow around his form. "The mistress is going to be devastated when she finds out." Tom jerked his thumb over his shoulder.

"Miss Whitaker doesn't know about the fire?" Daniel asked.

Tom shook his head. "Haven't seen her all day. Thought she was with you, sir, if you please."

Daniel felt a sinking dread. "Miss Green came alone. She told me Miss Whitaker rode toward the creek to check on a flock. She feared some sheep were missing."

Tom lifted his hat and furrowed his fingers through his hair. "Don' know nothin' about that, sir."

"Would she have crossed into the mountains to look for the sheep?"

"Could have." Tom glanced toward the fire, the light making his face shine. "Mountains are dangerous in a storm. She knows—" A deluge of rain swallowed his words. He yelled more that Daniel couldn't hear then ran for cover beneath the trees.

"Dan-yah," Charrah called over the torrent. He pointed toward the mountain.

Daniel nodded. His friend was right. If the women were on the other side of the creek, they needed to hurry.

They turned the horses, and Daniel heard hissing behind them as the rain poured onto the fire. Water dripped off the brim of his hat, running down his face and into his eyes. They rode back to the flock and crossed the creek. If Sarah was looking for sheep, this is where she'd have started.

Once they emerged from the trees, Daniel held up a hand to shield his eyes from the torrents of water. His coat was heavy, drips pounded loudly against his hat, and when he bent his arm, rivulets of water squeezed out of the elbow like a sponge. He looked both directions along the creek but saw nothing to indicate which way he should go. He shook his head. Even if there had been an enormous arrow pointing to her location, he wouldn't have seen it in this blasted rain.

He looked at his companion. Charrah seemed completely unbothered by the rain. He rose in the stirrups, eyes squinted as he scanned the rocky foothills.

This was ridiculous. Daniel felt overwhelmed by the enormity of the task as well as the futility. They could never find the women in these mountains, not with such limited visibility. The rain was loud in his ears. Even if they called, the women wouldn't hear.

He blew out a breath, spraying rainwater off his lips. Sarah could very well be warm and dry in her house. And Kiturra surely knew how to find shelter.

Charrah went still then pointed. "Miss Wita-ka. Horse."

Daniel squinted through the rain but saw nothing. He started forward anyway. The two had been hunting together often enough that he knew to trust his friend's excellent eyesight. A moment later, he saw it. The animal was tied to a tree. And it was definitely Sarah's horse. Daniel felt a spike of fear. She had crossed the river and was on foot in this torrent.

He dismounted and walked to the animal, looking at the saddle and the area around. At least the horse was tied up, which meant Sarah had left it purposefully. "How long have you been here, girl?" He caught the nervous animal's bridle and lay a hand on its neck. "And where is your mistress?"

He turned back to Charrah, who was watching him with a strange look as if saying, *You ninny, horses don't talk.* He ignored the look. "What do we do, Charrah?"

Charrah's brow furrowed thoughtfully then he dismounted. He must have taken Daniel's question as authorization to take charge of the expedition. His manner was sure and confident. Charrah untied Sarah's horse, leading it and the other two animals beneath a clump of trees then motioning for Daniel to follow as he climbed up into the rocks.

Daniel was glad *someone* knew what to do. He felt utterly at a loss.

After a moment of climbing, Charrah pointed to a spot beneath an overhang. He crouched down and sat beneath, leaning back against a boulder.

Daniel removed his hat and followed. "We just take shelter? Shouldn't we search?" They'd ridden frantically to get across the stream, but now they would just wait?

Charrah gave him a familiar look, exasperated with his inexperience. He pointed, then moved his hand downward, indicating a split in the rock, a natural path that they could see perfectly from their position above.

Daniel realized this was likely the way someone would come down the mountain. From this spot, they also had a good view of the horses. *Well chosen*, he thought, squinting to see through the rain. It was a good plan, he realized. The only choice, really. Sarah had no doubt taken shelter. She wouldn't be wandering around in the rain. And now they were on the same side of the rising water. He glanced at his friend. How would he have ever managed in this colony without this wise man's help?

Charrah's jaw was tight as he stared out at the rain.

Daniel realized his friend was worried. Had he expected Kiturra to return earlier? "Kiturra?" he asked.

Charrah shot him a look then went back to staring.

"She is safe," Daniel said. He knew the man couldn't understand him but hoped his voice held concern as well as conviction.

They remained beneath the ledge for another hour. Daniel found it hard to believe a downpour could last so long. Water wound through the rocks, making small streams as they flowed downward. The sound that had been such a din when it began had dulled, and the noise was actually soothing, lulling him into a sleepy stupor. He rested his elbows on his knees, leaning his head back, and wondered where Sarah was.

Seeing her horse had been both reassuring and disconcerting to him. She had come this way, but why had she left the horse? The obvious answer was that she'd climbed into the mountains. Had she seen a sheep and gone after it? He couldn't imagine what else would have drawn her away. His stomach tightened as he thought of the dangers she may have encountered. Were there men in the mountains? Wild dogs? He hoped she had her pistol. Sarah was not naïve to the threats, and truthfully, she was probably more capable of dealing with them than he would be. But still he worried.

He shifted, feeling a sharp rock beneath him. When would he learn to carry around a cushion? The seating arrangements in the colony had proven to be less than satisfactory for the comfort of his backside.

As quickly as it started, the rain stopped. Charrah stood, and Daniel followed him out of the shelter. He put on his top hat and held up a hand against the sudden brightness of the sun. Around them, he could hear the trickling of water continuing down over the rocks. The air smelled wet and fresh. He looked at the horses and saw they were comfortably eating grass beside the stream. Birds called from the trees. Rocks and trees shined. The entire mountain sparkled as if it had just been cleaned.

Charrah started toward the path. Now that Daniel had a better view of the area, he could see it was the best way up. Daniel slipped off his wet jacket and left it on a rock to dry. He stepped carefully over the wet ground, his boots sticking in the muddy patches.

They had only climbed for a few minutes when Charrah stopped.

Daniel looked to him, then followed his gaze. He blinked, breath suspended for a split-second as his mind caught up to the sight before him.

Sarah, her hat askew and her hair loose and wild, carried Kitura's baby in a pouch bound around her chest and shoulders. She walked slowly, supporting Kiturra with an arm around her waist. The dark-skinned woman hopped, her leg wrapped in a makeshift splint. Was this the same Sarah Whitaker who had left Francis Park in tears when he'd tried to introduce his aboriginal friend?

The men glanced at one another, neither knowing what to make of the scene, then they hurried forward.

When she saw him, Sarah stopped. A smile grew on her face. "Daniel."

Seeing her unharmed made his muscles suddenly weak. He had never felt so relieved to see anyone.

Charrah crouched down beside Kiturra, studying her foot. She put a hand on his shoulder and spoke quietly to him, her voice filled with exhaustion and pain. Charrah glanced at the baby, lifted his gaze to Sarah.

Sarah stepped toward Daniel. Her arm was wrapped around the baby sleeping against her chest. Rips and mud stains ruined what he thought must have been a beautiful gown.

"Thank goodness you're here." Sarah's expression was tense, brows pinched together in worry. "We must get her to Sarah Hills and send for a doctor." She tipped her head toward Kiturra then rubbed her eyes.

"Daniel, I found the sheep. They are in a canyon not far from here. And there's a fire. I don't know if the property suffered any damage, and . . ." her voice trailed off. She looked suddenly drained of energy.

Daniel pulled her into his arms, careful not to smash the baby between them. Her hat fell the remainder of the way off, and he rested his chin on her head. "We have a much bigger problem, Miss Whitaker."

She tensed, looking up at him. "What is it?"

From this angle, her lashes were so thick they looked like feathers. He tightened his embrace. "You are very late for our luncheon appointment." He sighed dramatically. "Do you have any idea what time it is?"

Sarah gave him a flat look that softened into a smile. She opened her mouth as if to say something, but Daniel thought they'd done rather enough talking for the moment.

He touched her cheek, and she blinked. Her brows raised and pinched together uncertainly. Daniel smoothed away the furrows with his thumb, cupping her cheek, his palm tingling when she leaned against it. He held her gaze as he bent closer.

Sarah dropped her gaze to his lips then back, her breath hitching. She closed her eyes, the dark lashes fluttering to her cheeks. And he kissed her.

His pulse surged at the touch. Sarah moved her hand over his arm, resting it on his shoulder, and he thought it could have well been a hot iron. Her lips were soft, just as he'd imagined. Finally, Daniel pulled back but didn't loosen his hold.

Hearing a cough, he glanced toward the others.

Charrah's brow ticked upward.

Daniel smiled in spite of himself. The man could speak volumes with the smallest movement. He turned back to the woman in his arms.

Sarah rested her head against his chest. She sighed, her body relaxing into his, and the sound found its way directly to his heart.

"We'll figure it all out, Sarah," Daniel said. "The sheep, the fire, all of it. We'll solve it together, all right?"

He felt her nod against his chest, her arms tightening around him, and for the moment, all was right with the world.

Chapter 20

SARAH LEANED BACK IN THE soft chair. A cushion propped at her side kept her elbow raised and helped support the baby. She glanced across the room at the bed, glad the woman had finally fallen asleep. Once Mrs. Webster had gotten over the shock of Sarah bringing the injured aboriginal woman home and insisting a bedchamber be prepared for her, the housekeeper had made a tea with white willow bark to ease some of the pain.

Sarah settled deeper into the chair, fatigue making her head ache, but her mind would not stop.

She, Daniel, and their aborigine companions had arrived at the house just after dark to find the entire farm in uproar. Tom had sent a group of men to search for Sarah in the forest on the far side of the property. Others had searched to the mountains, but the group hadn't encountered them. Since the creek had swollen, Sarah and Daniel's party had traveled quite a ways before they found a suitable place to cross.

Upon arriving home, Sarah had immediately dispatched men to retrieve the flock in the mountains. Once she'd learned about the fire and realized the shepherds had gone missing, she'd sent to town for the constable as well as the doctor.

Daniel remained by her side as she'd spoken to Tom and tried to piece together exactly what had happened. She was glad he'd been there. His presence was steady and strong when the world around had seemed to fall into chaos. Sarah allowed herself to swoon just the smallest bit as she remembered the kiss. How was it possible that the most perfect man had ended up on the bottom side of the earth, living right next to her?

Charrah and Daniel sat with the patient in the guest chamber while Sarah bathed and changed. When she entered, the men rose. Their motions were slow, and she could see they were both exhausted. She offered them each a bed for the night, but Daniel declined for the sake of propriety.

Sarah would not feel one bit sorrowful if she never heard the word propriety again.

As she thought, she patted the baby's coarse hair, thinking that it reminded her of springy wool. She untucked a little hand from the blanket. She'd discovered that when she put her finger into the baby's hand, he grabbed on tightly, and Sarah loved the sensation. It was silly, really. Probably a reflex. The child was sleeping after all, and he didn't know her. But the feel of the small body nestling close cast a pleasant warm glow over her. She closed her eyes feeling contented.

The hour was nearly dawn by the time Tom arrived with the doctor. The muddy roads and flooding creeks had slowed them down. Sarah woke when the housekeeper entered.

When Dr. Cobb strode into the room, Sarah rose. "Thank you for coming, Doctor." She dipped in a curtsey, blinking away her sleep.

"Miss Whitaker." His gaze dropped to the child she held.

"Her ankle is broken, I think. She's been in quite a lot of pain." Sarah stepped toward the bed and indicated toward the woman's leg, which rested on a pile of pillows. "Mrs. Webster gave her willow bark tea."

She turned back to the doctor, but the man hadn't moved. He stared at the woman in the bed then shook his head, looking back at Sarah. "Miss Whitaker, are you telling me I rode through the night to tend the injury of a *negro*? I wouldn't have my sleep interrupted for a felon; why would I for this creature?"

Sarah's chest went hot. She lifted up the baby, holding him upright against her chest as if to shield him from the doctor's offences against his mother. "I beg your pardon. I hardly think the identity of the patient is of concern. She is injured, and I am perfectly willing to pay—"

"Miss Whitaker, you of all people know how dangerous these aborigines are. After what they did to your own father . . ."

Pain and fear rose inside Sarah, typical feelings when she thought of her father's death, but the emotions were weak now compared to the anger she felt. The man had no right to speak so. The heat grew, and Sarah fought against the wave of furious words that had sprung into her mind. If she made the doctor angry, he would leave, and the mother needed him.

"I see your point, Doctor." Her words were calm in spite of her anger. She moved to the doorway and called for the housekeeper to bring tea and cakes. "You are quite right, of course. Riding for such a distance. You must be worn out. You do me a great service, and I will reimburse you accordingly." She smiled sweetly. "But as long as you've come all this way, you may as well tend to the woman's injury."

"For this patient, my fee will be double." He folded his arms, glaring.
"Of course."

The doctor took his time with tea, eating an extra slice of lemon cake before he grudgingly rose and considered the woman's ankle. He prodded and squeezed it, and the woman in the bed gasped with each touch.

"It hurts her," Sarah said. How could a man be a doctor without an ounce of compassion for a person's pain?

He pulled a kit from his bag and laid out cloth and wooden splints. "The bones seem to be aligned, so it's just a matter of keeping them immobile." He lifted the ankle, wrapping the bandages around the splints, as Sarah had tried to do earlier in the mountain. She thought he worked much less gently.

"And the pain?"

The doctor shook his head. "We've such a limited supply of medication in the colony. I'll not waste it on negroes or felons."

Sarah's stomach felt tight. A few days ago, she would have been in full agreement with the man, but now, she didn't understand why it bothered her so badly. "Sir—"

"I'm sorry, Miss Whitaker." He looked at Sarah's face, and his own scowl lessened a bit. "The willow tea is very effective. It will help her sleep."

Sarah accompanied the doctor down the stairs, paid him, and bid him farewell. She returned to the room, cracking open the door and peeking in.

The woman was awake. *How could she not be after the bone-smith's procedure?* She pressed her arms down on the bed, trying to sit up. Sarah settled the baby on the bed then helped the mother, propping up some pillows behind her and under her ankle. She called for Mrs. Webster to bring some breakfast.

When Sarah returned, the mother held her baby, stroking his cheeks and speaking quietly. Her voice sounded like a song. Sarah stepped quietly. She poured a glass of water and brought it to the bed. The baby looked up and gave Sarah a toothless smile.

Her heart grew warm, and she smiled in return. She reached for his hand, letting him clasp her finger for a moment. She gave the water to the woman, waiting to take the empty cup back to the side table. Pulling a chair closer to the bed, she sat. "I don't know your name," she said.

The woman watched her.

Sarah put her hand on her chest. "I'm Miss—" She shook her head and started again. "Sarah," she said, wondering if the woman understood.

The woman tipped her head thoughtfully, then smiled. "Kiturra." She leaned forward and touched Sarah's breastbone.

Sarah shook her head. "Sarah."

The woman shook her head, placing her hand on her own chest. "Sara." She leaned forward touching Sarah. "Kiturra."

This is silly, Sarah thought. How does she not know her own name?

She opened her mouth to try again, but Kiturra stopped her. She took Sarah's hand, and her eyes became solemn. She swallowed, blinking wet eyes. She lifted their joined hands, squeezing them together. Sarah saw that her small finger was missing its upper joint. "Sa-ra. Kiturra." She held Sarah's gaze as if she were willing Sarah to understand something important.

Even though the words were reversed and the woman's actions made no sense, Sarah understood. This moment was special, significant. Kiturra felt she was giving something of great importance, and in return, taking the name of a person she valued. The exchange of names bonded the two women. Her eyes burned at the tenderness of the gesture, and she nodded. "Sarah."

Later that afternoon, Sarah sat in the parlour listening to Constable Wayne's report. Daniel sat beside her on the settee across from the lawman. Tom stood on the side of the room with arms folded.

"We apprehended the fugitives just on the other side of the creek. Seems they were looking for a herd of sheep they'd stashed before the storm broke." The constable had a long mustache that he seemed very fond of pulling on. "Had a few weapons among them, stolen, obviously, but they didn't put up a fight."

"Surprised the blokes, we did." Tom nodded his head, looking very satisfied.

"Thank you." Sarah was too stunned to say more. Jack Smythe, Dick Hammond, and Marcus Payne were in custody for an escape attempt. An attempt that involved stealing a flock of sheep that they apparently planned to sell or live off.

"I 'eard those new convicts were trouble, even on the ship. Must've convinced Marcus an attempt at freedom was worth risking his life."

"And do you think the men were responsible for the fire too?" Daniel's voice was calm, strong, and at that moment, she felt like he was the only thing holding her together. She'd had very little sleep the night before, and she'd determined her fleece shipment for Captain Thackeray to be ruined. And her workers had betrayed her.

"I do, sir." Constable Wayne stroked his mustache. "Meant to be a distraction while they moved the sheep."

"Didn't plan on the rain, poor sots," Tom added. "Downright foiled their plans of escaping to China, it did."

Why would they do this? The fleece was a complete loss. Fleece she'd promised to Captain Thackeray. Sarah closed her eyes. Her chest felt heavy. And *Marcus Payne.* He'd been an employee of her father's, loyal for well over ten years. Few people had been at Sarah Hills as long as he.

"The men will be tried and sentenced within the week, Miss Whitaker," the constable said. "Once the date and time are set, you'll be notified. If you care to be present at the hearing."

"Thank you," she muttered again. She thought of Marcus's thick beard and crinkled eyes. The man had lifted her onto her horse when she was a child. He'd worked beside her for years. And now he would be hanged or, at the very least, sent to Van Dieman's land. Surely Daniel could see now why trusting a criminal was foolish.

At the sound of movement, Sarah looked up. The men had risen without her notice.

"Thank you again, Constable," Daniel said, shaking the man's hand.

Sarah thanked the lawman and bid him farewell then noticed Tom. He leaned back against the wall and looked close to falling down. She realized he'd gone for the doctor, riding all night, then returned home and joined the manhunt. "Mr. Gilbert, when did you last sleep?"

Tom yawned. "Night before last, my lady."

She nodded. "Go home. And rest tomorrow as well. I will see you at church Sunday."

"Thank you, my lady." He gave a grateful bow.

"You did good work today, Mr. Gilbert."

When the two men had departed, Sarah sank down onto the settee. A wave of fatigue washed over her. "It has been a long day, Mr. Burton."

Daniel sat beside her. "That it has, Miss Whitaker."

She looked at him, feeling shy now that they were alone. "I am glad you're here. I don't know what I would do if you were not."

He turned his knees toward her, stretching one leg straight. "I told you, we will solve this together."

Sarah blushed, looking at her hands. "You shouldn't have to worry about my problems. You have your own farm to manage."

Daniel scratched behind his ear. "Sarah?"

The way he spoke her name, his voice low and determined, sent a shiver over her skin. He took her hand, threading his fingers through it, holding their palms together.

"Sarah, I *want* to worry about your problems. I want them to be my own." He lifted her hand to his lips. "I want *you* to be my own." His breath was warm on her fingers. He leaned forward, his gaze locked on hers. "Sarah Whitaker, would you do me the honor of being my wife?"

Sarah couldn't draw a breath; her insides fluttered like a trapped bird. Daniel's eyes were earnest, hopeful, and in that moment, she knew there was nothing she wanted more than to be with this man. To marry him. "Yes," she whispered.

Daniel's face relaxed into a crooked grin. He pulled her toward him, his lips finding hers easily, as if kissing was the most natural thing in the world. Sarah slipped her hand up his neck, tangling her fingers in his curls. He turned his head, deepening the kiss, and she felt like her heart would burst from happiness.

He drew back, putting his arm behind her and pulling her against him. She laid her cheek on his shoulder, her forehead touching his neck, and let the sensation of being held in his arms cover her like sunshine. Daniel smelled like spice and cake. His body was warm against hers. His heart beat beneath her ear, his chest rising and falling. She sighed. This is what it felt like to truly love a person.

"Daniel," she said after a long moment, "I hope I bring more to our marriage than my problems."

His arm tightened around her, and he leaned his cheek on her head. "Why do you say that?"

"You said you wanted to make my problems yours, but I don't want that to be the reason you marry me. To solve my difficulties."

"There are hundreds of other reasons, Sarah. Thousands, in fact. For one, you are definitely the more intelligent of the two of us. Another, you know how to handle a gun. Not to mention, of course, your exquisite beauty."

"Stop teasing." She swatted his arm. "I am being serious."

He pulled back, turning her toward him. All joking was gone from his expression. "I am in love with you, Sarah Whitaker. And do you know why? Because you are a contradiction. A puzzle. A woman who wears work boots with a ball gown. A woman who is intelligent and opinionated but has a kind heart. Every day I learn something new about you, something that surprises me.

"Seeing you yesterday with Kiturra and her baby, knowing how difficult it must have been for you to save them but doing it anyway. *That* is why I love you, Sarah Whitaker. Because you are unpredictable and admirable, and I want to understand more about you—to keep discovering something new every day."

Sarah sat, stunned by his words. She'd not realized the depths of his feelings, and it felt like more than her heart could bear. She blinked, her eyes wet. "I did not expect . . . Thank you, Daniel. I don't think anyone has ever said such thoughtful things to me."

He smiled, his eyes soft. "If you do not wish for an answer, you should not ask such a question of a man in love, my dear."

Sarah felt a blush spread over her cheeks. She looked down, twisting her fingers. "I don't know why I did it, why I helped Kiturra and the baby." She glanced up.

Daniel watched her silently, so she continued.

"I haven't changed my feelings. I don't feel differently toward the aboriginal people; I still fear them. I hate them, Daniel. They killed my papá." She felt horrible speaking this way, but she didn't want him to think that by her actions the day before, she'd suddenly become a different person. She rubbed her arm, feeling like she was exposing a part of herself that she wasn't proud of. "I still hate them. I just don't hate them all." She looked up, expecting to see disappointment in his eyes, but instead his brows were furrowed thoughtfully.

"I understand," he said.

"You do? How can you when I don't understand myself?"

Daniel shrugged. "You told me trust is giving another person the ability to hurt you. Isn't love the same? That woman and child trust you, Sarah. And in return, you care for them."

She thought about his words. Were trust and love the same? They did seem to be very similar. But . . . her anger at the shepherds came forefront into her mind. She'd trusted, and look what had happened.

"Sarah, I need to tell you—"

"I am tired of trusting, Daniel." She spoke over his words, not wanting to hear his lecture. The true problem was exactly the opposite of what he believed it to be. She *did* allow herself to trust and then came the inevitable betrayal. "It happens again and again." She balled her hands into fists. "Marcus Payne—I've known him for ten years, trusted him, but I was wrong."

Daniel winced. "I'm sorry it happened."

"It happened because I was foolish. Criminals don't change. You see it, don't you?" She studied him, but his eyes had dulled. "Daniel?"

He gave a smile, though she could see it was forced. She didn't want to ruin the first moments of her betrothal by upsetting him.

"I trust *you*, Daniel." She tipped her head, hoping to elicit a true smile from him. Something changed in Daniel's expression, and for a moment, she thought she saw pain in his eyes.

He glanced toward the window.

Sarah was surprised to note that the sky was darkening. She could smell supper being prepared. It was much later than she'd realized. "I should check on Kiturra," she said, pushing herself forward.

"Don't you mean Sarah?" He spoke with a teasing tone, but it lacked its usual joviality.

"Do not make a jest," she said, acting as if she hadn't heard the change in his voice. "It was a very dear thing; I could tell it was meaningful to her." She glanced toward the door, pushing herself to her feet. Charrah was upstairs with Kiturra. Perhaps they were both hungry.

Daniel rose beside her.

"Will you accompany me?" She held out a hand.

Daniel smiled and took it. He kissed her fingers then tucked her hand beneath his arm, resting it in the crook of his elbow. "Always, my dear."

Sarah sighed. His moment of unease had passed. She leaned her head on his shoulder as they walked to the staircase vowing to be more careful about what she said in the future. He was sensitive when they discussed the convicts, likely because he cared for Bill Hawkins and his family the same way Sarah cared about Kiturra. She must remember it.

She shivered as a rush of nervous tingles flowed over her. She was betrothed to the man she loved, and no convict felon could ruin that.

Chapter 21

SUNDAY MORNING DANIEL JERKED AWAKE to a pounding at his door. He looked to the window, trying to push the fog of sleep from his mind. The sky was lightening, but it was not yet dawn. The pounding came again, and fingers of cold dread wrapped around his chest. He stumbled from bed and pulled on trousers. A caller this early could only mean bad news. *Sarah? Another fire?* Daniel's worry grew.

He snatched up a pistol from atop his bureau and hurried down the staircase. He didn't have a butler, and Winnie didn't come to the house this early. He took a breath and opened the door.

Charrah stood in the doorway, his arms folded.

"Charrah, what . . ." Daniel trailed off as he noticed the man wasn't alone. There were at least thirty men and women of Charrah's tribe in front of the house.

"Kiturra," Charrah said. He pointed toward Sarah Hills.

Daniel stared at him, trying to understand. Did he want Daniel to send for the woman? To fetch her?

Charrah turned, pointing toward a man. No, not the man, the object he held. Two long, straight branches attached with a large piece of leather. A travois, Daniel realized.

He groaned, rubbing his eyes. "Charrah, wait a few hours. We can't barge into Sarah's house before the sun's even up." He spread his hand over his head, making a motion of a rising sun.

"Kiturra," Charrah repeated. His tone was definitive. He wouldn't discuss the matter.

Daniel groaned again. Charrah wouldn't take this group to Sarah Hills without Daniel. The aboriginal people were aware of which places they were welcome and where they might be shot on sight. They were afforded no protection under the law, and some landowners considered shooting a black-skinned native to be the equivalent of ridding the colony of dingoes or other nuisances.

"Very well," Daniel said. "We will walk slowly, and I'll send a man ahead to notify her."

Charrah didn't understand the words, but he recognized the concession in Daniel's voice. He nodded. "Thank-you, Dan-yah." His stance remained strong, probably for the benefit of the others, but Daniel saw gratitude in his friend's eyes.

He yawned, scratching his hair. "I need to get dressed."

Charrah remained still, waiting for an explanation.

Daniel pulled at his night shirt and rubbed the whiskers on his chin. "I will not call on my fiancée looking like . . . a pirate."

Charrah rolled his eyes telling Daniel exactly what he thought of all of the gentlemen's trappings and efforts at presentation.

"I'll be out in a moment. Make yourselves at home." Daniel yawned again then returned inside to dress and shave.

As he studied the knot in his cravat half hour later, Daniel smirked, thinking how much easier his mornings would be if he wore only a loincloth and let his hair and beard grow wild. The idea was tempting for less than a second—until he thought of the sunburn.

He glanced out the window. The sun was just cresting the horizon. Maybe if they walked slowly, their arrival wouldn't be so terribly early.

When he returned outside, pulling on a jacket, Charrah stood in the same spot on the porch. He looked pointedly at Daniel's attire, and his look said, *Really?*

Daniel smirked at his friend, knowing Charrah's mocking was made in jest. He stepped down from the porch, walking to a group of his men.

Charrah walked beside him.

The ranch workers stood well away from the group, nervous looks on their faces. Daniel reassured them that the aborigines were friends of Charrah and would not cause any harm. He sent a man ahead on horseback to alert Sarah then turned to Charrah. "Shall we?" He made a sweeping motion with his arm in the direction of Sarah Hills.

Charrah shook his head. "Dan-yah horse."

Daniel nodded. "Good idea." Having Daniel so visible as the group trekked over the hills would be a wise move.

"Would you like to ride as well?" he asked. "Charrah, horse?"

Charrah shook his head. He tipped his head toward the others. He would walk with his people.

He rode slowly, the group of men, women, and children following. Daniel wondered why so many were needed to fetch one person. But they weren't armed, and he trusted their intentions, even if he didn't understand them.

They left the property by way of the road; the creek was still too swollen to cross. Daniel smiled, remembering the first time he'd come to Francis Park, the first time he'd seen the beautiful land that was now his. And the first day he'd met Sarah. His smile grew. Sarah. His fiancée. He could not imagine feeling happier. His chest felt like it was inflating when he remembered their kisses, their intimate moments and conversations. All the times before when he'd fancied himself in love, none even came close to the wholeness he felt with Sarah. She was everything he was not, yet they went together perfectly, like a broken piece of crockery that finds its other half.

A shadow moved over his blissful contemplations. He must tell Sarah. He must. But he told himself the timing had never been exactly right. He'd planned to on Friday night when he'd proposed, but the pain of Marcus Payne's betrayal was still raw. She'd been so hurt—so angry.

Daniel's bliss deflated. He was a coward. In truth, it was her reaction he feared, her anger. He feared losing her. Even the thought made his heart ache.

He scratched behind his ear. Sarah's trust was a privilege granted to very few, and he, the person she trusted most, was unworthy of it.

When they drew closer to the house, Daniel saw Sarah standing on the porch. Her hair was loose, and she wore a simple white morning gown. She held the baby. Even from a distance, he could see unease in her posture, and it worried him.

He raised his hand, and she waved in return. Daniel urged his horse forward, arriving before the others. He dismounted and bowed with a flourish, "Good morning, my betrothed."

Sarah smiled at his teasing. She stepped off the porch toward him as he handed the reins to a groom. "Daniel, what is all this?" She pointed with a look toward the approaching group.

He shrugged a shoulder. "Honestly, I do not know. Apparently Charrah thought each person of his acquaintance needed to accompany him to fetch Kiturra."

She clutched the baby closer, not seeming aware of the action.

Charrah approached with the old man Daniel had met in the forest, Obing. Sarah welcomed them politely, shaking both men's hands.

Daniel was proud of her dignity. He did not know what she was feeling, but her actions were gracious.

She stepped back, motioning for Charrah. "She will need assistance on the stairs," she said, turning toward the house. "Daniel, will you come too?"

"Always, my dear," he said in a low voice, hoping to set her at ease.

She gave a small smile for his effort.

Sarah moved aside the blankets, but Kiturra climbed out of the bed on her own. She hopped down the stairs with Charrah's assistance then through the entry hall to the front door. Sarah and Daniel followed, stepping out behind the couple.

When she saw her people, Kiturra stopped. She smiled but did not go to them right away. Instead she turned to Sarah.

Daniel stepped aside, giving the women space.

Kiturra touched Sarah's chest, right below her neck. She whispered something, and Sarah duplicated the motion, touching Kiturra's breastbone and whispering in return. Sarah's lip trembled, and Daniel's throat constricted as he saw her bid farewell to her friend. She held the baby tight.

Kiturra turned away but not before Daniel saw tears in the woman's eyes. Sarah was not the only one to be affected by their friendship. She leaned on Charrah and allowed him to lead her to the group. People greeted her with touches and soft words, obviously glad for her safe return. She lay on the leather of the unrolled stretcher, and men lifted the poles.

Charrah stepped onto the porch with a woman. They approached Sarah, and the woman held out her hands.

Daniel heard Sarah's breath hitch. She tightened her arms for an instant and pulled the baby forward, giving a kiss on his cheek. Her movements were slow, careful. She closed her eyes for a moment then placed the baby gently in the woman's arms.

The woman moved away, joining the group as they walked toward the forest. Apparently the aboriginal people weren't ones for drawn-out farewells.

Sarah wrapped her arms around herself as she watched.

"Thank you, Miss Wita-ka," Charrah said.

Sarah swallowed, breathing out a long breath. She shook her head, placing her hand on her chest, appearing to gather herself. "Sarah," she said after a moment. "And you are welcome, Charrah."

"Sarah." Charrah gave a solemn nod.

Sarah seemed to understand the importance his people placed on names. Charrah's look was one of respect. He nodded to Daniel and strode away.

The pair stood for a moment, watching the group depart, and suddenly Sarah turned to him, wrapping her arms around his middle and burying her face in his chest.

He stroked her hair, pulling her close. The smell of vanilla swirled around him. "Oh, my dearest," he whispered, wishing he knew how to comfort her.

After a long moment, she pulled back but didn't release him. She turned her head, resting it against his chest. "I am being silly."

"It is not silly to care."

"I am silly because I was pretending. I knew it wasn't real."

"Your affection was real, Sarah. It was not imagined."

"No. That is not it." Her voice was soft, hesitant. "When they were here, I pretended I had a family."

An ache pierced Daniel's heart. He held her close, his eyes burning as he saw the truth: the outspoken, guarded, independent woman in his arms was also a lonely girl, a girl who wanted more than anything to belong to someone.

When he thought he could keep his voice steady, he spoke. "We are to be married, remember? You and I, we will be a family."

She held him tighter. "We will be a family," she whispered.

Chapter 22

SARAH RODE OVER THE MEADOW at a gallop. With one hand, she held her hat on her head; her braid flew out behind. Early that morning, the convict supervisor had brought new workers to replace those she'd lost the week before, and she'd spent the morning showing them the farm. The men were good workers, he'd assured her. All three had worked for years at the government farm and had clean behavior records. While she was glad the men weren't fresh off the ship, she still told Tom to keep a watchful eye on them. And she planned to as well.

Nearing the Sarah Hills homestead, she slowed, smiling when she saw Daniel's horse in the corral with the others. They'd planned to go over Sarah Hills's ledgers today, assess the actual loss from the fire. The thought of all the wasted fleece made her stomach clench. She dismounted and hurried inside.

She found Daniel already in the study, ledgers and papers scattered around the desk before him.

When she entered, he rose and kissed her cheek. "I hope you don't mind I started already. I didn't know how long you'd be. Your books are in excellent order, Miss Whitaker."

"Thank you," she said as he turned back to the desk. "I don't mind in the least." Having someone to help her with the dull bookkeeping was a relief. While he examined the books, Sarah sat on the sofa and sorted through a stack of correspondence on the side table. She opened an envelope and read the card. An invitation to a garden party at the Government House. She smiled when she realized she would not have to attend alone.

Yesterday, she and Daniel had ridden to church together in her carriage. Of course, Molly rode with them, but their arrival still caused a stir among the people of Parramatta. She'd heard whispers as they walked into the church together, speculation that she quickly set to rest after the service when she confirmed the truth of their engagement privately to Dorthea Iverson.

By now, she was certain every person within a thirty-mile radius of the town had heard the news. Gossip traveled quickly in the colony.

She opened another envelope, but as she read the communication, her gaze wandered. Keeping her mind on the task was difficult. She'd much rather watch Daniel work. She noticed his lips move just the smallest bit as he read, and occasionally, he'd make a note on a piece of paper then tap the quill against his chin, contemplating. She smiled, pleased with the idea of discovering simple things like his little habits. What more would she learn over the years?

He glanced up and saw her watching.

Sarah started out of her daydreaming and hurried to the doorway to call for Mrs. Webster. "I should have sent for tea earlier," she said. "I am a terrible hostess today."

He dropped the quill into the ink and leaned back in the chair. "Tea sounds wonderful." He smoothed a hand over his curls. "And, Miss Whitaker, from the looks of things, the burned wool will not hurt Sarah Hills's profits too greatly this year."

"I am not worried about that," she said. "It's the wool itself. I'd promised it to Captain Thackeray."

"This is not the only sheep ranch in the colony. He'll be able to purchase elsewhere."

Sarah nodded. "I know. But not for my price."

Daniel's brows rose and his mouth formed an *O*.

"He depended on this wool, fine wool he can sell for a large profit while Spain is still under French control and Spanish wool is virtually impossible to buy in England. He plans to finance his retirement and stay in England with his family."

"But it is just one shipment? You have more in a warehouse in Sydney Town, I believe."

"Yes, it is just one shipment."

Mrs. Webster entered with a tea tray.

Sarah thanked her, scooting toward the table to pour out. "This shipment was the very finest. I waited as long as I could before shearing. The wool was thick, and all of the sheep were pure white." She brought him a cup of tea. "It felt important."

Daniel took it. "You felt like it was a gift, something you could do for a man who had been a great influence in your life."

She nodded. "That's it exactly." The sick feeling returned to her stomach as she thought about the lost fleece. She picked up a plate. "Lemon cake?"

The bell rang before Daniel could answer. The butler entered a moment later. "Mr. and Mrs. Pierce are in the parlour, miss."

Sarah wrinkled her nose. She looked at Daniel and saw his lip curl. "Should I send them away?" she asked.

He shrugged. "Will they just return?"

"They are rather like vermin." She huffed out a breath, making Daniel laugh. "Will you come with me?"

Daniel rounded the desk. He took her in his arms. "Always, my dear." He swept away loose tendrils from her cheek, slipping his hand beneath her ear and bending to kiss her. Sarah sighed, leaning toward him.

Daniel paused, his lips a breath away. "But let's make them wait a bit, shall we?"

The pair entered the parlour fifteen minutes later. Sarah twisted her lips to hold back a giggle. She knew her cheeks were flushed. Her lips tingled, and she wondered if they were swollen from kissing. A blush made her already heated skin burn, and she wished she'd thought to bring a fan.

Minerva had, of course, remembered. She waved her fan in front of her red face with forceful motions like she was striking a drum.

Mr. Pierce rose, his eyes going wide at the sight of the two of them then narrowing into a scowl. He took Sarah's hand, offering a bow, then after a slight hesitation, shook Daniel's.

They greeted Minerva, who only lifted her chin in acknowledgement of Daniel's bow.

Sarah had half a mind to throw them out then and there. She knew they still harbored ill feelings after the incident in the churchyard, but if Daniel could be cordial after their insults to him, they could do the same. She admired him all the more for his dignity in the face of such rudeness.

Sarah took Daniel's arm. She did not sit, nor did she order tea for her guests. "To what do I owe this visit?"

"It is true then," Minerva said, her eyes moving between the couple. "Miss Whitaker, you are engaged to this . . . person?" She spat out her words.

Daniel stiffened.

Sarah leveled a glare at the woman. "Madam, if you have come to my house to insult me or my fiancé, I will thank you to leave." She spoke in a cool voice that belied the anger simmering beneath the surface.

"That is not our reasoning at all," Minerva said. "We've come with a gift."

Sarah looked at the couple and saw them exchange a confirming look that made her scalp tingle. *What were they conspiring?*

Minerva slapped the fan into her hand, closing it, then took a folded paper from her reticule. She held it between two fingers and waved it toward Sarah.

Sarah released Daniel's arm. She stepped forward, snatching the paper. "What is this?"

"A convict manifest, my dear," Mr. Pierce said, spite in his voice. "From the *Bollerophon*. Perhaps you know the ship, Mr. Burton?"

Sarah turned to Daniel, confused. "Of course he . . ." Her voice trailed off when she saw his face had gone white.

Cold shot through Sarah, spreading from her chest, leaving numbness in its wake. *No.* She shook her head, the paper making a flapping noise as her trembling hands opened it. The silence in the room pressed against her ears, her eyes moving in and out of focus as she stared at the blotched ink and lines of words. She scanned down the column, reading the names of the prisoners and stopped. It was there. *Daniel Burton, transported for Larceny.*

Sarah's mind was numb. It couldn't be true. There was a mistake. But a glance at Daniel's expression confirmed it.

The paper stung her fingers, and she dropped it. Her head was dizzy, and she felt the blood drain from her face. She couldn't draw a breath. The air in the room became too heavy to pull into her lungs.

"Sarah." Daniel's voice sounded far away. He helped her to a chair.

She sat hard, head in her hands as she breathed jagged breaths. Her mind whirled, thoughts jumbling together half-formed. The image of Oliver Winchell sitting at the desk, ledgers open, leaning back in the chair solidified—but it wasn't Oliver at all. Daniel smiled at her from behind the desk. *Not again. Not him.* She touched her lips, still warm from his kiss. He'd used her, lied to her. She could hear blood pulsing in her ears.

"Sarah."

She realized Daniel knelt in front of her, his hands on her arms. She shook her head, unable to form words.

"Sarah, let me—"

"No." Her voice sounded strange in her ears. "Do not touch me." She jerked away, standing so quickly she pushed the chair over.

Mr. Pierce stood and helped his wife to rise. "We thought you needed to be informed. Of course, any thief knows, the quickest way to money is to marry a rich woman."

Sarah rushed from the room. Her head felt light, and she clutched the stair rail, steading herself.

"Sarah, please stop. Let me explain," Daniel's voice pleaded.

She spun, standing on the stair above him. "Let you explain? What is there to explain? You have been deceiving me all along. Lying to me." Her voice was rising with each word. "You let me . . ." Her throat closed, and she choked on the sob that pushed its way free. She pressed a shaking hand to her mouth. "I trusted you," she whispered.

"Please listen to me. I love you."

She squeezed her eyes shut. Another lie, and this one hurt the very worst. *Any thief knows, the quickest way to money is to marry a rich woman.* He'd seen right into her heart, known exactly how to manipulate her. *We are a family now.* She was a fool.

"Sarah."

"Go," she said. Her voice was cold as it had been moments earlier to her other guests. The world, in those few minutes, had turned over, and Sarah felt she was spinning like a leaf on the breeze with nothing to cling to. "Leave my house, Daniel Burton. I do not ever want to see you again."

Chapter 23

DANIEL TURNED HIS HORSE FROM the main road, riding beneath the canopy of trees onto Francis Park. His shoulders slumped and his heart felt heavy. The hearing for the Sarah Hills herders had been surprisingly short; as promised, Sarah wasn't in attendance. Even though he hadn't expected her, he'd still felt disappointed. Her absence made his own presence seem all the more out of place.

Word of his convict status had spread through the colonial society faster than lice in a prisonyard. People who had days earlier welcomed him into their homes with affection now regarded him with sidelong glances and disgust. Even Elizabeth Macquarie pretended not to see him when they passed on the road.

Sighing, he rubbed his cheek, realizing he didn't remember when he'd last shaved. The loss of the Exclusives' good favor bothered him much less than he'd thought it would. In fact, it was a relief not to worry that one day the truth would be exposed. He could have tolerated the disdain of the town easily, if only . . .

A familiar ache wrapped around his heart as he glanced in the direction of Sarah Hills, though of course he could not see the property through the trees. With Sarah beside him, he could have endured anyone's disapproval.

Daniel had hoped the hearing would provide some reassurance, some explanation from Marcus and the others that would prove Daniel was not like them. But it hadn't come. The men had spoken with little remorse of their actions, telling of their plans to escape, sell the sheep, and flee to freedom. No mistreatment on their overseer's behalf had spurred them; they'd simply seen an opportunity and taken it.

And Daniel was a fool to believe he was different. He'd convinced himself that even though he had made mistakes in the past, he was on a worthy path now. He'd thought he could help those around him, make their lives better. But the truth was he was an arrogant fool. He couldn't even help himself. Sarah's words haunted him: *Criminals don't change.*

He reined in the horse near the pond, watching the activity of the farm. Charrah's people fished in their small boats, the smell of cooking fires reached his nose, and the sounds of construction on the new barn came from beyond the trees. In the distance, he could see workers tending the flock on the hill.

The ache grew. He loved Francis Park. Loved the work, the land, the people. Francis Park had felt like his sanctuary, his salvation. He'd felt like a better man, hoped to make a fine life here.

He rode onward toward the house.

"Mr. Burt!"

He waved as Trudy called out to him from the doorway. How could he leave this behind? He dismounted and swept the child into his arms.

She wrapped her short arms around his neck. "You're back, Mr. Burt."

He blinked and swallowed hard, finding it impossible to speak as he carried her toward the house.

The Hawkinses looked up to him—Trudy thought of him as a hero, Charrah admired him and treated him as a brother—but it was all a fraud. *He* was a fraud, and the time had come to stop pretending. But before he did, he had to do one thing right.

Chapter 24

SARAH STOOD ON SOUTH HEAD, looking over the harbor and the town of Sydney. Behind her, the signal whipped in the breeze, signifying a ship in port. Below, the town glowed in the morning light. What had begun as a small settlement was growing as new people, bond and free, came to the colony. The town expanded outward from the harbor, spreading like spilled ink. She moved her gaze up the steep steps and winding alleys of the Rocks District. Colorful birds in cages hung outside the doors of the whitewashed cottages along the waterline. In the Government District, she watched the red coats moving in formation as the regiment drilled on the parade ground. She squinted, idly wondering if Conall Stewart was among them.

Looking toward the sea, she saw pink eucalypts growing on rocky shores. Whalers' and sealers' ships bobbed among the merchant ships, and here and there, she saw the red-and-white whip pennant of a convict vessel. The sights of Sydney were as familiar to her as any, but today, none of the familiarity brought her comfort.

She felt hollow, numb. The Pierces' visit had taken place a week earlier, and still her heart was cold. Gloom hung over her like morning fog rolling off the ocean and stealing the brightness.

"Sarah."

She turned as Captain Thackeray approached. She curtseyed, motioning toward the harbor. "The *Coeur d'Alene* looks magnificent."

He puffed out his chest. "Aye, that she does." He walked to stand beside her, his eyes scanning the view. "She just waits for a few more libations—and fair winds, of course. I'll miss this city, my girl. Fine people here."

She tried to smile but couldn't manage it. "I'm sorry about the wool."

He squinted, tipping his head. "The wool?"

"The wool that didn't arrive, the last shipment. Surely you got my note about the fleece burned in the fire." She let out a sigh, feeling the weight of his disappointment. "If only I'd sent it to the warehouse sooner. I—"

"Sarah, the wool arrived."

"Impossible. It burned, all of it. The storage building . . . I had no more to send."

"It arrived," he said slowly, studying her face as if just noticing something was amiss. "Sarah, are you well?"

"Oh, yes." She nodded, but the gloom seemed to grow heavier when she tried to act cheerful.

He continued to study her, but Sarah didn't have the energy to even feel uncomfortable beneath his scrutiny. She felt like she was wilting

"Come." He led her to a bench. "Sarah, what aren't you telling me?"

She shook her head. "I am a bit tired after my journey, I suppose."

He nodded, crossing his leg and resting an arm across the back of the bench. "Can you think of how a shipment of the finest Saxon-Merino wool arrived on my ship yesterday evening, addressed to Captain Alan Thackeray of the *Coeur d'Alene* from Miss Sarah Whitaker of Sarah Hills?"

"I told you, all my fleece was burned—" Sarah stopped. Saxon-Merino wool? "Daniel." Just saying his name hurt so badly that she drew in a quick breath, wincing. Daniel had sent the wool. *His* wool. But . . .

Captain Thackeray continued to study her. "There is more to the story, I see. Something has happened."

"He is a felon, sir."

He nodded. "I know."

Sarah gaped at him. "You know? But you befriended him. You seemed to . . . regard him favorably."

"A fine man," he said. "I consider him one of the finest of my acquaintance."

"But . . ." She opened her eyes wide, unable to believe what he was saying.

"I did befriend him. I also gave my blessing when he asked permission to court you." His voice dropped low as he spoke.

"Why?" She shook her head. "Why would you do that?"

"Because he's a good man, Sarah. A changed man."

She let her shoulders drop. "People don't change."

The captain lowered his foot, letting it tap for a moment as he watched a sea bird flying in a lazy circle far above the town.

"Did he tell you why he was transported?"

"Larceny," she said. "I read it in the convict manifest."

"He did not tell you himself?"

"I did not . . ."

"Ah. I see, you did not give him the chance."

Sarah frowned, darting a glance at the man. It seemed very much like he was taking the wrong side.

"Through a series of bad decisions, Mr. Burton found himself in a fair bit of debt. He placed a wager he could not afford to lose and took measures to ensure a win. He killed a racehorse."

Sarah's mouth opened.

"It was an accident. He'd been assured the herbs would make the animal sleepy, too slow to win the race, but the concoction was more potent."

"That is despicable." Sarah tried to sound indignant. She should feel disgusted, but she just felt . . . sad.

Captain Thackeray nodded. "Exactly what the judge thought. And what Daniel thought himself—and still does." He threaded his fingers together, leaning his arms on his knees. "He cannot forgive himself. And instead he forgives others."

Sarah averted her gaze. The captain's words disconcerted her.

"Daniel cannot undo what he's done, Sarah. But he can change his actions from now on."

"But I cannot trust him." She felt desperate to convince him. Surely he could understand why she'd been so hurt by Daniel's secret. "He kept the truth from me. He is a felon, and I cannot trust a felon."

"You cannot?"

"I cannot allow myself to. They are not honorable, even when they give the appearance to have changed. Oliver Winchell seemed to be a gentleman. Marcus Payne worked at Sarah Hills for over ten years. They speak lies, seeking only to deceive. And when they have your trust, they betray you." Captain Thackeray let out a long breath. He closed his eyes. "Sarah, do you know why I went to sea?"

She shook her head slowly.

He looked down at his hands. "I was an orphan, grew up on the rookery streets in London. I worked for a man—we all did if we hoped to survive—who fed me based on what I was able to steal from wealthy people's pockets."

Sarah stared at the captain. Her chest burned as she realized what his story meant. "You, Captain?"

"Aye, Sarah." He glanced up at the crow. "Course, I wasn't any good at stealin'. Police runners caught me lifting a lady's purse. Gave me a choice of prison or service. Said there's a captain at the docks lookin' for a crew."

"I'm sorry. I did not know."

"Nobody knows, 'cept my wife, of course. I'm not proud of my past. But I give my word of honor, since that day over fifty years ago, I've never stolen a farthing."

Sarah felt heavy as she contemplated the man's story. She'd never thought of him as anything less than an honorable gentleman. She was surprised when she found she still thought of him that way.

"A person is not what he has done in the past. He becomes what he chooses to do with the life he's been given. You must see that." He turned to her, leaning forward to catch her gaze. "We are all dealt a hand to play. As a child, you were brought to a foreign land where you had no friends, a rather irritable aunt, and news of your father's death. Instead of selling the land and returning home, you learned bookkeeping, you became an expert on sheep and crops. You cannot tell me *you* haven't changed, Sarah."

He lifted her hand, loosening the fist and held it in both of his. "People *can* change."

His words were true. She wasn't the same girl who arrived in the colony ten years earlier hoping to see a kangaroo. She had become a new person. The same, yet different. She had made mistakes along the way, so many mistakes, and yet she'd not made allowance for others to do the same.

She thought of what the captain said about Daniel. He was not the same man who'd fixed a wager by killing a horse. She knew it, and thinking over his actions, she could see that he had changed his path. He avoided places where he might be tempted to wager. He defended his workers. He replaced her lost wool. These were not the actions of a dishonest person.

Captain Thackeray pressed a handkerchief into her hand, and Sarah realized she was weeping. She leaned against his shoulder, and her emotions burst forth.

He wrapped an arm around her, patting her back.

Daniel believed in her. He trusted her, as imperfect as she was. He not only knew her faults but understood them. And from the first day, she had faulted him for every perceived error. From taking the land she wanted, to hiring her foreman, to befriending an aborigine, she'd seen only his flaws and tried to convince him to change. Daniel, in turn, had loved her for the person she was, not who he wished she'd be.

Captain Thackeray had said Daniel forgave everyone else, but he needed forgiveness too. And she'd failed him.

"Oh, Sarah," the captain muttered in a soothing tone.

"Captain." Her breath hitched as she sat up and wiped her eyes. "I have made a dreadful mistake." She rose. "I must go—"

He stood, smiling.

She glanced toward the harbor. "But I will wait and see you off."

The captain took her shoulders, turning her fully toward him. "Sarah Whitaker, I love you like a daughter, and so I will tell you what I'd tell my own children." He cleared his throat, his eyes wet. "Look to your future not your past, my dear. Bid me farewell, shed a tear if you must, promise to write, then leave this old man behind and go after the life that awaits you."

Sarah's throat was tight. "Thank you, Captain." She whispered the words.

"I'm proud of you, Little Minnow." He pulled her to him, kissing her forehead. "Now, off with ya. And I want a full report in your next letter."

"Aye-aye, sir." She embraced him once more then hurried away. Her heart ached, but it was a different kind of ache. Not the emptiness she'd felt earlier but a soft sadness that came from bidding farewell to a beloved friend. And the feeling was tempered with hope, pushing the emptiness from her heart and casting off the gloom. It was the last and dearest gift Captain Thackeray had given her.

Sarah returned to the inn and asked Molly to repack their clothes.

Molly looked at her with confusion. They had arrived only the night before. "But, my lady, are we not going window shopping? And what about the ship?"

"I'm sorry; I must return right away."

"My lady, have you been crying?"

"I—" Sarah's throat grew tight, but she had enough of weeping. Now she was resolved to action. She rubbed her eyes, realizing she still held Captain Thackeray's handkerchief, which threatened to send her off again. She fought against the emotion.

She considered how to answer Molly then remembered the captain's words. She looked at the woman for a moment, making up her mind. "Molly, I do not mean to be presumptuous, but I saw you speaking to a man in town last week."

Molly's eyes became immediately wary.

"Is he a friend of yours?" Sarah asked.

"Yes, my lady," Molly answered slowly, her face nervous, but a blush bloomed on her cheeks, confirming Sarah's suspicions.

"Do you think he might want to work for me?"

Molly's eyes went wide. "Yes, my lady, I think he'd like that very much."

Sarah nodded, turning to leave. "I'll wait for you at the carriage." Once she left, she allowed a smile at Molly's bewildered expression.

She stepped out of the inn and nearly bumped into the colonial secretary.

"I beg your pardon, Miss Whitaker." He swept off his hat and bowed.

Sarah curtseyed. "Mr. Campbell."

"I heard you were in town to see off the *Coeur d'Alene*." He looked irritated, as usual, to have to speak to a woman about business matters.

"Yes," she said, not wishing for a long conversation with the man, not after their last meeting.

"Very good," he said. "I came to tell you the property you'd, ah, inquired about a few months ago is available for purchase."

"What property?"

"The land beside yours, formerly belonging to a Mr. Daniel Burton."

Francis Park? Sarah's felt a chill go over her spine. "I don't understand, sir. Mr. Burton is living on the land. He's built a house there."

He shrugged. "Apparently he's gone. The grant papers arrived at my office just this morning."

"But where did he go?" Daniel wouldn't abandon Francis Park. She couldn't believe it was true.

"That I don't know, Miss Whitaker."

"And what of his workers?"

"I expect they've been turned over to the convict supervisor in Parramatta." He hissed out a breath and patted a handkerchief on his forehead. "Really, miss, you know how these things work. Now do you want the land or not?"

Daniel was gone? Where was he? How would she find him?

"Miss Whitaker, it is dreadfully hot out here in the sun. If you don't mind—"

"Yes. I want the land." Sarah's mind raced through options. She could think of nowhere Daniel would go. He couldn't return to England. Had he found a ship bound for America? She didn't know of any set to sail in the next few weeks aside from the *Coeur d'Alene*, and Captain Thackeray would not keep something of that magnitude from her.

"You can pick up the papers in my office, miss."

"Pardon? Oh yes. Thank you, Mr. Campbell."

He gave a curt bow and left.

Sarah chewed on her lip, and the answer came to her. Sergeant Conall Stewart. He would know where to find Daniel. And if not, he'd surely help her search.

After a few inquiries, Sarah and Molly were directed to a low stone building. She spoke to the soldier at the door, who asked her to wait then hurried inside.

A moment later, Conall stepped through the door grinning. "Och, Miss Whitaker, Miss Green. A fine sight indeed. And what can I do for ye lassies then?"

Sarah did not bother with pleasantries. "Sergeant, Mr. Burton has left Francis Park. Do you know where he went?"

Conall's smile weakened. His eyes became serious. "Aye, miss. I do at tha'."

"And will you tell me?"

"If ya don't mind me askin', why do ya wish to know?" He folded his arms across his chest.

Sarah was surprised by his manner. She'd never seen the sergeant without his typical booming cheerfulness. He seemed to be choosing his words with caution.

"Sergeant Stewart, I have made a mistake." She twisted the handkerchief in her fingers, the scrap of cloth giving her courage. "I said things I regret, and I must find Daniel and make it right."

He blinked and lifted his brows. He seemed to be considering. "He's gone to Bathurst, across the mountains."

Sarah's heart sank. She glanced at Molly. *Bathurst?* The idea of leaving the safety of the ring of mountains was terrifying. "Oh." She pressed her hand to her mouth.

"Ah, Miss Whitaker, don't go cryin'," Conall said. "'Twill be all right."

"Sergeant, please. Can you help me to get to him?"

The man's grin returned. "Aye, that I can."

❉

Three days later, Sarah rode with Conall up the winding road to the convict farm. She held a lead rope, and another saddled horse followed behind.

On either side of the road, she could see acres of farmland. Pumpkins, potatoes, cabbages, turnips—all growing in rows, all being tended by felons wearing the coarsely woven gray-and-yellow uniforms.

Bored guards stood along the road, anywhere they could find shade, keeping watch over the workers. They snapped to attention when Conall passed.

The pair reached the farm buildings and located the main house, leaving their horses with a groom.

"Ya goin' to be all right, miss?"

Sarah hadn't realized how tightly she'd been holding her shoulders. "These are not my favorite people, Sergeant," she said in a low voice. "If it was not absolutely necessary to speak to them, I would happily avoid them for the remainder of my life." She forced herself to relax.

Conall nodded. "I agree with ye wholeheartedly." He knocked.

A butler admitted them and showed them to a sitting room, and a few minutes later, Mr. Pierce joined them. Sarah and Conall rose when he entered.

"Sergeant Stewart, Miss Whitaker. I apologize. Mrs. Pierce is away at present."

He motioned for them to be seated.

"That is just as well," Sarah said. Her skin crawled at the sight of the horrid man and the memory of their last meeting. "I'm here to speak with you."

"I see you've come to your senses, miss. Found a respectable companion. No doubt you're here to thank me for the enlightening bit of information I delivered last week?" He sat back, a smug look on his face.

Conall's hands balled into fists on his legs.

"No, that is not the reason for my visit, sir. I've come to discuss a business matter."

"Ah." He waved his hand. "By all means."

"I'd like to take on one of your workers. A Mr. Bill Hawkins. He was assigned to the farm only a few days ago from Francis Park. The convict supervisor's office tells me his transfer will not leave you understaffed." The man's eyes were narrowed, but he didn't speak, so Sarah continued. "Mr. Hawkins was my foreman before he went to Francis Park. He's experienced with sheep and knows my farm. I want him back." She held her tongue, wanting to condemn the man for his cruelty, separating Bill Hawkins from his family out of spite. The convict supervisor had told her of Daniel's request and the measures he'd taken to keep the Hawkinses' together.

Mr. Pierce gave a casual shrug. "I don't particularly wish to part with the man. He's a good worker. Don't see many of those these days. I'm afraid I'm going to deny your request."

Sarah swallowed the bile in her throat. The man was just trying to goad her. She lifted her chin, forcing herself to speak civilly. "Please, Mr. Pierce. A favor."

"I am not inclined to, Miss Whitaker." He stood. "Good day to you both."

"Och, Mr. Pierce," Conall said. He hadn't risen despite the rudeness of remaining when his host stood. He leaned back in the chair. "Is tha' any way to treat a lady, I ask ye?"

Mr. Pierce looked properly affronted. "I beg your pardon, sir. This affair is none of your concern."

"Aye, true enough. My concerns are soldiers and the like. As a matter o' fact, Mr. Pierce, it puts me to mind o' somethin' one o' the men said. Believe he mentioned ye. Said yer the man to ask about a seamstress. You've been quite often a' the docks, ya see, with different lassies. When he asked yer business, ye said ye were lookin' for a woman to mend yer clothes." Conall spoke casually, but the way his eyes narrowed left no doubt as to his meaning.

"Sir, I take offense to that outrageous accusation." Mr. Pierce's face was a striking color of burgundy. Veins bulged in his neck.

"Nothin' to be ashamed of. A lost button here, ripped seam there. Happens to all o' us." Conall leaned forward. "Perhaps I'll ask Mrs. Pierce if *she's* a recommendation for a mender."

Twenty minutes later, Bill was brought into the room. Mr. Pierce hadn't returned with him, which Sarah thought was a relief.

Bill looked between the two, frowning. "Miss Whitaker?"

"Mr. Hawkins," Sarah said. "I'm here to offer you a position."

His frown turned into a scowl.

"I understand why you might be hesitant. I separated your family."

He did not change his expression.

Sarah could see the man's hurt and knew she was the cause of it. "Mrs. Hawkins has taken a position at Sarah Hills with Trudy."

His scowl fell away, and he cocked his head.

Sarah took a step closer. "I want you to work with me. All of you. I was wrong before, and I apologize." She held out her hand.

Bill looked from her to Conall then reached forward, clasping it nervously. "I don't know what to say, Miss Whitaker."

"I hope you will say you forgive me."

"I do."

She smiled. "Thank you. And you must forgive Mr. Burton. I know he wanted you to be with your family."

Bill nodded. "Aye, he put in a request with the convict supervisor to keep us together, but Mr. Pierce . . ." He glanced back as if to ensure the man wasn't listening.

Sarah felt a wave of anger at Mr. Pierce. That the man would purposely go after Bill's family, separate them as an act of revenge, was horrible, even for him.

Conall smacked Mr. Hawkins on the shoulder. "Bill, let's get ye home to see yer wife and that bairn. Then, Miss Whitaker and I need ye to help us plan."

Chapter 25

DANIEL WRESTLED A FENCEPOST INTO the hollow he'd dug then reached for the shovel, filling in the dirt and rocks to hold it in place. Sweat dripped from his face and rolled down his back.

It felt good to exert himself. He could push his body but leave his mind blank. *Work hard. Don't think. Don't feel. Don't remember.* It had become his mantra.

He grunted as he pushed the shovel into the dirt. He'd found over the past weeks since he'd started work as a stockman that if he pushed himself to the point of exhaustion each day, he could drop to sleep without his memories consuming his thoughts. The pain of his body distracted him from the ache in his heart. *Work hard. Don't think. Don't feel. Don't remember.*

He straightened, pressing fists into his lower back, and looked over the red dusty ground. The land beyond the mountains was endless, and he'd only seen a small part of it, an expanse of rust-colored dirt scattered with yellow rocks and scraggly bushes.

For just an instant, his mind flashed to the lush green of Francis Park, and the image was accompanied by a rush of emotion—pride and love of the land, the people, and the work. The emotion was followed by an ache that made him inhale quickly. It had all been a lie. He hadn't just lied to Sarah; he'd lied to himself. He'd almost believed the idea that he could make a life in Francis Park like any honest man, that he deserved the respect of his workers, the pride that came from working with his hands, that he deserved—

He drew his thoughts back, pushing the shovel into the hard ground. They had moved dangerously close to painful territory. *Work hard. Don't think. Don't feel. Don't remember.*

He pulled on his shirt, the movement giving a small breeze over his sweaty skin. He scratched his cheek. His rough whiskers itched, but he didn't care to shave. He didn't care to wear gentleman's clothing and fine silk hats. Not anymore. Daniel was through pretending to be a person he was not. He had the life he earned now.

A moment later, something caught his eye. He raised a hand, squinting against the sun. He typically worked alone, sometimes going for days without seeing another person. Through the blurry heat waves, he saw a group approaching on horseback. He frowned and reached for his rifle. He didn't imagine many prisoners escaped on horseback, but in the back country, he knew to be wary.

He watched them approach. Five riders and three . . . packhorses? He squinted closer. The riderless horses were sleek and muscular with long legs. They looked like racehorses. *Who would bring those animals to the middle of an uninhabited land? And where could they be going?* They were at least twenty miles away from the small settlement of Bathurst and traveling in the wrong direction.

He studied the riders. The men were coming directly toward him. Their leader suddenly broke off from the rest of the group, galloping forward. Daniel held his gun tighter. A long braid flew out behind the rider. Daniel jerked his head back, shock making his thoughts incoherent. *Sarah was here? But . . .*

Memories he'd tried to keep at bay were loosed and flooded him, bringing with them an entire range of emotions. Daniel fought to breathe. With great effort he pushed the feelings away.

She dismounted and hurried forward. "Daniel, we found you."

He saw hesitation as she took in his appearance, but it lasted for only a second. "Miss Whitaker." He inclined his head.

She looked taken aback by his greeting.

Daniel held himself tightly; the fear of re-opening his wounds nearly paralyzed him.

Sarah's brows rose and pinched together. Behind her, the others drew near but stopped a distance away. Daniel glanced toward them.

"I brought Bill Hawkins and Sergeant Stewart to help me find you," she said, breathing heavily from the hard ride. "Molly, of course, and her new husband, Arthur."

He looked at her. Her lady's maid was married? Bill was here? Had he returned to work at Sarah Hills?

"I also brought horses," she continued. Her brows pinched tighter. "For you. They're racing horses. Bill says they're very good. You can keep them here if you like, or . . ." She paused as if waiting for a reply.

His mind spun.

She chewed on her lip. "And I wanted to thank you for your wool. For sending it to Captain Thackeray. I am so grateful to you."

Daniel finally found his voice. "Why have you come?"

Sarah opened her mouth then closed it. She lowered her gaze. "Daniel, I'm sorry."

She looked up at him, tears in her eyes. "I was wrong. I said you betrayed me, but it isn't true. You gave me your trust, and I broke it." Her voice cracked, and she swallowed. "It is I who betrayed you."

She held a handkerchief, wringing it in her hands as she looked down at the ground. "I came to apologize, to ask your forgiveness, but mostly to give you mine." She lifted her gaze. "I love you—not just in spite of your past but because of it. Your experiences, good and bad, have made you who you are. And who you are is the man I am in love with."

Daniel's heart pounded. His throat felt like a rock was lodged in it, and he swallowed hard. Could her words be true? Had she forgiven him? He was a convict felon, the very thing she abhorred and feared. He'd deceived her, and here she was, offering the acceptance he ached for. Did he dare accept it?

"You traveled all this way to . . ." He squeezed his eyes shut, shaking his head. "What did you think would happen, Sarah? Did you think I'd forget what you said? That in spite of everything, I'd return with you? Marry you?" He didn't sound angry, just incredulous.

She gasped, her chin quivering. "I'd hoped you would."

He closed the space between them with a quick step, pulling her to him. "Good. Because that is exactly what I plan to do." He flipped off her hat, letting it tumble to the hard earth, and pressed a kiss to her lips. A kiss free of secrets, worries, and questions. He felt light and whole, the self-loathing about his past had vanished, and he could fully give himself, all of him, with his mistakes and faults to this woman.

A cheer arose from the group on horseback. Daniel cupped her face in his hands. "Miss Whitaker, I'm afraid I do have a complaint to lodge."

Her brows pinched together, worried.

"The day we met, you said you were not going to rob me, but Sarah, you have stolen away my heart." He brushed a kiss over her lips.

Her lashes fluttered, and she sighed. "And I intend to treat it very nicely."

"I have every confidence that you will."

Epilogue

SARAH PULLED ON THE REINS as her horse galloped over the meadowland of Sarah Hills, heading for home. The animal's hooves pounded on the wood of the new bridge leading over the creek to Francis Park.

As she passed the pond, she waved to the aboriginal women on the bank. They tended small smoky fires, where they cooked the fish as they caught them. She searched for Kiturra but didn't see her or Jandy. Of course, the boy would be with his father. He was a man now. He'd proudly pointed out his missing tooth a few months earlier. Sarah grimaced when she thought of the painful procedure. It was part of the coming-of-age ceremony, Daniel had explained. But she still didn't like the idea.

Reining in, she dismounted, wincing and laying a hand on her protruding stomach. Horseback riding is not comfortable when one is in a family way, she thought.

She hurried inside and found Winnie sitting on the drawing room rug, a child on her lap and another playing nearby. Toys were scattered about the room.

Seeing her, little Hortensia lifted her arms, indicating she wanted to be held.

Sarah bent down with a groan and lifted her, kissing her cheeks as the little girl wrapped her arms around her neck. "Have they returned?" she asked Winnie as the woman lifted her own baby.

"Yes, my lady. Just over an hour ago. You'll find them in Mr. Burton's office, I think."

Sarah nodded, taking the doll Winnie held toward her. The baby had been reaching for it.

"Trudy is preparing tea," Winnie said. "She'll deliver it promptly."

"Thank you." She carried the baby on her hip as she walked through the entry hall, smiling at the child's drawing of a sheep she'd propped up on the table beside the stairs.

"Mamá!" Alan jumped to his feet as she entered the room. His red curls bounced as he ran to her, throwing his arms around her legs.

She patted his head. "And how was your journey? Did you behave for your father?"

"Yes," he said, looking toward the desk. "Papá bought me a sweet."

"You must have been very good indeed." She met Daniel's eye and smiled.

He rounded the desk to join them. He took Hortensia, offering the baby a sweet of her own from his pocket.

"How was town?" Sarah sat on the sofa.

Alan sat beside her, his drawing pad on his lap.

She put an arm around her son and turned to her husband. "Were you able to find all the items on my list?"

"We were indeed." Daniel sat next to her. The baby's mouth was sticky and dripping from her sweet, but he didn't mind at all. "Mr. Grimes also sent home a jar of pickles. Seemed to think you'd appreciate it."

Sarah rolled her eyes at Daniel's laugh. The grocer, bless him, sent pickles with every single order.

Trudy brought a tray of tea and carefully set it on the low table.

Daniel thanked her. He poured a cup and handed it to Sarah. "The extra furniture order arrived as well." He handed a cup of milk to Alan. "Sarah Hills Inn is going to need more rooms at this rate." She saw the pride in his eyes.

With the end of the war and the discovery of gold, more and more people came every day to Australia. Sarah Hills was a convenient stopping place between Parramatta and the mountains. Daniel had taken to hotel management, turning the inn into the finest establishment west of Sydney. And his racehorses were known across the colony. Sarah settled back, sipping her tea and basking in the bliss of her young family.

She turned and watched her husband wiping Hortensia's face with a napkin. She could not imagine there was ever a finer man than Daniel Burton.

"And the lambs?" he asked. "How are the flocks today?"

"All is well. Between Bill managing Francis Park and Tom at the farm, I have quite a lot of free time."

"I am glad of it. You look tired," Daniel said.

She nodded. "I think I will take a nap before supper." She set her teacup on the low table, and Daniel helped her to her feet. "Will you join me?"

He grinned, taking her hand and kissing her fingers. "Always, my dear."

About the Author

JENNIFER MOORE IS A PASSIONATE reader and writer of all things romance due to the need to balance the rest of her world, which includes a perpetually traveling husband and four active sons, who create heaps of laundry that are anything but romantic. Jennifer has a BA in linguistics from the University of Utah and is a Guitar Hero champion. She lives in northern Utah with her family. You can learn more about her at authorjmoore.com.